# RISE OF AN AMERICAN GANGSTRESS

Buy

for Melodrama

# RISE OF AN AMERICAN GANGSTRESS

Kim K.

*Rise of an American Gangstress.* Copyright © 2012 by Melodrama Publishing. All rights reserved. Printed in the United States of America. No part of this book may be used or reproduced in any manner whatsoever without written permission except in the case of brief quotations embodied in critical articles or reviews. For information, address Melodrama Publishing, P.O. Box 522, Bellport, NY 11713.

www.melodramapublishing.com

Library of Congress Control Number: 2011946167
ISBN-13: 978-1934157534
ISBN-10: 1934157538
First Edition: December 2012
10 9 8 7 6 5 4 3 2 1

Interior Design: Candace K. Cottrell
Cover Design: Marion Designs
Model: Kamale

# ALSO BY KIM K.

# PROLOGUE

The darkened alley was desolate, except for a few gutter rats and a mangy dog in search of a meal. The stench of urine, beer, and debris permeated the narrow passageway. There, two individuals fought the fight of their lives.

Bloodied and bruised, the men went pound for pound on a cold winter's night, the air thin from the low temperature. Nasir and Shoe-Shine desperately tried to reach for the Glock 9 that had fallen to the ground just inches away from their scuffle. As they struggled, Nasir, in his peripheral vision, noticed Fancy creep up, and instantly he was relieved.

The shiny pistol in her hands trembled as she raised it.

"Fancy, do it!" Nasir demanded. "Hit 'im up. Now!" He knew he could only outbox Shoe-Shine for so long.

Fancy was indecisive and paralyzed with fear, the decision to end the life of someone she once loved weighing heavily on her mind. Guilt gripped the nineteen-year-old, and her body began to react to the situation. As she gripped the handle of the pistol, her fingers locked up, and her heart expanded in her chest. Small beads of sweat began to trickle down her forehead into her eyes, temporarily blurring her vision.

*What if I hit the wrong person?* she thought.

When Fancy didn't do as he commanded, Nasir said, "Yo, what the fuck you waitin' on? Lullaby this nigga!"

Fancy swallowed hard. She couldn't believe she was in this situation once again.

And then she heard, "If you want it done, you gotta do it!"

She looked from blood to lover.

Shoe-Shine continued, "Fancy, don't think. Just do it just like we planned!"

Both men looked at each other, eye to eye. Covered in each other's blood, they'd both given orders to Fancy to execute the other, and now their lives were in her hands.

Fancy closed her eyes and squeezed the trigger once, and felt her body jerk.

Blaow!

And then twice.

*Blaow! Blaow!*

Only one of the three bullets had struck its intended target.

His eyes grew large from a combination of shock and fear, until eventually they showed sorrow and disappointment. She didn't want it to end this way, but he left her no choice. If she was going to rise in the drug game, then she knew she had to get her gangsta on.

"Finish him off! Do it now!"

She looked down at someone she once loved holding his waist where the bullet had entered. She couldn't see any blood, but she could see the pain and agony etched on his face, his chest heaving up and down as his eyes pleaded for mercy.

She raised her gun again but then slowly lowered it. She couldn't do it. She couldn't kill him. The fear in his eyes scared her. He wasn't ready to meet his Maker.

"I can't!" she screamed, and burst into tears. "I'm not built for this."

"You ain't gotta do it," he pleaded. "You ain't gotta take orders from this nigga!"

8

"Fuck you, nigga! You ain't runnin' shit!"

The strong arms that enveloped her gave her quick comfort. He stood behind her and lifted her arm that held her gun.

"You can, and you will do it," he said. "You were born and bred for this. Make it happen!"

As she stared at the body slumped against the dirty concrete, she now felt nothing. It was at that point that she knew she has crossed the threshold into becoming an American gangstress.

# CHAPTER 1

That early July morning, as she now remembered it, almost seemed like a dream. She remembered being picked up from the airport by her father, Alexandro, in his black-on-black Bentley Phantom coupe, then speeding down the Northern State Parkway to their six-bedroom home in exclusive Great Neck, Long Island, and waving to her mother, Belen, who stood regally by the iron, high-brow double doors.

And then things got fuzzy.

The barrel of the assault rifle aimed straight between her perfectly shaped almond eyes. The narrow eyes of the assailant spoke louder than his words.

His eyes said, "Move, bitch, and you're dead." His mouth said, "FBI! Get on the fuckin' ground!"

There was a lot of noise and pushing and shoving. She remembered being knocked around quite a bit. Her knees were scraped, and she had a small cut on her elbow that was leaking blood all over the imported stone pavers of her family's front deck.

One agent twisted her wrist so hard, she thought it would snap like a twig under the weight of a fallen oak.

"Owwww!"

And then she heard a sound she would never forget. The click-clacking of the handcuffs sent chills down her spine. As she was restrained she felt like a captured creature.

Laying face down on the concrete, she thought, only briefly, of her thirteen-hundred-dollar pair of Christian Louboutin's being scuffed up.

She searched the scene, looking for a sign of familiarity. Where were her parents? All she saw was dozens of strangers—law enforcement—descending on the property. Everyone was hyped—amped up off pure adrenaline. She overheard someone saying this was the apprehension of the decade that was sure to make headlines.

Finally she saw her father being loaded into the back of an ambulance, his white T-shirt saturated with blood.

*What the hell?* she thought. Was the loud boom she'd heard earlier a gunshot? Had her father been shot? Was he dead?

Next, she saw her mother being stuffed into the back of an unmarked car, her massive weave tossed around, and no shoes on her feet. It took two agents to force her in the backseat. Belen only stood five-one, but she was solid muscle and had the strength of a woman half her age.

The scene was too much for Fancy to take. She needed to check out.

✳✳✳

"Ma'am . . . ma'am, you need to wake up now."

The LPN named Gloria had stood vigilantly over Fancy for the past two days as she came in and out of consciousness. The IV had been inserted in her arm after she refused to eat or drink anything after 12 hours of intake.

Fancy just lying in the hospital and refusing to speak to anyone, including hospital staff, wasn't helping her situation. Law enforcement had brought her in five days earlier after she'd fainted.

And the hospital didn't know if she had any health insurance.

"Ms. Fancy, the hospital needs this bed. You're being discharged today. I need you to lie still while I remove your IV. Nod if you understand me." Gloria felt sorry for the young girl.

The hospital and all of Long Island was abuzz with the gossip of the notorious kingpin living right under everyone's noses. Rumor had it that Alexandro played golf with the mayor of New York City and even hosted fundraisers for most of the politicians at his Long Island mansion. Now, he lay a couple floors down in ICU after being shot twice by one of the agents. The news reported that the agents had identified themselves and told him to freeze, but he still went for the gun he had tucked in his waistband.

Alexandro was lucky to be alive. Agent Oscar Giuliani had aimed and only missed his heart by one millimeter.

Gloria didn't get a chance to see the mother up close and personal. Only her image on television with her head tucked in between her thighs as she hid from the cameras. Belen was taken straight to Central Booking to be arraigned shortly after she was detained.

After Gloria removed the tube, she ushered a mute Fancy out of bed.

"Do you have someone to pick you up?"

Fancy dropped her eyes to the ground, fighting back tears. "W-where"—She stopped short, her throat burning from not speaking for days. "Where are my parents?" she finally managed to squeeze out.

Softly, Gloria replied, "Your father is here in ICU. You won't be able to see him, so I advise you to not even try. The agents guarding his door are gruff, to say the least. You'd think they had Osama bin Laden up there. The press have been camping outside 'round the clock, trying to get the scoop. Of course, I didn't give them an interview on account of your condition. And your mother is in some jail, I guess. I really don't know much about that how that process works."

"What is it that you do know?"

Gloria thought she'd heard a hint of attitude in the young girl's voice. Her sentence was wrapped in a life of privilege and entitlement. Surely, this drug dealer's daughter didn't think she was better than the LPN. Gloria shook off her thoughts and told herself not to judge.

"Well, as I said, I don't know much, other than your parents are being charged with federal racketeering, money laundering, and conspiracy of some sort. Some sort of drug dealing."

Just in case the young Ms. Fancy was trying to pull the privilege card, Gloria reminded her of who she really was.

Once again, Fancy lowered her eyes. Not out of shame, but out of deep thought. Finally, she said, "I need to use your phone."

Gloria wrestled with whether or not to lend Fancy her cell phone, especially since they weren't permitted in the hospital. The more time she spent with her, the more she disliked her. She couldn't put her finger on it, but there was something about the awakened, more alert patient that now rubbed her the wrong way.

And it wasn't what the papers and news media were alleging about her parents. She felt that everyone had a past. She certainly did. Just last year she'd gone to a Baptist church, got dunked in some water, and all her sins were washed away. She had a clean slate and promised she would try not to get too holy and start being one of those Christians who believe they're holier than Jesus Christ himself. Nah, that's not who Gloria felt she was. But this Fancy girl had an aura about her that sucked all the air out of a room.

Reluctantly, Gloria pulled her cell phone out of the tight white polyester pants she was wearing and handed it to Fancy.

"People still use these?" Fancy asked, as she dialed Sita, their maid.

"Excuse me?"

As Fancy dialed her telephone number, she replied, "Your phone—I wanted to know if people still use this old model."

Gloria tried to respond, but Fancy put up her index finger to silence her and began her conversation with someone on the other line.

"This is Fancy . . . I borrowed it from someone in the hospital . . . I prefer not to use my phone . . . I'll be all right . . . I should be there in an hour.

"I have no idea what's going on. . . they shot my father. . . I'm told they won't let me see him . . . Our lawyers will get to the bottom of this. That's an ignorant question. Right now I'm thinking you're a little pathetic . . . I don't believe anything I'm told. Oh, grow up!"

Fancy tossed the phone back to Gloria and began to gather her things. She was still a little fatigued but was slowly getting her strength back. There was so much going through her head that she needed alone-time to sort things out and proceed accordingly.

She thought about ruffling some feathers to try and see her father, but she knew that would be in vain and would only exacerbate things. The main concern was that he was still alive. Her father was a fighter, and on the strength of that alone, she knew he would pull through. She knew her only savior would be her father's team of lawyers, who would put all the necessary paperwork in place to at least get her parents a bail hearing, if not the whole case dropped.

It was laughable to Fancy to think that her parents were involved in anything illegal, especially something as low-class as selling narcotics. Her parents were educated pillars in the community, so only a misunderstanding could explain why federal agents descended on their property.

Fancy thought she knew who the culprit was. Last year her father had severed all ties with a business partner, Bradley Westinghouse, after they had lost a lot of money investing in a restaurant/nightclub in the Hamptons. For Bradley it was sour grapes after Alexandro pulled the plug on his expense account and wrote the business off as a loss.

Fancy thought he had to be behind this soap-opera drama that had unfolded in her hometown, on her front steps.

Gloria placed her hands on her hips and stared intently at Fancy. "You're welcome!"

"Pardon me?"

"You could at least say thank you for using my phone." Gloria's beady eyes narrowed. "After all I've done for you all these days your ass was laid up in this here hospital bed, you have the nerve to be so dismissive."

Fancy stared at Gloria as if she were seeing her for the first time. She felt like she understood where her sudden outburst of anger was coming from. Her father had always said that when you block a person's goal that rage won't seep out; it will implode.

"Listen, this is your job, which means I don't owe you anything. You're supposed to attend to my comfort and well-being, so don't hate on me. You choose a low-paying life of servitude." Fancy reached in her purse and tossed her two crisp hundred-dollar bills. "Feel better now?" She shrugged.

Gloria allowed the money to cascade to the floor. She was furious that the pompous, spoiled brat was speaking to her like she was her hired help, after all Gloria had done for her the five days she was convalescing in the hospital. She gave her sponge baths, put a cool rag over her head when she would break out into cold sweats, and gently woke her up from her numerous nightmares. And this was the thanks she got?

*Well, fuck it,* Gloria thought. *I could hit below the belt too.* "You gonna need this here two hundred sooner than you think. I've seen people like you come and go in this world, and it always ends badly for them. And it will end badly for you and your parents too—Ain't no judge ever gonna give them their freedom."

"I'll buy their freedom!" Fancy snapped, thinking about the five-million-dollar trust her father had set up for her when she was only three years old.

"There ain't enough money in this world to buy them out of the trouble they're in."

Fancy thought the statement was so farfetched that it was absurd. To her, money could buy anything. "Then I'll buy new parents."

# CHAPTER 2

**F**ancy really didn't mean that last quip about buying new parents. She sometimes said things for shock value. It was a defense mechanism when she felt like she was being unjustly attacked.

She took a taxi back to her house straight from the hospital. She needed all the amenities and luxuries that her home held in order to get her mind right. She thought she would be met with a slew of press and paparazzi like O.J. Simpson and was a little peeved that the property was empty. She knew she should not have bought into what the nurse had to say.

Fancy walked through her threshold to find destruction and chaos. The house was ransacked without any regard that it was someone's home and sanctuary. Furniture was turned over, dishes were broken, and closed crevices were opened up and exposed.

Fancy needed Sita, their maid, to put things back in order. She couldn't think straight with a house full of clutter.

Next, she ascended to her bedroom, where to her horror, her vintage crystal lights were broken, clothing was strewn about, and her most prized jewelry had apparently been seized or stolen by the federal government. She didn't know which, but she would get down to the bottom of it.

For an hour, she walked mindlessly throughout the large house, unable to believe the devastation that had taken place. Priceless paintings were missing from the walls, and expensive vases were either broken or just missing. Every item of clothing with either a tag on it, or worth value, such as mink coats, was all gone. She stared in disbelief at her closet that used to hold nearly five hundred pairs of art, which was how she liked to think of her shoe collection. All of her size eight Manolo Blahnik, Jimmy Choo, Fendi, Prada, and Christian Louboutin shoes were seized. To Fancy, the house now was a mere shell. The guts were ripped out, leaving only the skeletal remains.

The government seized every flat-screen television in the house, which totaled eleven. This was more than a nightmare. *This is almost worthy enough for suicide,* Fancy thought. It was that bad.

Fancy didn't hear Sita come in until she was right behind her.

"Miss Fancy," she said. "I'm here now. What can I do?"

The simple question, to most, would have sounded sincere, but Fancy wasn't most, having been raised by a man who taught in parables and lectures.

"Why would you ask such an asinine question when you see this fuckin' house in shambles? Clean it up, stupid!"

"Yes, Miss Fancy. I clean it up." Sita didn't dare make eye contact, and so she bowed her head.

"And call the rest of the staff in, and have their asses here *pronto*. And if you need additional help, hire them. But I better not get asked one silly question by you or anyone else about how to get this house back in order. The first person to ask some dumb shit is getting fired. Do you understand me?"

Sita only nodded.

"Speak!"

"Yes, Miss Fancy. I understand."

Fancy pushed further. "You understand what?!"

"I understand no ask stupid questions, or I get fired."

Fancy exhaled. "Very well. You're excused."

Sita was half-Mexican and half-Dominican. She immigrated to the States with her parents when she was only nine years old. Quickly she learned to speak English and began working as a domestic one year later. Now fifty-three, she'd never owned a green card. She had three children, all sons, who were born in the United States.

Sita had worked for Mr. and Mrs. Lane for fifteen years. And even though she pretended to close her ears and eyes to what went on in the family business, she knew it was only a matter of time before things began unraveling at the seams.

Next on Fancy's agenda was contacting Jacob Levin, her father's senior counsel. She had to go inside his office and search under mounds of broken desk parts, a slew of books, and shards of broken glass, only to find the Rolodex was yet another item missing.

"Ain't this a bitch!" she mumbled. Reaching for her cell phone, she Googled the firm and was immediately connected. "Jacob Levin, please."

"Who may I ask is calling?"

"Fancy Lane."

Long pause.

"Is he expecting your call?"

"Under the circumstances, he should be."

"Excuse me?"

"Yes, yes, he's expecting my call."

Fancy was put on hold before hearing a familiar voice.

"Fancy, how are things?" Jacob said.

His baritone voice was deceptively misleading. He sounded as if he was tall, dark, and handsome, but he was short, slightly overweight, well dressed, and balding.

"Well, I've had better times."

"Yes, I'm sure. How was Europe?"

"Oh, it was over the top. Fabulous. I had an amazing three weeks! I wish I would have stayed the whole summer, but Pop-Pop was missing me and wanted me home. I met so many interesting people, all of whom promised to keep in touch."

"When I was your age I traveled abroad as well, and it was, to date, the best years of my life. You know, right at that age when you feel old enough to make your own decisions but still young enough not to have all the adult baggage that holds you down?"

"Exactly! Overseas I didn't have a care in the world. I ate the best foods, stayed in the best villas, and met the best people in the world." Fancy's pitch rose as she relived her special moments. "And I can't even begin to tell you about shopping. Europe gets all the new collections from the designers at least seven weeks before the States."

"Is that a fact?" Jacob chuckled, knowing how much women loved to shop.

"Yes, that's factual. I have garments from Europe that my friends can't get their hands on. I tell you, I've had the time of my life."

"And now this?"

Fancy could have gone on and on about her travels, but knew she couldn't be selfish at a time like this. "Yes, now this. That's why I'm calling. I'm sure you've heard the crazy rumors the news media is spewing about my parents. The freakin' federal government treated me like I was a criminal." She lowered the tone of her voice to reflect how she should be feeling. "One minute I'm enjoying a summer breeze on my face, the next a gun is practically shoved in my mouth! A freakin' gun!"

"Yes, I'm sure this has been traumatic for you—"

"They tossed me on the dirty ground, handcuffed me, and shoved a foot in my back. I was mortified. I'm telling you, Jacob, it was all too distressing. Did you know I had to be hospitalized?"

"And your father was shot," Jacob reminded her. "Twice."

"Yes, I was getting to that," Fancy stated tersely. "I'm told he's in ICU, and they won't let me see him."

Jacob couldn't blame Fancy for being self-centered. He'd known her half her life and had watched her parents dote upon their only child, giving her diamond earrings and expensive toys instead of hugs and kisses. Fancy didn't understand there wasn't any *I* in *we*. All she knew was *I*.

"Well, did you try?" Jacob knew the answer, but decided to have a little fun.

"Why would I do that? Exert unnecessary energy when I could channel it more effectively? You know that's my father's philosophy. I decided to come here, check on the house, and call you to get this sorted."

"Me?"

"Yes, you. Do you know that the FBI has seized all of my shoes, clothing, and all other valuables we had in this house? They're savages! I need you to place the necessary calls to get my things released."

"Fancy—"

"And I want you to get me to see my father," Fancy blurted out. She realized how egotistical she must've sounded and didn't want Jacob to scold her or tell her parents that she was insensitive toward their plight. "And my mother too."

"Fancy, I can't help you or your parents in this situation."

"I don't understand. My father pays you good money to do a service for him."

"He pays me to handle his business affairs, and I do that very well, Fancy. I'm a corporate lawyer who—"

"You're a lawyer!"

Jacob buttons weren't easily pushed, so her assertions weren't really fazing him. He proceeded, delicately.

"I am a lawyer as we both know, but as I was saying, I only handle your father's corporate affairs. What Alexandro needs is a criminal defense attorney who has knowledge of federal statutes. I've been waiting for you to call. I have a referral. His name is Michael Sheinberg."

"And I have a headache. I thought this would be much simpler. I assumed, since I've been incapacitated for nearly a week, that you would have all of this sorted. My mother should have been arraigned on bail, and my father should not be under police guard while in ICU. I can assure you that, once my father gets released, you shouldn't expect to keep your position with him for long."

The threat wasn't even absorbed by Jacob. He knew Fancy was delusional. What he couldn't reconcile in his mind was, Is it better to keep your child sheltered from the intricate details of your illicit lifestyle, or should they be kept abreast so that when the shit hit the fan they would know how to jump in the driver's seat and take charge? Jacob realized that he would have to come to terms with an answer, and quickly, since he had a thirteen-year-old son and could end up in the same predicament as his client.

"I don't think you understand the gravity of the situation. Your parents need help. Powerhouse legal help far beyond the scope of my capabilities. Trust me, I know what I'm doing. Call Mike Sheinberg and then go and see your father. And whatever you do, do not discuss anything with anyone. Do not trust anyone, Fancy, only your parents. Do you understand what I'm saying? No discussing your parents' case on the telephone, and be leery of any new people who might try to come into your life."

"And what about getting my things back?"

"Fancy!"

"No! I want to know if Mr. Sheinberg will help with that too."

"Fancy, I doubt that the FBI took your shoes, unless the house was seized, which it wasn't. I think that's something for the local police. It sounds to me like your house was burglarized after the federal government left."

"Burglarized?"

"That's what it sounds like. The FBI isn't taking TVs and dresses unless there's a court order, which I'm sure will be coming down soon. So, if I were you, I'd take whatever you hold dear to your heart and find a new place to stay."

"Have you lost your mind?" Fancy couldn't contain her anger. Her throat was swelling with venom. "I've lived in this house all my life! It's mine! And you're telling me to pick up and leave because of a misunderstanding? My parents are innocent!"

Fancy slammed the phone down before taking down Michael Sheinberg's number. She was thoroughly disgusted with Jacob and no longer considered him an ally. And if he wasn't a friend, then he was an enemy. Therefore, she couldn't trust anyone associated with him. In her mind, Sheinberg was a fruit from a poisonous tree.

She decided that she would find her parents a great lawyer on her own, but first she needed to get the house in order and get to the bottom of who robbed their home.

# CHAPTER 3

Fancy watched as the staff of housekeepers ran around tending to the ransacked house. Every room was pillaged, and she knew she would have to replace nearly every fixture, appliance, and amenity that was once there.

She was furious that she had come home to this and felt lost without the man of the house. Her father Alexandro was the problem-solver; the one person she and her mother could always turn to.

"Miss Fancy, telephone." Sita walked into the den holding a cordless receiver.

Fancy was in deep thought. "Take a message."

"They say it's important."

Fancy snatched the telephone from Sita and allowed her voice to reflect her mood.

"Who is this?"

"This is your Aunt Bee."

"Who?"

"Your Aunty Brenda. Your mother's sister. You remember me, right?"

"Absolutely not."

There was a pregnant pause.

"Well, I've spoken to your mother, and she wanted me to come and check on you."

"You spoke to Mommy?"

"Yea, and she wanted me to come and check on you. What's your address?"

Fancy smirked. "I don't need a babysitter."

"No, it ain't even like that. She just wanted me to come holla—"

"What did I just say?" Fancy said, her voice curt and dismissive.

"Little girl, you better watch your tone. I'm trying to help your stupid ass 'cuz you family."

"Get off my phone line. I don't give a fuck who you say you are. I don't need you, and I never will."

"Let me tell you one muthafuckin' thing, bitch! You better watch how the fuck you speak to me 'cuz I will come and fuck your li'l ass—"

*Click.*

*Life is too short to entertain such ignorance,* Fancy thought. Besides, she knew for a fact that her mother did not commingle with her side of the family, always calling them ghetto and classless.

Fancy realized the best thing for her to do was to prioritize, because right now, she felt like things were closing in around her. She needed to find a lawyer for her parents so she could get them bail, and Alexandro could jump back into his head-of-the-household role, something she appreciated now more than ever.

Fancy loved being pampered and allowing the man to make all the important decisions, but she also loved her freedom and independence. As it stood, so many thoughts were infiltrating her mind at the same time, she didn't know which to follow first.

She decided that the only way to get through this ordeal was one step at a time. She would get the house in order today, tomorrow she would work on new counsel, and from there, things should start falling in place.

As she heard vacuums turning on and off and dishes being loaded and unloaded into the dishwasher, the familiar smell of cleaning products permeated the house, comforting her. She knew in her heart of hearts that things would eventually come back to normal.

She reached for her cell phone and saw that she had 137 missed calls. She scrolled through the call log and wasn't compelled to call anyone back. Not even her best friend Rosario, who was in Los Angeles with her boyfriend for the week.

Fancy wondered if the news had traveled as far as California. She sat down, propped her feet up on the ottoman, and looked online through her phone to see if she could find any articles written about the arrests.

After perusing a few articles, which she thought were outlandish, she went to check to see how the cleanup was progressing. As she walked from room to room, she saw that the hardwood floors were sparkling again. The overturned furniture was now back in place, broken glass was vacuumed away, and most of the evidence of an FBI raid was gone. Her mind suddenly began to relax and de-clutter.

She went to find Sita, who was in the butlers' quarters, preparing to wash laundry. Sita's blouse was slightly open as she leaned over the hamper, and Fancy immediately spotted the transgression.

"Where did you get that chain?"

Sita's hand immediately went up and placed her hand over her chest, covering the diamond heart.

"What?"

Fancy immediately slapped her hand off her chest. "Where did you get this? This is my mother's chain, you thief!"

"No, Miss Fancy. This is mine. She give it to me."

Fancy knew that hell would freeze over before Belen started doling out ten-thousand-dollar chains to anyone, let alone staff. "You Mexican liar! I'm calling the police!"

As Fancy flew through the house, things became crystal clear. Jacob was right. The feds didn't seize her shoes, clothes, or the flat-screen televisions. Sita and her crew had come back into the house and looted.

"Your ass and your *hombres* are getting deported! You watch—"

The firm grip on her forearm shocked Fancy. She didn't realize that Sita, small in stature, was so strong. What was more shocking was the butcher knife pressed firmly up against her throat, resting slightly on her carotid artery.

"You call the police and I kill you!" Sita mumbled, her tone low and sinister. "You understand, Miss Fancy?"

Fancy nodded.

"Answer me!"

"Yes."

"Yes, what, Miss Fancy?"

"Yes, I understand. I won't call the police."

The crazed look in Sita's eyes was something out of a horror flick. It sent chills down Fancy's spine and left her immobile. She couldn't move if she wanted to. She watched as Sita backed out of the kitchen, eyes glaring. She stood paralyzed as she heard all the cleaning equipment being shut down and doors being opened and shut.

It wasn't until she was completely alone that she collapsed to the ground and cried her eyes out. She had no idea what had just happened, but she didn't like it one bit.

# CHAPTER 4

The relentless ringing of Fancy's cell phone jarred her back to reality. She slowly picked herself up off the floor.

*Get it together, girl. You're not going to let an immigrant get the best of you,* she thought.

Scrambling for her iPhone, she looked down to see the telephone number come up as unknown. Her heart skipped a beat. She knew it had to be one of her parents.

"Hello?"

"Hey, angel," her father's voice whispered through the phone. He sounded weak and so distant. "Are you okay?"

The tears began to stream down Fancy's face, but she wanted to be strong for him. She realized that there were so many questions she could pose, but she felt it was best to just listen.

"Yes, I'm fine. I should ask, how are you doing?"

Alexandro tried to chuckle. "Well, I've been better, but I'm a lion. You don't have to worry about me. I'm more concerned about you and your mother. Have you spoken to her?"

Fancy shook her head vigorously before realizing she needed to vocalize. "No, not yet. I missed several phone calls, and I'm sure she could be one."

"Where are you?"

"I'm home."

"Good. This is my one phone call, and Daddy needs you to do me a favor. Remember when you were twelve we went to our special place?"

Fancy thought back to when she was a child and her father had taken her out back, just beyond their pool in the floor of their pool house and showed her a "magic" door. He said it was their secret and for her not to share it with anyone. Over the years she had forgotten all about what she thought was a childish game.

"Yes, I remember."

"Good. Go there now and get what's there. There will be instructions, and you'll know what to do. Okay, sweetheart?"

Her heart began to race. What type of game were they playing? She felt that it was risky, and yet it intrigued her. She knew better than to ask any questions and not to speak openly over the telephone.

"I'm walking now . . ."

While holding the phone to her ear, she ventured toward the magic place. Entering the pool house, she walked toward the wall on the far left that held towels.

On the surface, that's all it appeared to be, but if you hit it in just the right place, which was the upper paneling on the third shelf, it would unlock a door to reveal a small hidden room.

Fancy hit the paneling and she heard a faint click, and like one of her favorite childhood fables, the door unlocked as if the genie had said, "Open, Sesame." To her intrigue, there were two suitcases neatly stacked in the small cubicle.

"Do you see anything?" Alexandro patiently asked.

"Yes."

"Good. Listen, take what's there, and I want you out of that house now. I'm now allowed visitors from immediate family. Come and see me tomorrow, and I will give you further instructions. Understood?"

"Out of our house? But where will I go?"

"I don't want you to tell me over the phone, but you're a smart girl. I raised you. Wherever you go, do not use your credit cards, and stay off your cell phone. In fact, toss it now. Pick up a new one and don't contact any of your friends until you come here first."

"But, Pop-Pop! This is crazy!"

"No, baby. It's necessary."

"You're behaving as if I'm a criminal."

Alexandro exhaled. He understood that this was too much for her to absorb in such a small time frame, but he didn't have time to coddle her.

"Fancy, we don't have much time. Do as I say, and it will work out for all of us. You can help your mother, yourself, and me, but I need you to get out of there. You're not safe. You understand?"

"But I need to call the police!"

"The police? What are you talking about? What's happened?" Alexandro was practically squeezing his words out. He felt so frail.

"Pop-Pop, Sita is not who we thought she was! She's stolen all of our televisions, my shoes—"

"Fancy, that's all bullshit." Alexandro tried to keep his voice level, but his spoiled child was proving to be slightly denser than he'd expected. And he knew it was only his fault. "Trust me, baby, they can keep all of that. It means nothing. When I get out of here, you'll have the world again, but I need you to focus."

Fancy didn't like being dismissed. She felt her situation was dire, and in her mind her father was acting a little selfish.

"I am focused," she shot back. "All you care about is yourself! Sita pulled a knife on me, and she should be in jail!"

"Fancy!" Alexandro snapped. "Get the fuck out of that house now, and come and see me tomorrow. If I hear one more stupid-ass remark come out of your mouth, I swear to God, when I get out of here, I will slap some sense into you!"

Two things struck Fancy. First, her father had never raised a hand to her. Ever. And, second, he never used profanity, not even to her mother. He was always talking about how a woman should be respected and treated. She had to admit, his edgy demeanor was scaring her.

Fancy hated to do it, but she hung up. She didn't tolerate such disrespect. From anyone. And whenever she felt threatened or backed up against a wall, she would fold. For good measure, she shut her cell phone off and retrieved the two heavy suitcases. She pulled them out and sat down Indian-style on the floor.

When she opened the first suitcase, all she saw was presidents. Benjamin Franklin, to be exact. She was raised as a child of privilege, so even though she didn't have stacks of cash handed to her, she did have a large bank account and led a life of opulence. But she was still concerned by why her father had two suitcases filled with a large amount of cash.

She saw a note addressed to her and read it.

My Dearest Fancy,

If you're reading this it's because either your mother and I are both jammed up—which means we are incarcerated—or my attorney has read our will and we're both dead. Either way, you're on your own. If we're dead, we were most likely murdered by someone close because you know your mother and I would never allow anyone but someone we love to get at us. That means you are to trust no one. Not one living soul on this earth.

I want you to take this money and leave town, go far away and start over. That means a new identity, new life, new friends, the whole gamut. If we're both alive and we're locked down, I still need you to leave our home because most likely it's been compromised. If you're reading this, it means that I have told you where to look and the feds haven't found it. There's ten million dollars in here. Enough money for all three of us. I want you to contact Gary Scheck. He's a federal criminal defense attorney. He will know what to do for your mother and I. Bring him a $250,000 retainer, and he will do the rest. He has connections, but they cost. Buy a throwaway phone that you only use for him. Buy three more; one for your mother, one for me, and one for my wishes. Come and see me, and I will give you further instruction.

And, Fancy, don't be afraid. You're my daughter, and I wouldn't give you more than you could handle. Believe it or not, you were bred into this lifestyle. And just so I'm clear, believe everything everyone is saying about your mother and I. That way, you'll be sharp as a blade.

P.S. Destroy this letter, ASAP.

Love, Daddy

Fancy stared blankly at the letter as her teardrops stained the paper. What was her father saying? That her parents were drug dealers, like the nurse had said? That her whole life was a lie?

She stared at the mounds of cash. She knew she had to follow her father's directions. She rolled both suitcases into the house and placed them by the front door. Next, she ran upstairs and began to pack her must-haves. There wasn't much left, but she did manage to find a couple pairs of designer jeans, La Perla underwear sets, and some house slippers to hold her over in the hotel until she could find a permanent place to stay and also go shopping. She planned on tearing up the mall, dropping at least one hundred grand, but only after her parents' release.

After packing, she hopped in the shower and decided to stay the night. She was exhausted from all the drama from the day. Her father's revelation alone was enough to drain her. Not to mention having her life threatened by someone who had been around her family for over a decade.

✳✳✳

She awoke a couple hours later drenched in sweat; the faceless demon dragging her down to hell was too much for her to bear. Lying in bed alone in their big house wasn't as peaceful as she had remembered. She began to hear all type of noises. From the attic to the basement, she could hear movement.

She placed her feet on her plush carpet and exhaled. What had her parents gotten her into? She knew if she dwelled on it long enough, she would lose her mind. She had ten million dollars by her front door with instructions to disappear, leave her former life behind and sneak around like a criminal. *It just isn't fair,* she thought. And she couldn't wait to visit each parent and begin pointing the blame. She needed them to know how her life was now ruined.

The short walk to the kitchen was a familiar one. Fancy grabbed a glass of orange juice, and before she could take a sip, the front door was knocked off its hinges with a battering ram, making her glass slip out of her hand, splattering juice and glass everywhere. It felt like a movie scene as the events seemed to go down in slow motion. The shock and horror on her face couldn't be faked. Fancy instantly feared for her life.

"FBI! You know the drill! Get the fuck face down!"

# CHAPTER 5

The cold interrogation room was agonizing. Agent Anthony and Agent Ledger refused to allow Fancy to get dressed, dragging her out of the house in boy shorts and spaghetti strap tank top. With her legs and arms exposed, the vents felt like they were spewing ice daggers straight into her veins. But she refused to complain, not wanting to give them the satisfaction of knowing they were making her miserable.

"Now why would someone who has ten million dollars in their possession not purchase a one-way ticket to Rio?"

Fancy refused to answer.

"Where did you get the money?" Agent Anthony asked. "Did your father give you this money? Or was it your mother? We're still trying to figure out who's the brains of the organization."

Fancy still sat silent, shivering.

"You know, when we came tonight to seize the property, we had no idea what we'd find. It's like Christmas up in here. That's how excited our boss is. Hell, I think we'll get bonuses off this case and a higher pay grade."

The agents had been at it for hours, trying to glean any information from the naïve teenager. They purposely had the air pumped up, knowing she was scantily clad in her bedclothes. They wanted her to be as uncomfortable as possible, a tactic agents used against suspects, thinking the elements would cause them to fold. So far, all they were getting was the silent treatment—even after they'd threatened her with life in prison if she didn't roll over on her parents and save herself.

"I want a lawyer."

And that concluded their interview.

Fancy was booked on one count of conspiracy to launder money and sent to Central Booking, where the judge set a low bail. Only, she was penniless. From there she was shipped to the Metropolitan Correctional Center in Lower Manhattan, known as MCC, to await a second arraignment. She didn't know it, but it was the same place her mother was housed.

Fancy spent the next nine days crying her eyes out until the magistrate judge released her on her own recognizance. Since she and her mother were in two different units, neither knew that the other one was only yards away. The prison allowed her to be released in the government-issued sweat suit and Pro-Keds sneakers. Her doobie wrap was no more. At intake, they made her wash her hair and body with a harsh soap to kill any lice that might be present. Her naturally long hair was put into two braids that hung down her back. The hairstyle took years off of her life. She looked all of fourteen years old, as opposed to seventeen. She'd lost five pounds in less than a week, and her vibrant eyes were sunken in.

She didn't have any cash but was issued a round-trip MetroCard that allowed her to get on the city's mass transit system. It would have been useful if she'd had somewhere to go. Her home, along with all the cash, her pocketbook, cell phone, and any remnants of her past, had all been confiscated by the federal government. The only thing she had was her black ass, and right now it wasn't worth two cents.

✳✳✳

After walking around aimlessly for an hour and ending up in Battery Park City, just blocks away from the World Trade Center, Fancy felt if she could slap her own face, she would have. She had no idea why she didn't think of the one person she knew who could get her out of her situation. Her best friend, Rosario, had to be frantic about her whereabouts. Fancy knew that she should be home by now from her short vacation in California.

Rosario lived about four miles from Fancy's former house. She would have called Rosario's cell phone but couldn't recall the number from memory. Fancy figured she could live with Rosario until her parents were released. They had an enormous house just as Fancy had, with several guest rooms that she could easily move into. She reasoned she could wear Rosario's clothes, since they were ultimately the same size, unless, of course, Rosario's parents took her shopping, which shouldn't be a problem. Her parents would certainly repay them.

Fancy tried to think of the quickest way to get there. After asking questions, the fastest route via mass transit was to take the Long Island Rail Road, which to her dismay cost seventeen dollars one way. Getting to Rosario's house on the LIRR wasn't an option. She simply didn't have the cash or means to get there, so she needed to go to plan B. A taxi.

It didn't take long for a yellow cab to nearly run over two people before stopping abruptly in front of her. She got in and rattled off the address. The Iranian looked at her through his rearview mirror, trying to read her. And then he said, "Get out. I'm not going to Long Island. I get off at one o'clock."

Fancy was startled. She looked down at her clothes and realized she must have looked shady. She began, in her posh accent, "My parents will pay you double if you bring me home. My father is a very important businessman."

Fancy actually believed every word she had said. She did believe Rosario's parents would pay him double, and she also believed, at one time, that her father was a very important businessman.

Perhaps the cab driver was easily convinced, or maybe conviction in her voice made her appear to be trustworthy. The driver flipped the switch on his meter and proceeded onto the BQE toward eastern Long Island.

Intermittently, she would burst out into tears as the grave reality of her situation would come full circle. Now that she had experienced jail, she knew firsthand what her parents were going through. Especially Belen. Fancy knew she needed to get them out, but now with the money gone, she didn't know how. She reasoned that she would have to dip into her trust fund to pay Gary Scheck and was sure that once her father was released he would reimburse her.

"You ran away?"

Fancy looked pitiful. She looked up, and their eyes met. She sighed and wondered if she should tell him her story. She desperately needed an outlet. Someone who could possibly offer some advice but who also wouldn't have any attachment or connection to her or her family. Then she remembered what her father and Jacob Levin said, which was to not trust anyone. She shook her head. He didn't believe her.

"How old are you? Thirteen?" He didn't wait for an answer before continuing. "And you're in the city by yourself?"

Fancy realized that without makeup and proper attire, she did look juvenile. She decided to play along, if only for sympathy.

"I got lost."

"What?" He let out a hearty laugh. "And ended up way across town? Yeah, I bet. I bet you were chasing some boy double your age."

"No, I wasn't."

"Please. Don't tell your parents that story! That you got lost. Listen, I have two kids, and if either one of my daughters told me some crazy shit like that, I would put them on punishment until they reached eighteen. If I were you, I would just tell them the truth, and I'm sure they will understand."

Fancy allowed him to ramble on and on for the whole ride. By the time they pulled up in front of Rosario's house, she wanted to run to a quiet place. The fare was seventy-seven dollars, and he reminded her of her promise for double.

"Yes, I remember. Stay here, and I will go and get it."

Confidently, she stepped out of the taxi toward the front door. She was exhausted, but it was all worth it when she walked up to the front door and knocked.

The wind chime melody rang out.

When Mrs. Hutchinson answered the door, she was a sight for sore eyes. Fancy ran and embraced her and almost didn't want to let her go. Firmly, Mrs. Hutchinson loosened Fancy's clutched hands from around her thin waist.

"Why, Fancy? What are you doing here?"

"I should have come sooner. So much has happened," she gushed. Her heart was palpitating, and she could feel tears welling up in her eyes. "These people are insane. They grabbed my parents."

Mrs. Hutchinson took two steps back. "Yes, we've heard. The embarrassing incident has been all over the news."

Fancy read her body language. "You do know they're innocent, right?"

Ignoring the question, Mrs. Hutchinson got right down to the point. "What do you want?" Her voice was snippy, and her eyes were direct. Not the warm eyes Fancy had remembered.

"I wanted to know if I could stay here."

You could hear the desperation in her voice. Her eyes darted around the imported furniture as her skin was enveloped in the cool breeze from the central air conditioning.

"It won't be long, I promise. Just until my parents are released."

Mrs. Hutchinson began shaking her head vigorously before Fancy could finish her sentence. "Absolutely not, Fancy." She placed her hand on

Fancy's shoulder and began to usher her out the front door. "And I would appreciate it if you would not come around here again." She hesitated for a moment. "And don't contact Rosario. You and my daughter no longer have anything in common."

The heavy solid wood door slammed shut in Fancy's face. She stood furious, broken. She rang the doorbell once, then twice, then continually. She began to bang and then scream and then holler until finally she collapsed on the front steps.

The cab driver witnessed the whole scene. He thought he had seen a mother turn her child away for reasons he didn't know. He was furious that he would get stiffed for his fare, but his heart tugged for the minor. He decided to give her a few minutes before getting out and demanding his money from her parents.

Five minutes later the police car pulling into the driveway jolted her out of her thoughts. She swallowed hard and then stood to her feet. The imposing figure was known to almost every resident in Nassau County. Officer Nolte stepped out of his patrol car wearing his riding boots, aviator shades, and toting his pistol.

"Young lady, you're on private property."

"Hi, Officer Nolte." Fancy had known him all her life. He'd come over to the house for barbecues, card games, and sunbathing by their pool. He'd even joked that he was her godfather and that if anything was to ever happen to her real father he would step in and help out.

"Did you hear me? You're trespassing."

"I only came to see Rosario," Fancy whispered, finally feeling the full magnitude of her situation.

Officer Nolte saw that the yellow cab hadn't left. "Get in the back of the cruiser," he demanded.

"Am I being arrested?"

"If that's what you want, it could be arranged."

She swallowed hard. "No, sir."

"Then do as I say."

Quickly, with her trembling hands she reached for the handle and slid inside. As Officer Nolte walked over to the cab driver, she feared that she was going to be arrested for petty larceny. She couldn't hear what they were saying, but suddenly the cab driver backed out of the driveway and peeled out.

Shortly thereafter, the police cruiser backed out of the driveway, and their eyes met through the rearview mirror. He looked through Fancy as if he didn't know her. His disapproving stare made her feel worthless.

"Why are you coming around here, to our neighborhood?"

"I live here."

"Not anymore, you don't! Last I heard, the federales seized the address you use to reside at, so you don't live here." He snorted. "And DON'T come back. I don't tolerate people like you around here."

Fancy wanted to ask him so many questions. Like, why was he treating her so disrespectfully? Instead she buried her head into her hands and began to cry her heart out, her gut wrenching with emotion. She felt like she was on the brink of imploding.

"Save the tears for your parents' jury!" He sneered. "If I catch you out here in my town again, I'll arrest you. Do I make myself clear?"

The lump that had formed in Fancy's throat continued to rise. She tried to swallow back her emotions, but instead she vomited all over the backseat of the cruiser. As her stomach convulsed, Fancy thought she had come down with an illness. Truth be told, she was in the middle of an anxiety attack. She was fatigued and overwhelmed.

When Officer Nolte noticed what she'd just done, he went berserk. "You gotta be fuckin' kiddin' me!" he ranted. "Do you know how much that'll cost to get cleaned? Huh, bitch?"

"I'm sorry," she whispered, more scared than sorry.

The tires on the cruiser came to a screeching halt. "Get the fuck out!" he bellowed. "I was going to take you back to the railroad, but after pulling this stunt, you can walk your ass there!"

"I didn't do this on purpose!"

"Shut up! And you better walk directly to the train, or you'll be fuckin' sorry."

Fancy reached for the door, but there wasn't a handle. Officer Nolte immediately jumped out and pulled her out of the car. She took off running for a few blocks before she got winded and began to walk.

It was at that moment she felt she was being followed. She peered over her shoulder, only to find that the yellow cab was trailing behind. He had never left.

"Get in."

"I don't have any money."

"Get in."

Fancy thought about her options. She had all of a five-dollar MetroCard and was approaching a railroad she couldn't afford to board. She didn't have anywhere to go, and it seemed she didn't have any friends either. She was starving, mentally drained, and most of all, she was scared. She went to reach for the door handle to the backseat.

"Get in the front. I'm no longer on duty."

"But I could just sit back here."

"And I could get a fine, if you do. You've already cost me money. Either come sit up front, or take the railroad. It's up to you."

Reluctantly, she walked around the car and slid into the seat.

"Buckle up."

The car headed toward 495 West at a slow, steady speed. For a long moment, neither said anything to one another.

Finally, he asked her, "Where you headed?"

Fancy dreaded the question.

Where was she headed? She didn't have a boyfriend in the States; her last relationship was with Balthazar, who lived in the UK. She was blocked from seeing her best friend, and after the way she was treated, she was embarrassed to try and contact anyone else who lived in her neighborhood. The police had all of her credit cards, bank cards, and any cash she had on her person. Her only hope was to get her hands on her trust fund money, and fast. Still, she had no answer.

Fancy shrugged her shoulders.

"You don't have any place to go?" he probed. "No relatives, friends?"

She shook her head vigorously. "I have no one."

Fancy thought she saw a smile, however slight, through her peripheral vision. She didn't know what that meant. Was he amused that she was broke and stranded? Or was he willing to help her out with some cash to hold her over?

"I could use some cash so I could get something to eat and book a hotel room." Before he could refuse, for good measure, she added, "And I promise I'll pay you back every cent . . . with interest."

The cabbie decided to entertain the thirteen-year-old. "Now where are you going to get the money? And I just witnessed your mother toss you out, and you just admitted to having no one."

She wondered if she should tell him about her trust fund, but then she remembered how she was not to trust anyone. "I'll get a job."

He chuckled. "Aren't you too young to work?"

"The question should be, can I work? I've never had a job in my life," she replied sourly.

Finally, he heard a hint of maturity in her voice. "You're not thirteen, are you?"

"Nope. Add four years to that."

It was at that moment his intention shifted. Originally he was going to drive her to his sister-in-law's place of business. She ran a home for young girls all under the age of seventeen. He was going to see if they could put her up for a few days until her parents cooled down and accepted her back. Now, looking at the desperate, almost adult beauty, he wanted to test the waters.

"Well, I have a small place in downtown Brooklyn. It's not as nice as what you're accustomed to, but it doesn't seem like you have many options."

"There is the other option of you giving me some cash to get a hotel room and some food, as I suggested earlier."

"There's also the option of you getting the fuck out right now." He chuckled. "But that's the thing with options. They're usually indicative of the circumstance."

Fancy wished she could close her eyes tight and make the past three weeks disappear. She just didn't know how to respond. Could she really stay the night in some stranger's house? A cab driver at that? What if he tried to touch her? Or kill her?

"If I come with you, you better not try any funny business. And I will only stay a few days."

"Oh, if you come with me, we're fuckin'," he stately matter-of-factly. "I'm not having it any other way. You give me free pussy, and I give you free room and board. And you can eat whatever you want. I will keep you around as long as the sex is good. The moment I get tired of you, you're gone."

She had to blink several times. And then a few more times, trying to hold back tears. Was he seriously speaking to her like that? She was usually the one giving orders and talking down to people. He was treating her like he was renting her for a service.

"Pull over!" she screamed. "Let me out of this piece of shit!"

He shrugged. "I'll let you out at the next exit."

They were approaching Exit 30 on the Long Island Expressway. Calmly, he hit his right signal and proceeded down the ramp. At the first light, he made a left and pulled over on a busy intersection.

Fancy looked around and wondered where would she go from there. There certainly wasn't any mass transit around, and even if there was, she still didn't have a roof over her head.

For a fleeting moment, she entertained his proposition before hopping out of his taxi and slamming the door. "Pervert," she yelled.

"Fuck you!" he retorted.

Out in the fresh air she walked slowly, trying to get a semblance of normalcy. Then she stopped to stare at her reflection. She had definitely seen better days. The prison-issued sweat suit and discount sneakers made her cringe. It was at that moment she realized she was down and out. She needed Jacob.

# CHAPTER 6

t took close to five hours for Fancy to make it to his office. She did a little hitchhiking, took a city bus, and then transferred to the A train to Fulton Street/Broadway Nassau and walked to Wall Street. The sun was beating down on her back, and she was sweating profusely in every crevice imaginable. As she approached reception, she was met with a look of total confusion coupled with shock.

With sweat beads running down her face, she held her head high. "Jacob Levin, please."

A blank stare, and then, "He isn't in."

"Let's try this again—Jacob Levin. And tell him it's Fancy Lane."

The hard, cold stare Fancy displayed gave the receptionist pause. She picked up her telephone and whispered into the receiver.

Seconds later, Fancy was shown in to see Jacob, who sat behind a massive cherry wood desk, his small frame swallowed up by the mammoth furniture.

When he saw Fancy, if he was shocked by her overall physical appearance, he didn't show it. Years of practicing law had disciplined him for such affairs. Inwardly, he had to admit, she looked like dirt, but the moment she smiled and displayed her two deep dimples, his heart melted, and he saw the beauty he remembered.

"The saga continues, eh?" he remarked.

Fancy collapsed into the buttery leather chair and lost it, crying for a solid three minutes before he needed to rush her melodramatic moment along. He had shit to do.

"Well, it's not as bad as it seems," he stated. "I'm sure things will work out in the end."

Fancy didn't find his words comforting at all. In fact, she found them condescending and dismissive.

"What did you just say?" she roared. "You have no idea what I've been through."

"Calm down."

"No, *you* calm down!"

He snickered. "I am calm."

"You know, in a time like this, you could be a little more sympathetic of my plight. I've known you almost all my life. Now everyone who I thought loved me and my family has turned their backs on us."

Fancy was really hurt. Not to mention, he was the last resort. If he didn't help her out, she felt she would die. She was so hungry and almost lethargic. She hadn't had anything to drink or eat since she was released. And with the heat up in the high 90s, it was rough.

"I'm not turning my back on you," he began. "But, as I told you, I'm not the type of lawyer your parents need. Did you go and see your father yet?"

She realized he didn't know about her arrest. "I was arrested right after you and I spoke."

"Arrested? For what?"

She didn't want to tell him about the money. The more she thought about having all that money at her disposal, disobeying her father, and allowing the government to get their hands on it when they weren't even looking for it, the more foolish she felt.

"They came to seize the property, and I was still in there."

"They can't arrest you for that, Fancy."

"I put up resistance. I couldn't help it. I was upset."

He chuckled. "Well, you always had your mother's temper. But I hope you realize that was a foolish thing to do. Just as hanging up on me before calling Michael Sheinberg."

She nodded in agreement. She now had a laundry list of foolish things she'd done.

"I'm here because I need you to help me get my hands on my trust fund money early. I'm not supposed to get it until I'm twenty-five."

He exhaled. She was turning out to not be the sharpest knife in the drawer. "Look, Fancy, please go and see your father. I'm sure he's made arrangements for you to be all right. I'm sure he has set aside something for your well-being."

"So you're not going to help me with getting my money?" Near hysterical, Fancy's voice elevated into a high pitch. She knew he was referring to the ten million her father had entrusted her with.

"I hate to be the bearer of bad news but, sweetheart, there probably won't be any trust money. If the government has seized all the properties, all vehicles, they will freeze all assets—bank accounts, money market, CDs, stocks, bonds, and your trust fund. Anything that was invested in or purchased through any of your parents' organizations are considered fruits of a poisonous tree. That's the way it goes in the real world." His voice hardened. "Go see your father."

Her face turned beet-red, and her fingers felt cold and stiff. She thought she was going to check out again, but her mind was too busy coming to terms with the news. She was broke. Broke? There wasn't any coming back from that.

"I need to see my father," she whispered in desperation. "He'll fix this."

Jacob saw the fear in the young girl's eyes. He knew that within a couple days she would have her hands on a substantial amount of money, but she needed to see her father. He remembered that Alexandro told him that if he ever got jammed up, he had a nest egg for his only child that was untraceable.

"Is there anything I could do for you in the meantime?"

Fancy swallowed her fears and said, "I need to go shopping."

Jacob sent his secretary to Saks Fifth Avenue with a seven-thousand-dollar budget. She bought Fancy a week's worth of clothing, shoes, intimates, and toiletries. He also booked her a room at Gansevoort Hotel in SoHo, a trendy area for people her age, for two weeks. He figured that would be enough time to visit her parents and get squared away.

He did it for two reasons: The first was that if—and that was a thin if—her father did get out, he would be repaid handsomely for helping out his only child. And the second equally important reason was that if he didn't, and her father got out, his life would be as good as over. Alexandro would bury anyone who harmed his princess. And that wasn't an assumption. It was a cold fact.

# CHAPTER 7

Fancy spent the next couple days going in and out of sleep and ordering room service. She'd fallen into a slight depression, despite Jacob putting a Band-Aid over her problems. But then reality began to infiltrate her brain. She knew there wasn't any money—no nest egg to save her and her family—thanks to her foolishness. And from what appeared to be true, she no longer had a trust fund to buy her and her parents' way out of their legal problems. She was terrified that she would have to spend additional time in jail for something she really didn't have any part in. She was never around for the drug-dealing meetings her parents must have held. She didn't order any hits on rival cartel members, nor did she have any input on how the money was spent. Her only crime was being their daughter.

Slowly she began to resent that her parents had kept her sheltered from the family business. Had she been privy, she would've had the wherewithal to not stay home with ten million in the foyer. *Stupid. Just plain stupid,* she reasoned. But she also knew that she shouldn't beat herself up over the past.

On the fourth day at the hotel, she got up early to make the hike to see her parents. First she would go and see her mother, and then reluctantly, her father, who had been discharged from the hospital and placed in MCC. She dreaded what Alexandro would say once he found out what had happened to his cash.

# KIM K.

### ✳✳✳

The corrections officers were stone-faced, cold, and mechanical in their delivery of instructions. Everyone was rude and grumpy, and compassion was lost on the guards. At this point, Fancy didn't expect much. She'd gotten thrown into the real world quickly.

Fancy sat at the visiting table of MCC, which housed both male and female pretrial and holdover inmates, looking like a reality TV star. The form-fitting Diane von Fürstenberg dress and six-inch stilettos belied what was truly going on in her life. Her naturally curly hair was washed and flat-ironed straight, and hung just a couple inches above her ass, and the pale pink polish shined like glass on her manicured fingertips.

She wasn't in a great mood, but she was hopeful. In order to pull herself out of bed, she continued to tell herself that her parents would know what to do. They had acquired great wealth, and that had to take ingenuity and intelligence. The fact that it was accumulated illegally was no longer germane.

She figured that her mother would be frantic, almost catatonic, after the ordeal she'd gone through. Her concerns were for both her parents, but she knew her father was a pillar of strength and could hold his own. As she sat at the small, round table wringing her hands, every sound, movement, and smell gave her an uneasy feeling.

Slowly, inmates began to trickle in, and she finally saw her mother. Their eyes met, and to her amazement, Belen came out of the back pen all smiles. Which made Fancy smile. She had expected to see her mother with a tear-streaked face, gaunt eyes, and disheveled appearance.

Instead, she saw hope. Belen's weave was pulled back into a loose ponytail, and she didn't have any makeup on. Her dark chocolate skin was glowing against her bright, white teeth. Growing up, kids in Fancy's classrooms could hardly believe that Belen was her mother. She was several shades darker than Fancy, and their young minds weren't sophisticated enough to glean facial features. Fancy had her mother's high cheekbones and almond-shaped eyes, and she had her father's complexion, soft hair, and dimples.

They embraced, and Belen almost didn't want to let Fancy go. She took a step back. "You look gorgeous, sweetheart."

Those words provoked tears. Fancy began to cry as Belen wiped her tears away.

"Shhhh, it's all right. I promise you, they can't keep me in here forever."

Fancy began to shake her head vigorously. "I want you to come home."

"Come on now, baby. It ain't that bad. Don't let these people see you in this vulnerable position."

Fancy shook her head briskly. Her heart swelled up and felt like it was about to explode. Suddenly, she collapsed on the table and buried her head into her hands and let out a much-needed cry.

The outburst shook up the whole unit, and within seconds, two COs surrounded Fancy and demanded that she knock it off.

"Miss, you gotta control yourself, or you'll be asked to leave the visit."

"Fancy, please stop this." Belen leaned in close. "I got things I need to discuss."

When Fancy couldn't contain her emotions, one of the COs began to tug on her arm. "Come on," he said. "You outta here."

Belen pleaded, "Just give her one second. I promise she'll get it together. Just two minutes."

Both guards stepped back to give Fancy a moment to compose herself.

Belen continued, "Fancy, I've been there for seventeen years of your life. For this moment, I need you, sweetheart. Please, for me, stop crying."

Fancy began to control her breathing, until eventually the sobs slowed to a soft whimper. "I can't see you like this in here. I need you home, Mommy."

"In due time. Please stop. Don't let these people get to you. You're a Lane. We don't break."

If ever a motto could make her dig down deep and suck up her fears, it was that one. Since she was a child, whenever things would get rough at school, or when she had her heart broken by her first love, her father would always say the same line.

"You're a Lane. We don't break."

He'd explained that a lane is a line, and that although it could splinter, another one would resurface. So, to him, lanes were infinite, therefore, they couldn't be broken. She didn't know how solid his logic was, but she had to admit that it had gotten her through a lot of rough nights.

"How are you holding up?"

"My body is in here, but not my mind." Belen grabbed Fancy's hands into her own. "What's been going on? I thought I would have seen you sooner. I was worried sick."

Fancy paused then replied, "Mommy, things are spinning out of control for me. Things that I can't handle. Did anyone tell you that they seized our house, all of Pop-Pop's vehicles, your vehicles, anything of value?"

"No one had to tell me that information, Fancy. I expected that."

Fancy stared blankly at her mother. It was as if she'd finally realized there was a secret society that she wasn't privy to. Her parents knew the rules and how things would unfold. You would think the feds arrested her mother twice a week. Belen was reserved, calm, insightful, and most of all, she still had enough strength in her to lend some of it to her daughter.

"Well, did you expect Sita to come back to our house and burglarize it?" Fancy didn't know why she wanted a rise out of her mother. She felt she had been through so much because of her parents' actions. For weeks she had been in tears and turmoil. She was homeless, tossed in jail, starved, propositioned for sex, and humiliated. She wanted to see some real emotion out of Belen.

"They took all my clothing. Yours too."

Belen never flinched. "Didn't we always teach you to expect the worst from people who aren't in our circle? The only two people on earth to trust are me and your father. That's it. No one else. So to answer your question, yes, I did expect it. Sita is a mother and a grandmother, and she did what she had to do to provide for her family—which is all that matters. *Family.* I'm almost glad she took what she needed before the government got their damn hands on it."

Fancy didn't understand her logic and was sure that the next news she shared would get a reaction. "Speaking of family, your sister called. She wanted our address. Did you tell her to come and get me?"

"Brenda?" Belen rolled her eyes. "You know I didn't do no such thing. That bitch was trying to get over there and make a come-up. I'm glad you didn't fall for that one. Listen, stay far away from her and her wolf pack of ghetto hoodlums. You're not built for the type of chaos they will bring to your life."

"I was trying to tell her to get lost when Sita pulled a knife on me."

Fancy braced for the wrath that never came. "I'm glad she didn't use it. Well, *she* should be glad she didn't use it."

Fancy listened incredulously. "Well, Pop-Pop isn't so cavalier about what was done to me."

"Your father was always overprotective of you," she said dismissively. "Speaking of your father, did he give you any messages for me?"

"No, not yet. We only spoke briefly."

"Why briefly?"

"Because it was on the telephone."

"You haven't gone to see him yet?"

"I'm going next."

"Fancy, he's the head of the household. You should have gone to see him first. You should know these things." Belen sighed. "You will be our only form of communication. We need you to wise up."

"Train a child in the way he should go, and when he is old, he will not turn from it," she said, reciting from *Proverbs*. Fancy resented the implication that she was a dumb ass. Her parents weren't *that* smart. After all, they did get caught.

"So this is all our fault. You're taking your sweet time to come and visit us after all we've done for you." Belen laughed. "First smart thing you've said thus far."

"No disrespect, Mommy, but I'm not in jail, you are. And, as you said, it is your fault, so don't go playing the blame game. You need to get a grip."

There was a pregnant silence that seemed to stretch an eternity.

"You might remember this parable. Your father told it to you when you were a child. You won't remember the circumstances surrounding the reason he told you this, but when you were six years old, there was an assassination attempt made on all of our lives. Your father and I didn't know where the hit came from. You were frightened, and only he could soothe you."

Belen leaned forward in her seat, an action that demanded Fancy's full attention.

"A rancher had an old stallion horse that fell into a well and cried out for hours while his owner tried to figure out what to do. Finally, the rancher decided that the horse was too old to save. He called over his neighbors to help him bury the horse in the old well. Immediately, they began to shovel dirt into the well. When the horse realized what was happening, he cried out. As the dirt began to pile up, he quieted down.

"A few piles of dirt later the rancher looked down and saw that with every shovel dropped on the horse's back, he was doing something extraordinary. He would shake it off and take a step up. As they continued to shovel the dirt, the horse climbed higher and higher, until he walked free out of the well. Two days later the horse returned to stomp his owner to death in his shed."

Fancy thought she felt a glint of amusement coupled with cynicism. It took her a moment to get the moral, which was life will throw a whole lot of troubles at you. She could either shake it off or let it bury her. She realized her mother was saying that the jail bars couldn't hold her. One day she would walk out of there, and people, perhaps even Fancy, would have hell to pay.

Fancy was furious. She had tried to play their game and lost. She decided to change the subject and pull the sympathy card.

"I was in jail, Mommy. Jail. For two weeks I was housed here. They pulled me out of the house practically naked and I can't"—Fancy felt a strong pressure on her hands. Her mother had tightened her grip on their once loving embrace. "Owwww!"

Both women looked at each other eye to eye, Fancy, with a look of confusion, Belen, a look of malice.

"I don't have time to coddle you." Belen continued to squeeze Fancy's hands until they felt like each bone could break. "For once, this isn't the Fancy show. Your father and I are in jail, facing life. We're going to die in here if we don't make the right moves. Now get the fuck outta my face and go see Alexandro. I expect you back here in two days with some good news. Do you understand me?"

Fancy couldn't speak. The cold stare in her mother's eyes and icy tone had freaked her out.

Belen released her grip and stood to leave. She didn't need a verbal response. She knew she was understood.

✳✳✳

If Fancy thought she would get hugs and kisses from Alexandro, she had another thing coming. She sat before her father with bloodshot eyes, shame and guilt written all over her face and body language.

"Is it all gone?" he asked, knowing the answer. "All of it?"

She nodded.

The anger and rage he had held within for nearly three weeks exploded into an aggressive bang against the steel table.

Startled, Fancy jumped back. Her hands began to tremble, and her lips quivered. In all her seventeen years, she had never seen her father so angry. And the look in his eyes said he was even past anger. His pupils were dilated, and his eyes widened, giving him a crazed and deranged look.

She cut her eyes toward the COs—who, by the way, didn't reprimand Alexandro for his outburst—looking for help.

"You think they could stop me from coming across this table and smashing my fist into your face?" Alexandro's voice was raspy and strained. "Don't you ever disrespect me again. Do you hear me?"

Fancy stared at a man she no longer knew. Who was this individual? He seemed like a monster in her father's skin. He'd lost a lot of weight after the shooting. His face was sunken in, and he looked frail and weak. All she wanted to do was run out the door as she fought back tears. But she knew that wasn't an option. Instead, she put on a brave face, sat still, and listened intently.

"Yes, Pop-Pop."

The inflection in her voice, the innocence, made him acquiesce.

"You know our options are limited, and I cannot stress how you not only fucked me and your mother, but your future as well."

"But what about my money? I could use some of it to make bail." Although Jacob had told Fancy that the money was most likely gone, she refused to believe it until she got confirmation from her father.

He exhaled. "You have money, huh? Is that what you think?"

She blinked twice, fighting back all her emotions. "My trust fund. The five million dollars. I could use some of that."

"It's gone, Fancy. Gone. Muthafuckin' seized by the government. We're done. We're penniless. Broke. That means you too."

Fancy felt her world close in. Broke? She didn't know the meaning of the word. She grew up in private schools, with drivers taking her to and from dance classes. They vacationed in Aspen and the Hamptons domestically, and spent weeks in France and Italy just for the cuisine.

"Well, isn't there anyone you could borrow money from just to float us through until we come up with a plan?" she asked, her voice laced with desperation. "Jacob has been helping me. He's put me up in a hotel for a couple weeks. I don't have anywhere to stay."

"Baby girl, I had a plan, a good fuckin' plan. Which was the ten million that we no longer have. I'll put in some calls to see if I could get you enough money to hold you over until I touch ground again. Right now, things are bleak. My associates will most likely not take my calls, something you should prepare yourself for. People will distance themselves from us."

"I've already experienced that. I went to see Mrs. Hutchinson, and she wouldn't allow me to see Rosario and also tried to get me arrested."

She could see the pain in her father's eyes from the disrespect. He held back his personal feelings because he thought logically.

Alexandro knew that everything that was happening, the way people would treat them, including their daughter, was warranted in his line of business. Had the shoe been on the other foot, and the feds were issuing down indictments, he would've cut off any and all ties too. It could've been his own blood. The drug game was about survival. And when someone takes a fall, you have to chop off the leg to stop the spread of the cancer.

"I see." He nodded. "Well, as I said, I'll make a few calls. In the meantime, how much longer do you have in the hotel?"

"A little over a week."

"That cheap bastard could have put you up longer," he mumbled to himself. "Okay, if all else fails, you'll have to go to Brooklyn and see if your Aunt Brenda will allow you to stay with her. Just until your mother and I—"

"Mommy said no."

"Your mother is bitter. She and her sister have bad blood between them, so she's not giving you reasonable advice. Where else are you to go once you have to leave the hotel? I don't have any family, and we now don't have any money."

Fancy looked down at her perfectly manicured fingers. "Do you think Jacob would let me move in with him?"

"And his wife and kid? Fancy, use your brain."

Briefly, Alexandro wondered had he wasted all his money sending her to private school, because at the moment she appeared as dumb as the day is long. And then something swept over him, which made him grit his teeth.

"Has he tried to sleep with you?"

Fancy's eyes flew open in horror. "Oh God, no! It's not like that. He said he could only help me out but so much, and that when I came to see you, that you would make me whole again."

Alexandro nodded. He knew Jacob was speaking about the stash he once had.

"Listen, do as I say, as our options are limited. Go and see your Aunt Brenda and tell her that I said you'll need to stay there. She'll let you in."

"But, Pop-Pop—"

"Don't argue with me." His voice was low. "And go back to see your mother. Tell her that the safety net got up and walked away—She'll understand what I mean—and that we'll have to use legal aides. There's no other way out of this."

Fancy left the visit knowing one thing for certain. She wasn't ever, ever going to stay with her aunt in Brooklyn. That jungle wasn't going to be her future.

# CHAPTER 8

The dimly lit hotel room wasn't dark enough for Fancy. She thought she could, but she realized she could never get used to seeing Jacob naked. Every time his stubby little fingers touched her skin, she was repulsed, and every time he crawled on top of her with his pale white skin and protruding belly, she wanted to vomit.

She wanted to cry out to God for mercy when he pushed his irregular-sized penis into her. His small frame belied his massive penis that would rip her insides apart. It was humongous—pink and heavy. He was always rough and sweaty, and quite disrespectful in bed. The litany of names he would assault her with was unbearable for someone raised in the manner she had been.

"Black cunt, suck my dick," wasn't exactly music to her ears. But she did what she had to do to stay in the sanctity of the hotel room, with unlimited room service, and an expense account at Saks Fifth Avenue to boot.

**✳✳✳**

Fancy never did make it back to see her mother or revisit her father, and before she knew it, another month had passed. She did write Belen a short note repeating what her father had told her about the safety net being gone and using the legal aides. She was in survival mode and had to fend for herself. Jacob was working on her case and had promised to pull a few strings to get it dismissed on a technicality. Although he wasn't a criminal defense attorney, he said her case was bullshit and just a scare tactic.

On this particular afternoon he walked through the hotel room in a dark mood. He came to have sex Monday through Friday on his lunch break, and he never had a problem getting it up. His dick was always stiff and at attention. And for a man his age, she deduced he had to be on Viagra.

*Damn those pharmaceutical companies,* she thought.

Fancy dreaded his visits. Her vagina was always still store from the previous session. Usually, she was pissy drunk before noon and would soak in a bath before his arrival. She even purchased some lube, hoping to minimize the friction, but nothing worked.

She watched as he placed his briefcase on the table, took out a few items, loosened his tie and said, "I'm going to tie you up and whip you like Kunta Kinte. I don't want you to scream too loud, so I'll have to gag you."

"What?"

Fancy wasn't sure she had heard him correctly. And then she glanced over and saw the skinny black leather whip along with two sets of handcuffs. What was equally disturbing was the red ball gag with its black spiked straps. Visions of being beaten bloody like a slave flooded through her young mind.

"You've got to be joking."

"We have fifty-nine minutes. Now turn around," he commanded, cracking his knuckles. "And, Fancy, I never joke about how I spend my money."

Jacob was letting her know that he'd paid the cost to be her boss. That hotel room and all the other amenities weren't free. And he would rather she not forget that.

"I've taken all your shit, Jacob, but you've gone too far with this one." She quickly jumped up and began putting on her clothes. "If you think for one second that I would allow you to desecrate my body in such a vile manner, you've bumped your fuckin' head."

If he was angry, he didn't show it. He simply put his toys back into his briefcase and began to quietly leave.

Suddenly, she panicked. "Where are you going?"

He didn't say one word.

She started to remove the clothing she'd just put on. "You don't have to go. We can still have sex. Rough sex if you like, just not that."

Silence.

In desperation and out of sheer panic and fear, she blurted, "Okay, you can do it. Just this once."

When he turned to face her, the demonic look in his eyes sent chills down her spine.

The beating lasted well over his hour lunch break. Today, he treated himself to the whole afternoon off. He took great pleasure in whipping her like a slave, reliving American history. He always wanted to fuck a black woman, but growing up, he'd never had the gumption to approach one. Nor did he ever want to be seen with one. But sneaking around behind closed doors was an aphrodisiac. Here, he could be the master, and she his in-house slave. Whatever his command, kink, or fetish, any pleasure he had, was fulfilled.

When Jacob closed the heavy hotel room door, Fancy couldn't move. Every inch of her body had been violated in the worst way, with thick whelps scattered all over her neck, back, arms, ass, and torso. It even hurt to close her eyes.

As she lay in bed unable to move, she wondered who she hated more—him or herself.

The loud banging jolted Fancy out of her sleep. She opened her eyes but quickly shut them as the room began to spin. She tried to get up but was weighed back down with pain. She tried to speak, but even that was a task. All she wanted was an escape.

Before she could object, her door was opened, and two hotel staff came walking in uninvited. She heard the intrusion before she was able to pry her eyes open to see two tags that read Manager and Senior Manager.

The senior manager said, "Ms. Lane?"

"Yes?"

"Checkout time was two hours ago."

"What? I don't understand."

"You don't understand 'checkout'?" she asked, her voice snarky and laced with sarcasm.

"I don't understand why you're here. Hasn't my room been paid in full?"

"If that was the case, Ms. Lane, would we really be here?"

Fancy's heart rate began to increase from stress. She couldn't believe what was happening. Not now. Not in her condition. Not again.

"I need to make a telephone call, so I could get the room paid for." Fancy forced herself to sit up, exposing her partial nudity.

The senior manager snorted disgust. "That won't be necessary. This room has been re-booked. You have thirty minutes to vacate the premises before we call authorities. Good day."

The shock of the situation actually helped numb her body. She was able to run around and pack the numerous bags of clothing she had accumulated from Jacob, but not before first trying to contact him to no avail. Finally, his secretary said that he and his wife had left the country on vacation. Stupidly, she wondered if non-payment was an oversight.

# CHAPTER 9

Fancy sat outside of Starbucks in SoHo, sipping an overpriced latte, with five massive suitcases at her feet and less than two hundred dollars in her pocket. It was a harsh reality for her, but she finally realized that she had done numerous things wrong. And if she didn't start to think things through, with a more realistic outlook, she would continually get the rug pulled out from under her. It was at that moment that she decided to head into the belly of the beast. Brooklyn. She reasoned that it would only be temporary, until she was able to get a job and secure her own apartment.

The cab ride was one filled with anxiety. Fancy didn't know what to expect, but she was taught to expect the worst. Which wasn't comforting.

She watched as the boutiques, stores, and loft apartments turned into corner store bodegas and seedy tenement buildings. Crowds of men were congregated on corners wearing heavy jean shorts pulled low around their waist, with either red or blue bandannas, and white tees. The women all strutted around half naked in skintight outfits, large tattoos adorning their bodies, and gaudy weaves.

If she had any tears left, she would have cried. Instead, she asked herself, what would her father do? How would he handle the situation? And if she knew one thing for certain, it was that he would be brave, and that's what she planned on being.

The cabbie pulled close to the curb and shut off the meter. He turned to face her. "You pay cash or credit?"

"Cash." Fancy began searching for her wallet.

"You live in this neighborhood?" he asked, his eyes scanning his surroundings in disgust.

"I don't know," she replied curtly. And then she bravely added, "I hope so." She peeled off three twenty-dollar bills.

"Do you need change?"

Actually she did. She needed every penny she got her hands on, but she also needed assistance. Reluctantly, she told him he could keep the change.

"Would you be able to wait a few minutes, just in case I need a ride back into town? I need to go up and see if my aunt is home."

"How long will you be?"

"Just a couple minutes."

"Anything over five minutes, and I cut the meter back on."

Fancy was annoyed but didn't let it surface. "Okay, no problem. And I'm going to leave my luggage until I get back."

Fancy stepped out and headed toward the building. Three guys, dressed thuggish in Fancy's opinion, began to stare at her intently.

"Yo, ma," one said, "you wearing the shit outta that dress."

"You comin' to see me, shorty?" another one asked.

One male stated, "Leave the gorgeous young lady alone. Pardon these hoodlums, beautiful."

Fancy looked up and saw someone she was instantly attracted to. He looked just under six feet tall, broad shoulders, six-pack abs, full pink lips, and he had a presence. His deep cinnamon complexion had a glow, and his shiny, low-cut, jet-black hair made him look Indian. If it weren't for the two-inch scar from his bottom lip to his chin, she would have labeled him a pretty boy.

Fancy didn't engage in their banter. She just pushed past the mob and made her way to her aunt's home. Standing in front of door 3C, she heard lots of commotion. She looked around at the old, worn tenement building and wondered how people lived like this. She knocked. And then knocked again. Until her gentle knock became a loud bang.

"Who is it?"

"Fancy."

The door swung open, and there stood someone who was the spitting image of her mother. Although a little worn, her features were the same. Two small twin girls were sitting on the floor playing with a broken Easy Bake oven.

The woman's eyes adjusted on Fancy, and then her lips pursed together into a smirk. "Who you lookin' for?"

"Aunt Brenda, it's me, Fancy."

The cold stare never softened. "What do you want?"

Fancy lowered her eyes. "My parents told me to ask you if I could stay."

"No, the fuck they didn't! That bitch mother of yours—"

Fancy thought quickly. "I meant to say my father wanted me to come here. With you. He said to tell you that he'll take care of you."

"Take care of me? How he gonna do that and he fucked up?"

"If you know my father, then you know he still has resources. Right now, the feds are on his ass, but as soon as they fall back, you and I will be looked after." She didn't know where the words came from. All she knew was, she had to survive.

Brenda wasn't falling for her game so easily. She placed her hands on her hips. "I told ya ass you was gonna need me one day. Told the same shit to my sister! And look at her dumb ass."

"It's not over for my mother, Aunt Brenda. And you'd be a fool to think so. Either you could look out for me and my parents will bless you accordingly, or I could go and stay with my friend Rosario, and her family will be compensated. I was only trying to look out for you first because we're family."

"Ain't no need for you to stay anywhere else but here." Brenda's body softened. "That's why I called ya ass, but you were talkin' crazy, like we weren't blood."

"I was under a tremendous amount of stress."

"I know that's right." Brenda moved to the side, so Fancy could enter.

The putrid smell in the apartment assaulted Fancy's nostrils. She made a lemon-sucking face and took two steps back. "I need to get my luggage from the taxi. Could you help me?"

Brenda shook her head vigorously. "Now I said you could stay, but you have to pull your own weight around here." She coughed violently and then screamed, "Al-Saadiq, go and help your cousin bring up her shit!"

Fancy saw a thirteen-year-old kid emerge with no shirt on, shorts hanging off his tiny waist, and dirty white socks. The scowl on his face was an indication that he wasn't at all happy.

"Why I gotta do it?" He then looked at Fancy. "I don't even know her!"

"Boy, what the fuck I said? Keep it up, and I'ma put my foot in ya ass!"

Begrudgingly, Al-Saadiq put on his sneakers and pushed past Fancy. The two went back downstairs, where the taxi driver, true to his word, had cut his meter back on.

Fancy now owed an additional twelve dollars. She was pissed. "Why would you cut your meter back on?"

"I have living to make. I tell you the rules before you go." He shrugged his shoulders.

Fancy paid the driver because she didn't have a choice. Her last possessions on earth were in his trunk.

As they pulled out her luggage, she couldn't help but look around for the sexy stranger from earlier. She was hoping he would still be outside and ask if he could help her with her bags, but he wasn't anywhere in sight.

# CHAPTER 10

Upstairs, Fancy was treated to a front-row seat to a cramped, roach-infested apartment. They walked in to a putrid smell. Dirty clothes littered the sofa, and sneakers, socks, and heavy jeans were tossed about. A ten-speed bike with a broken rim was propped up against the narrow hallway, leaving a smidgen of room to pass. And the stained off-white walls were decorated with cheap picture frames and posters of Young Jeezy, Jay-Z, and Jennifer Lopez.

Fancy's legs felt like they'd turn into cement. She couldn't step in any farther; she felt stuck.

Brenda saw her expression. "You just gonna stand there looking silly?"

Fancy, never knowing how to filter her comments, replied, "How can you live like this?"

"What the fuck you just say?" Brenda stretched her neck in Fancy's direction. "I know I didn't hear what I think I heard 'cuz to me it sounded like you said how could I live like this."

"That's exactly what I—"

Whack!

Brenda didn't allow Fancy to finish her sentence. She didn't tolerate any disrespect from anyone. "You might have gotten away with that shit with your momma, but if you learn one thing today, it's gonna be that I ain't your momma!"

Holding the side of her face, Fancy wasn't easily intimidated. Her parents taught her to always have a voice and say whatever she felt. She refused to be abused.

"How dare you put your hands on—"

*Whack!*

Her aunt slapped her again. "This is my muthafuckin' house, bitch! I'll tear your little spoiled ass to pieces before I let you disrespect me!"

Fancy, her eyes welled with tears, refused to fight back. Actually, she didn't know if she knew how to fight back, other than with words. "Wait until my father gets home. Just wait and see what he does to you."

Brenda was going to slap her again, but she knew her words would hurt more than any physical abuse.

"Your drug-dealing mommy and daddy ain't coming home, ever! Never, bitch! So you wait!"

"You're a liar!" Fancy screamed the words so loud and with so much conviction, three of Brenda's five children came scurrying out of the room to see the drama.

Brenda loved to put on shows. Once the kids were at attention, it upped the ante.

"You're a smart girl," Brenda replied mockingly. "You know as well as I do that the police don't arrest innocent people. You know that your parents were more crooked than that bicycle rim."

All the kids laughed, encouraging Brenda.

"Belen and Alex might have fooled everyone in their neighborhood, but out here we keep it one hundred. It was only a matter of time before your moms fell off her throne. And you know why she's fucked up right now?" Brenda didn't expect an answer from Fancy. "Because she never gave a fuck about anybody but herself, and what goes around comes back around."

Fancy wanted to turn around and run back out the front door. She really couldn't take any more abuse. And it especially hurt coming from family.

"Your mother wasn't shit." Brenda looked off then smirked as if she'd just remembered a disturbing thought. "She was a selfish, greedy bitch. All these years she's allowed my kids to suffer, to live here in squalor while they made money hand over fist. You think she would throw me a bone? Give me some money to get on my feet?"

Brenda walked over to Fancy and got up in her face. She inched up close in her personal space, pointed her finger inches from her eyeballs and stated, "I knew this day would come. I'm just glad to be here to watch her fall. And your parents will pay out their asses for my help. You better believe that one, baby."

Fancy stood in the middle of the living room, dumbfounded.

No dinner was prepared in the household. Fancy watched as everyone passed each other like strangers. She listened as the refrigerator would open and close, but no one ever came out with any food.

She sat idle on the worn, smelly sofa until, to her surprise, Brenda's oldest son came home close to three in the morning, reeking of alcohol and weed.

He stared at Fancy, which turned into a glare, slightly intimidating her. "Move," he demanded.

Fancy hesitated, as if she had a choice in the matter.

"Yo, you slow or something? I said get the fuck up. I'm tired."

Fancy stood, looked around, and then sat on the uncomfortable chair.

Nasir kicked off his sneakers and stripped down to his boxers in front of his cousin. He walked to a hallway closet and came back with a balled-up pillow and sheet and made himself comfortable on the sofa. Within seconds he was snoring.

Fancy watched as he tossed and turned on the lean, lumpy sofa. His off-white boxers, which looked like they had seen better days, were now displaying his butt crack. She looked on at his muscular frame. Anything to help pass the time.

She had no idea how long she would be in that godforsaken place, if her parents would get released, or if things would go back to normal.

When Nasir shifted again, his long, heavy penis poked its head through the slit in his boxers. The vision was more than Fancy could tolerate. At first she turned her head, repulsed that she was staring at family. But after a few minutes she found herself unable to turn away. She watched as his chest heaved up and down peacefully, as if he didn't have a care in the world. She wondered how could someone in his circumstance be able to find peace, even in his sleep? That thought worried her, and she began to quietly cry. Would this lifestyle be her new existence?

Through her tears, Fancy could see activity. There was an infestation of roaches crawling up and down walls, one even falling from the sky to land on her exposed arm. When this happened, she leapt to her feet in horror, doing what appeared to be a rain dance. The nastiness of the household made her skin crawl, but nothing prepared her for what happened next.

Right before daybreak, her stomach couldn't hold out any longer. She was starving. She finally convinced herself to eat in the disgusting environment, even if only a sandwich. In desperation she walked to the kitchen, clicked on the light, and saw two mice on top of the countertop nibbling on crumbs. Her heart stopped for a second. She was mortified. She wanted to scream out, but the horror snatched her breath away.

Slowly, Fancy backpedaled out of the kitchen and out the front door. She needed to think and clear her head.

Outside, in the fresh air, the sun was just rising. She walked aimlessly around the neighborhood and came up on a park. The streets were busy with adults going to work and panhandlers begging for spare change.

Within minutes of sunrise the air became sultry. She was so hungry and almost dehydrated as she hadn't had food or water in almost twenty hours. She saw the golden arches in the distance and headed that way. As she passed by a corner store with an outside newsstand, there, splashed across the *Post* newspaper was a picture of her parents. She gasped.

"After a long investigation, federal agents have confirmed that a federal magistrate has issued more indictments on members of the Lane Cartel. Sources say several more informants came forward with information after federal authorities arrested Alexandro and Belen Lane, a prominent Long Island businessman and his wife, on several felony counts. The two were apprehended at their sprawling mansion after picking up their daughter from JFK Airport, who was allegedly on holiday in Paris, France. Off record, police wouldn't confirm or deny if the daughter's trip had anything to do with her parents' organization.

*"The big break came in the case after an unnamed informant tipped off the police to the ringleader, Alexandro Lane. The informant was subsequently murdered before Alexandro Lane could be brought to justice. But the police had set up surveillance and uncovered that Lane's wife, Belen, was second in command. The police won't confirm or deny that the couple had anything to do with the murder of the informant."*

"Ma'am, either buy the paper or get lost," the Pakistani storeowner demanded.

Fancy looked up at him with contempt. "Why would I buy this trash? It's filled with lies!" She tossed the paper and forgot about purchasing something to eat. Instantly she'd lost her appetite.

When she got back to her aunt's house, the two middle children, fourteen-year-old Lisa and thirteen-year-old Al-Saadiq, were sitting on the floor in the living room watching the news discuss the apprehension and arrest of their aunt and uncle. She caught the tail end of the story.

"What did they say about my parents?" Fancy asked.

Al-Saadiq was eager to reply. "They snitchin'."

"I know. They have someone cooperating with the government. What else did they say?"

"No, they said your parents are snitching on each other," Lisa said. "They trying to cut a deal, but that's so whack. Like, if it was me and somebody snitched on me, I'd have my brother kill them." The wise preteen knew a lot for her age, and none of it was what she should know. She didn't know algebra, but she knew how many dime bags fifty dollars could get you.

"Shut your little grown mouth," Fancy said. "You don't even know what you're talking about."

"Yes, I do. You just mad that don't nobody like you, ugly girl!"

Lisa would have been an easy target for Fancy to take out her frustrations on, but the sensible side of her wouldn't go there. Lisa and her siblings were products of their environment, and they hadn't chosen their parents.

# CHAPTER 11

Fancy was so used to getting her way, when Al-Saadiq told her not to wake up his mother under any circumstance, she ignored him, marching straight toward the back until she came across her aunt spread-eagled on her full-size bed, snoring. She had on a flimsy nightie and a scarf tied tightly around her head, and the room was in disarray. Beads of sweat were sliding down Brenda's face as the temperature in the house steadily approached ninety degrees.

"Aunt Brenda." Fancy waited a few seconds before calling out once again, this time more aggressively. "Aunt Brenda!"

Brenda snorted a few times before opening her eyes. Immediately, she had an attitude as she saw the accusatory glare in Fancy's eyes.

"Did you just wake me up?" Brenda asked, as she slowly tried to focus. She didn't have to ask the time because her body told her it was early.

"I think you should come with me to see my par—"

Brenda roared, "Get the fuck outta my room!"

Fancy wasn't having it. There wasn't any way she was spending another night in that hellhole. She wanted to sit face to face with her Aunt Brenda and her parents and work out better arrangements. They needed to know of the conditions she was living under, that there wasn't any place for her to sleep. And she wanted her aunt sitting inches away from her father when she told him how she was assaulted. She knew that her father would snap Brenda's neck for putting her hands on her.

"I'm not leaving until you tell me what time we're going to see my parents."

Brenda couldn't believe her ears. After yesterday's smackdown, the spoiled teenager still had the gumption to challenge her. If she wasn't dead tired, she would have given Fancy another Brooklyn beat-down.

"Bitch, is you stupid? You better get the fuck up outta my room with that bullshit. We ain't going nowhere. Keep fuckin' wit' me, and I'ma show you how to play."

Fancy thought for a moment. She sized up her aunt—lazy, rude, and bitter. She realized waiting for Brenda was a long shot.

She turned on her heels and walked back up front. Her cousin Nasir was now up. Well, technically, he had his eyes open and was watching television. He glanced at Fancy, who miraculously, he'd never officially met. Fancy studied his face. He didn't look like her Aunt Brenda, or his other siblings.

"Who are you?"

"I'm Fancy."

"Fancy? From where?"

"From Long Island." Fancy hesitated, not really understanding the relevance of his question.

"Nah. Who are you? You up in here walking around like you run this joint. I'm sayin', who let you in?" He rubbed his tired eyes. "Didn't I see you yesterday?"

Fancy was somewhat excited that he'd remembered her. "I'm your cousin, Belen's daughter."

"Oh, I thought you looked familiar. Yo, what's up with her anyway? She ain't been around in a minute."

Before Fancy could respond, Al-Saadiq said, "She locked up." Then he snickered. "Feds got her and Uncle Alex all over the news for drugs and murders."

Nasir sat straight up and focused on his little brother. His voice was crusty and deep. "Word? I was OT for a couple months, making paper. I just got back yesterday. My moms ain't tell me shit. Probably ain't wanna talk over those phones, ya know. I'm Nasir, by the way."

Fancy didn't have a clue, but she nodded anyway. "Nice to get reacquainted with you, Nasir."

"No doubt," he said with the confidence of a star athlete. "So what's really good?"

"Well, there isn't anything good, Nasir. My parents are in jail, I'm homeless, and I want your mother to go with me to visit them, but she won't get out of bed."

"Shorty, you buggin' with that shit."

"I am?"

Nasir looked in her eyes and saw an innocence that was foreign to him. He focused on his cousin. She looked tired and desperate.

"My moms ain't built like that. Before my pops got murdered, he got locked up and did a short bid, and she never held him down. It was on to the next one." He pointed toward his siblings. "Hooked up with his friend, and out popped Lisa and Saadiq. And then hooked up with his enemy and out popped the twins, Ava and Asia."

"But she's my mother's sister. That has to count for something."

"And where has your moms been at? My moms ain't real big on forgiveness, and whatever those two are beefing about is some ugly shit. And I doubt Aunt Belen catching a bid is going to mend it."

"Well, what do you think it will take to mend it?"

Nasir wanted to snap on her and ask how the fuck should he know, but he knew she was green. This was her first rodeo, and somehow he felt sympathetic.

"Look, check it. Send your moms a kite and ask her what's up. If not, then you go in person and politick. But get it through your young mind,

Brenda ain't going with you. That's a wrap, shorty."

"That's bizarre. What kind of kite?"

He chuckled. "She'll write to you telling you your next move."

At that moment, Fancy once again felt hopeless. Without warning, she burst into tears, startling her little cousins.

Nasir watched her for a moment. His heart began to soften when Lisa ran over to Fancy and began to pat her back.

"Don't cry, cousin," she said. "Your mom will come home to get you soon."

Nasir knew that if his moms was locked up, he would feel just as helpless. He reached for his jeans and pulled out two five-dollar bills. "Yo, Al-Saadiq," he said. "Go to the bodega and order two ham, egg, and cheese sandwiches."

"For who?"

"For me and Fancy. She gotta be hungry."

"Ooh, I want one!" Al-Saadiq sang.

"Me too," Lisa joined in.

"Y'all got cereal in there?"

"No, we don't. Mommy don't get her check until tomorrow."

Nasir reached back into his jeans and pulled out two tens. "A'ight, bring us all back a sandwich, and bring me back my change!"

"I don't eat pork," Fancy commented. Actually, she still didn't have an appetite.

"A'ight, order her turkey then."

Suddenly, she looked at Nasir quizzically. "I thought your mother raised you and your brothers Muslim?"

"I *am* Muslim. Why? 'Cuz I'm fuckin' with that pork?"

"Something like that."

"I don't fuck with that pork on the regular. Besides, Allah will understand. He ain't petty like that, ya know." Nasir stood up and stretched his limbs, letting out a loud grunt. He realized that Fancy wasn't anywhere close to stopping her tears.

He went to the bathroom and hopped in the shower to give her a few minutes to herself. When he emerged, she was still whimpering.

"You can't do that shit all day," he said, his tone level and matter-of-fact. "I feel your pain, but you gotta suck it up. Nobody ever promised that life would be easy. We play the hand we're dealt."

"This isn't supposed to be my life."

"Says who?"

"What?"

"Who told you that you wouldn't go through ups and downs? Just be glad that the first quarter of your life was a sunny day at the park. Now comes the rain."

"Don't minimize my life like that. It's insulting and condescending."

"Look, fuck all that smart shit you talking. Those slick words don't impress me, nor does it change the fact that you up in here, and we're now seven deep in a two-bedroom apartment. Now condescend that."

"I'm sorry, Nasir."

"For what?"

"Sounding like a spoiled brat, when all you're trying to do is shed light on my situation."

"No apology needed. I feel your pain. If anything happened to my moms, I'd flip the fuck out. And you got both your parents to worry about."

"Do you know much about situations like these?"

"Like court cases and shit?"

"Yeah. Could you walk me through what to expect?"

Nasir shrugged. "Expect the worst. That's how things go down in the drug game. You gotta plan for those rainy days and live like there's no tomorrow. If you do, when things go right, it's just biscuits and gravy."

"From what you just said, it means you're believing what the news is reporting, just like your mother."

"Real is real, and my moms is a realist just like me. But where we differ is her delivery. She could be more sensitive to your situation. Like me, I feel you. I know you really don't know shit about how your parents were tossing it up, and I don't know the details, but the only way to get answers is to ask questions."

Although Fancy dreaded going back to the jailhouse, she knew she didn't have a laundry list of options.

✳✳✳

The next night, Nasir allowed her to sleep on the sofa while he went out and purchased an air mattress. Fancy wondered who was actually getting the better deal. It didn't take her long to realize that, under her aunt's roof, she wouldn't have any luxuries or amenities.

When she awoke the next morning, her heart lurched. "Where are my suitcases?"

Nasir looked at her quizzically and then turned back over to continue his sleep.

Sheer panic overtook her body as she leapt up and went straight toward the back. Her aunt's door was closed, and to her annoyance it was also locked. *Has this lock always been here?* she thought. She thought about knocking and then relived her last incident and thought against it.

She walked into the kids' room and shuddered at the four kids piled up in two twin beds. She began searching through the small, untidy room. In sixty seconds, she knew her suitcases weren't there, but she couldn't stop searching.

She shook Lisa. "Have you seen my suitcases?"

The sleepy teen yawned wearily and tried to focus. "Huh?"

"My suitcases. Have you seen them?"

"They in the living room, right?"

She snapped. "If they were there, would I be asking?"

Lisa just stared at her cousin blankly and then pulled her oversized bloomers out of her butt crack.

Finally, Fancy gave up. She showered and then returned to the living room to wait on her Aunt Brenda.

It took Brenda hours to emerge from her bedroom. And Fancy didn't have to ask. She came prancing out wearing Fancy's hot pink Citizens of Humanity skinny jeans, with her white bebe top and white studded Jimmy Choo stilettos. She hadn't even showered. And she was toting a small plastic bag, which she tossed Fancy's way. It contained the clothing she didn't want or couldn't fit in.

"What are you doing in my clothes?"

"This here shit look better on me than it ever would on you, so don't play yourself."

Fancy jumped up in her face, but Brenda's look backed her down.

"I want my clothes back. All of them!"

"You ain't getting shit." Brenda reached for her Newport cigarette.

Fancy pushed past her aunt in an effort to retrieve her things from her room, but a strong hand grabbed her by her hair and, in one swift movement, body-slammed her to the ground. Fancy couldn't believe that her own stiletto was being used to stomp her into the dirty flooring. She tried to fight back, but Brenda was too skilled, so she did her best to try and block most of the blows.

Fancy was in the fetal position when Nasir finally got up and pulled his mother off her.

"Yo, what the fuck you doing?"

"Get off of me, Nasir. I'm giving her an ass-whipping she deserves."

"She ain't your kid, though."

Nasir helped his cousin to her feet before turning to his mother once again in disgust. "What you beating on her for anyways?"

Through a tear-stained face, Fancy managed to whisper, "She has my things, all of my clothing."

"You out here wildin' over that bullshit?" Nasir looked his mother up and down and shook his head. "Give her back her shit. You damn near fifty—"

"I ain't giving her back shit. And if y'all don't muthafuckin' like it, you know where the door is. This my fuckin' house!"

Brenda knew she looked too cute. She wasn't about to return anything. She hadn't worn anything that expensive in over two decades, so to her Fancy could kiss that shit good-bye. She walked out into the afternoon sun, her head held higher than usual.

"Don't worry, shorty. When I make some extra paper I'll take you shopping to cop a few things. Nothing crazy, but I'll do what I can."

Fancy could only nod. She knew her cousin couldn't afford the things she was used to wearing. But the fact that he offered his assistance made her feel somewhat optimistic.

# CHAPTER 12

Her parents had now been locked up for a few months, and things looked bleak. There wasn't any money, and they both had legal aid attorneys.

Answers. That's what Fancy planned to get from each parent. She had just about gotten used to the fact that they were both incarcerated, even used to the COs and inmates. She even began to get used to both her parents needing her. As someone who'd grown up in a household where everyone doted upon her, she never realized that being the caregiver would be so empowering.

Belen came walking out in her orange jumpsuit looking older than her thirty-eight years, now that the federal correctional department made her remove her weave. Her naturally thin, shoulder-length hair was braided back in unflattering cornrows. Her face looked ashy, and her eyes looked bloodshot, like she hadn't slept in weeks. Belen's midnight-black eyes did not light up when she saw her daughter, and she seemed perturbed about something.

"Mommy, what's wrong?"

"These bitches in here done got on my last fuckin' nerve," she spat as she sat down.

There was a new masculinity to her voice that was foreign to Fancy. Not to mention her newfound foul mouth. But Fancy understood. Her mother had to survive, just as she had to. She, too, had found an urban persona that was keeping her one step ahead of the game. She rationalized that it didn't matter what came out of her mouth, but what was inside her mind.

"If this one bitch keep fuckin' with me, I'ma catch a new charge."

Fancy hesitated. "Why let it get that far? Didn't Pop-Pop always say if a dog snaps at you, you have to put it down? If not, that snap will escalate into a bite. Why wait for her to handle you, when you could handle her first?"

Belen looked strangely at her daughter and got a chill. Did years of private school not shield her from the obvious messages her parents inadvertently were teaching her? Belen didn't know whether she should be proud or disappointed. She realized that the new Fancy was for the best. It was a new chapter in all their lives, so Fancy would need to be able to handle herself out on the streets without her parents' protection.

"Fancy, remember your place. I appreciate that you're trying to help, but I don't need advice from you. What I need is for you to follow directions and pass messages between your father and me. Instead, you walk out the door, and I never know when you're coming back." Belen cleared her throat. "I never thought I would give birth to a daughter who's so useless."

In all her life, Belen had never spoken to her in such a cruel manner. The harshness and tone had injured Fancy's feelings. She thought of herself as many things, but never useless.

Slowly, Fancy lifted her head and met her mother's eyes, which were glaring at her. Immediately she felt guilty. The unkind yet honest words struck a nerve. Her eyes began to well up as she gently wiped away one lone tear from her cheek. "I'm sorry, Mommy."

Belen wasn't letting her off the hook that easily. "You act like you're the one locked down."

"Huh?"

"You heard me." Belen's tone was low and menacing. "You were always spoiled and selfish."

"I'm crying for you," Fancy lied.

"For me?" Belen laughed. "I don't need your tears, Fancy. I need you to help me get out of here."

"Anything. Anything I can do to help."

"How many times have I heard those same words come out of your mouth?"

Fancy felt like she was being raped. Her mother was stripping her down to her bare bones. She decided to play the sympathy card. "I've said it a few times, but you have to understand, and before you interrupt me, I really want you to put yourself in my shoes. Aunt Brenda, Mommy, is a crazy lady. I think she's bipolar. She has these psychotic mood swings and takes out all of her frustrations on me. She's stolen *all* my good things and she hits me. Look"—She pointed to her bruised arm, which her mother had overlooked. "She's punched on me for no reason whatsoever. And it's all because she hates you."

Belen's beautiful black eyes hooded over with contempt. "You think I give a fuck about material things right now? I'm locked down in a cage like an animal, and you wanna talk about a few bumps and bruises? You need to be grateful you got a roof over your head 'cause, if you want to trade places with me, I'll be glad to oblige you. They talking about giving me the death penalty—You heard me? The fuckin' death penalty—for murders I didn't sanction."

"Oh my God!" Fancy clutched imaginary pearls. This was the first she'd heard this news. "Okay, you're right. I'm silly. Everything else is inconsequential. What can I do?"

"When you go see your father, ask him what he's gonna do."

"About what?"

"Getting me out of here, moron!"

Fancy thought for a moment. "How is he going to do that?"

"Don't concern yourself with these details. All you need to concern yourself with is doing everything I ask. And anything you and I talk about, you're not to repeat to anyone, including your Aunt Brenda. You hear me?"

"I hear you because you're speaking," Fancy snapped. She wasn't going to keep being spoken to like she was retarded.

"Now I said I need you to ask your father what the fuck he plans to do 'bout my situation. If he wanted to, he could get me up outta here."

Fancy was hurt and confused. "You mean, with the lawyer?"

"Just ask him that question and come back and tell me exactly what he says verbatim, you hear me? Just ask the question and listen. That's all."

"So tell him that you want him to—"

"No. Don't let him know that the question is coming from me. Say it like you're concerned for your mother and you want to know what the fuck he's gonna do to fix shit."

"But I don't like the idea of lying to Pop-Pop. I thought you two always taught me not to keep secrets or lie to you."

Belen wanted to slap Fancy into next week. She also wanted a cigarette and a bottle of champagne, but half those requests weren't happening.

"Do you love me?"

"Of course, I do. What kind of question is that?"

"I love you too. And I know your father loves me as well. So, as I said, ask him what I've asked of you, and come back to see me the very next day."

"I'll try to come back soon, but I don't have any money to get back here. I was hoping that you could get me some. Maybe make a few phone calls. Could you call Jacob for me?"

Belen looked at Fancy incredulously. "Get you some money? Do you realize what you just asked me? Am I not sitting in fuckin' prison?"

"Wait a minute. You're still my mother, and I'm still a minor." Suddenly Fancy was tired of being abused. "Who are you? Really? 'Cause right now I don't even know you."

Exhausted, Belen hung her head. It would take a lifetime for her to answer that question. Oddly, living the double life and keeping their true identity from people was what had kept her marriage together. The lies, deceptions, and cover-ups kept Belen and Alexandro entertained. Every time they met a couple on vacation or chatted up the clerk at a store, it gave them great pleasure and satisfaction that they were getting away with leading their double lives.

"A minor, huh? You're right. We've sheltered you and treated your big ass like you were a baby. We lived our fairytale at your expense, and now I want you to grow up and be someone you're not. You can't be me. At your age, I was orchestrating deals with men twice my age. I was running this town without a care in the world. I didn't run to Mommy for money; Mommy ran to *me* for money. We fucked up, Fancy. And if we're fucked up, that means you're fucked up. It might sound harsh, but it's real. Your parents are gangstas. That's the truth. And you're fucked."

"If you want me to help you, then you have to start being straight up with me. How do you expect Pop-Pop to get you out of here without any money for a good lawyer?"

Belen didn't look amused, but she knew she wasn't in the best position. "Well, he could be a man and step up to the plate."

Fancy smirked. Her father was a man and then some. "What do you mean by that?"

She whispered, "He could plead guilty and take the weight; say that I didn't have shit to do with any of the allegations."

Fancy was startled by her mother's wishes, but she wanted to know more. "You want him to say he's guilty and risk spending the rest of his life in jail, as in having my father never see the light of day again? As in, have him die alone in jail? Or, better yet, have him murdered by our government?"

Belen wasn't fazed by her daughter's tone. "Would you rather I take the weight and die in this bitch?"

"Let me ask you a question," Fancy began, ignoring her mother's question. "Are you innocent? Was it all Pop-Pop?"

"I dabbled," Belen said, minimizing her role. "But he was the kingpin."

Fancy didn't show any emotion. She wanted to hear the whole backstory.

"Tell me who my parents are."

In a low, monotone voice, Belen began shedding light on their situation. She told Fancy that when she met her father she was fifteen years old. He was only fourteen. By the time he reached sixteen, he had three corners on lock. She said she'd never condoned how he got his money but never blocked his growth either. It was the usual way of life in the hood. She went on to explain how he went from selling nickel vials of crack to pushing ki's of cocaine from New York to Miami. Soon his cartel was getting coke off freight boats that passed through the Panama Canal. Alexandro had even met and done business with Pablo Escobar.

As her husband's organization expanded, so did the risk. The more he tried to go legit with sound investments, the more haters came out the woodwork. Sometimes, in order to maintain control and keep his family safe, Belen explained that Alexandro had to deal with a few thugs. And by "deal with," she explained, he had to put a few contracts out on someone's life. Soon, upwards of twenty people were getting dealt with a year. Those type of numbers on bodies caused people to start running their mouths.

Belen explained that she warned Alexandro to get out of the game years ago, but he was addicted to the power and the danger. He dismissed her and her words of advice, and now indictments had been passed down and he was taking her along on the ride. She explained that her only real crime was knowing what he did for a living. She'd never gotten her hands dirty. Ever.

"Real men don't let their wives languish in jail, Fancy. You need to speak with him and tell him to fold and get me out of here."

Fancy wanted to ask both her parents what she felt was farfetched, but nonetheless, the rumor was put out there. "Do you think that Pop-Pop is snitching as the news reported?"

"He'd take a lethal needle in his arm before he would ever turn state's evidence."

Fancy knew in her heart that to be true but she still probed further. "How can you be so sure?"

"Because people's lives depend on his silence."

Fancy swallowed hard. "Really?"

"His associates would snatch those he loves up and have the FBI searching for body parts like Jimmy Hoffa."

Fancy didn't realize her hands were shaking, but they were. She realized that if her father snitched, his associates would surely hurt her mother. And there wasn't any way her father would ever take that chance.

Belen didn't stay for the full visit. In her mind Fancy was useless. She hated to be so cold, but she was facing life. And if they added the murders, she'd have a few life sentences on her jacket. She'd have to die several times before she'd be up for parole, so coddling her daughter just wasn't high on her agenda.

Fancy was now on a different mission. She now also viewed her father differently. How could he allow his wife to sit behind bars when her only crime was knowing about his organization and falling in love?

# CHAPTER 13

The intake procedure was the same when Fancy went to visit her father. Although the visit with her mother had left her confused and almost hopeless, she hoped her father would do the right thing and get his wife released from custody.

She sat hopeful as he was led inside the waiting room. Their eyes met, and he smiled, a winner's grin, and she instantly felt reassured. She knew that he would listen to what she had to say. Slowly, her tense shoulders began to relax.

As he approached, she stood to her feet. He didn't hesitate to give his daughter a full embrace. She wanted to hold onto him for dear life, but the corrections officer intervened, and they were separated. She did her best to not repeat what had happened with her mother, but a few tears did escape her eyes.

"Don't cry, Fancy," her father said lovingly.

Fancy was quiet.

"It's too complicated to lay it all on you right now. But soon all this will blow over, and things will get back to normal."

"How? We don't have a house to go back to. The federal government seized all of our things."

"Fancy, that's only materialistic. That house doesn't make us. I'll buy us a bigger, better house. A house that will make that one look like its ugly cousin." Alexandro tried to make his daughter laugh, but she continued to cry at her bleak outlook on life. "Don't waste your tears on this situation. I promise, everything is going to be all right."

"How, Pop-Pop? I've ruined our lives by not leaving with the money when you said. And Mommy doesn't say it, but she resents me for being so careless with it. She's so scary now."

"The money is gone. No need to keep reliving it." Alexandro rubbed his chin and looked off, past Fancy. "And what do you mean by scary?"

Fancy shrugged. "She's changed."

Alexandro nodded. "Rightfully so, baby girl. This is a lot to take in. But I don't want you worrying. Belen is clever and strong. She can handle herself under any circumstance. All I care about is your welfare."

"You don't have to worry about me. I'm fine."

His eyes washed over her. "How did you get those bruises?"

"I don't want to talk about it. I'm here for you." Fancy didn't want to get under her father's skin as she had done with her mother. She didn't want to seem selfish or useless, as her mother had stated.

Her father's eyes showed concern. "Who put their hands on you?"

"You promise not to get upset?"

"What did I teach you?"

She smiled. Growing up there was always a lesson, but she used to think it was all in fun. Now she realized it was some sort of preparation. "You said to never get upset. Get even."

"Exactly. Now speak."

"It's Aunt Brenda." Fancy shifted in her chair. "She's difficult to live with, to say the least. And she keeps reminding me that I'm living under her roof for free and ain't—excuse my language—shit free in life. She's taken what little bit of clothing that I had left. I'm forced to wear this same outfit because, as you know, I don't have any money. But I'm not complaining, Pop-Pop, especially considering your situation. And I promise, I'm looking for a job, so I could get some income to help take care of you and Mommy and afford you a real lawyer."

"That's a lot of responsibility, even for someone as intelligent and gifted as you," he complimented, which made her smile. "What I want you to do is think about enrolling in college next semester. You should be eligible for financial aid. Find a college that has dorms. I've been checking into Long Island University. They have a Brooklyn campus, so you won't need a vehicle. Major in something that you like and will give you great pleasure. And in the meantime get a part-time job, just something that will allow you to pay for your campus living. I don't want you worrying about your mother and me, or our legal situation, bills, lawyers, nothing. You're still a child, and I should have kept that at the forefront of my mind." He caressed her hand. "It's my fault what happened in the house with the money. I put too much responsibility on you, and I'm very sorry. You're my girl."

"And what about Mommy?"

"What?"

"Is she still your girl?"

"She's the love of my life. How could you ask such a question?"

"Well, I want her home, Pop-Pop. Jail isn't any place for her. I'm telling you, she's losing it."

"Things will work out."

"Don't talk to me like I wouldn't understand. What are you doing to ensure she comes home?"

Alexandro looked at Fancy sideways. "Did your mother tell you to talk to me?"

"No, not at all. I just can't stand to see her so depressed. I was thinking that maybe you could work something out on her behalf."

Alexandro stared at his beautiful daughter for a moment and then smiled. He loved her so much and hated the position she was placed in. All he ever wanted was the best for her, and to keep her out of harm's way.

He went over his movements repeatedly in his head and thought he could have done a couple things differently. As he looked and saw pain and confusion in Fancy's eyes, he knew that he would give his life to make her happy.

"On behalf of your mother?" Alexandro asked amusingly. "Belen will be all right. She can handle a little jail time."

Fancy was annoyed. How could her father think any woman would *want* to handle jail time, however small the timeframe? "Pop-Pop, you will make everything right, won't you?"

"On my life, I promise you that." He took his hand and lifted her chin, so she could look in his eyes. "Haven't I always taken care of my girls?"

He had a way of being so gentle with Fancy. It was a feeling that she missed dearly. She wondered if it was a good time to hear his side of the story.

"Could I ask you something?"

"Of course."

"Why are you in here? Really? You told me to believe everything people are saying about you, but I don't want to believe hearsay. I refuse. I want to hear who my father really is from my father."

"If I told you those crackers are trying to frame me, would you believe me?"

She hesitated. "I would *want* to believe you, but right now I couldn't."

"And why is that?"

"I don't know."

"Yes, you do. Think."

She realized that he was testing her, pushing her to dig deep and come up with her own answers. "Because the actions don't support your words."

"And what else?"

"Instinct," she said, almost gushing with excitement. "My instinctive nature is telling me that something isn't right."

"Always listen to that inner voice, Fancy. It might save your life one day. You hear me?"

She nodded.

Alexandro went on to tell Fancy a slightly different story than the one Belen had told, beginning with how her mother was the head of the Lane Cartel.

"See, this is why we have to do things the smart way. The feds got so many snitches telling the real story. It was your mother calling the shots, not me."

Fancy's mouth fell open. "Mommy?"

Alexandro nodded. "I did what I had to do to keep her at the top and keep the triggermen from getting at us, but baby girl, these feds ain't stupid. They want me to flip. They're offering me a get-out-of-jail-free card."

"What?" she gasped. Was her father snitching? "I can't believe this."

For Fancy the original thought that her father was a kingpin and her mother was somehow involved was hard enough, but to now hear that her mother was some sort of queenpin and her father was second-in-command to her was more than farfetched.

"Have I ever lied to you?"

She answered honestly. "I don't know."

Alexandro looked hurt. "Listen, this is a lot to handle. There's more news that I'll tell you, but only when the time is right. Don't worry about your mother. I'll fall on my sword before I allow anything to happen to her, or you."

"I just want to be clear that you are not cooperating with the government against Mommy. That's what you're telling me, right?"

"Look in my eyes." Alexandro lifted Fancy's chin. "I would do a hundred life sentences or fry in the electric chair before I would ever turn snitch."

Fancy exhaled.

"Mommy believes in you. She said so."

Those were her parting words of comfort. Fancy didn't have much more to say at the moment. She felt torn between her parents as if she were a pawn in a chess game. She wasn't playing; she was being played.

"Don't tell your mother about my disclosure to you. If she wants you to know, allow her the opportunity to tell it to you herself."

Fancy was tired of being hurt and confused. Her brain felt like scrambled eggs, and her body like soggy noodles. Slowly, she began not caring about too much other than survival.

# CHAPTER 14

"Let me tell you one muthafuckin' thing, bitch—If you ever put your fuckin' hands on my daughter again, I will have you buried where you stand. Don't think my reach is confined to this jail cell. And all her shit, return it, if you know what's really good."

That was the message Brenda received from a very angry Alexandro. The tone in his voice was enough to make her black hair gray. She wondered if his reach was that long. She didn't want to find out. She'd leave his little princess alone . . . for now.

She went to her closet and began pulling out all of Fancy's things. She stopped when she came upon the beautiful pair of Christian Louboutin shoes. Her whole being wanted to keep them. She wrestled with the idea and then relented. She knew the spoiled brat would run up on the visit and say, "She gave me everything back except my favorite pair of shoes." No, she could have all her shit back. It just wasn't worth it.

✳✳✳

When Fancy arrived back in the apartment, she saw all of her outfits piled up on the sofa. She was relieved, until she started to look through them and saw that they were stained with funk, deodorant, cigarette holes, and some God-forbidden white stains that she didn't want to know about.

She grabbed a plastic bag, dumped all of her clothing in it, and marched right back out to deposit them at the cleaners. She only hoped they could make them look good again. Next, she was on shoe duty. Her aunt had only had her things for roughly three weeks, yet each pair of shoes was worn down nearly to the sole. She certainly walked hard, as they say. Fancy had to pay fourteen dollars per shoe to get new lifts and heels, but when shoes cost five hundred and better, it was worth it.

She'd now spent the last bit of money she'd saved by doing errands for her cousin, Nasir. He'd give her two dollars to prepare his favorite meal, five dollars to iron out his jeans, ten dollars to go to the laundry mat and wash his clothes. He could easily have gotten any one of his chickenheads to do those errands for free, but he knew she needed to have some sort of cash in her pockets.

Exhausted and hungry from the long day, she grabbed a hero sandwich and grape soda—it was either that or roach-infested Chinese food—and settled down on the sofa. It was exceptionally hot outside, and inside wasn't a respite. Her only solace was that she had the house to herself. With four kids screaming and acting crazy all day, she jumped on any chance she got to be alone.

Bored, she began looking through Nasir's movie collection, all of which were basically in the urban genre. She started off with *Casino*. And then *Scarface*, *Once Upon a Time in America*, *The Godfather*, and last, *American Gangster* with Denzel Washington.

That last movie resonated with her, and she couldn't understand why. Was Alexandro an American gangster, just as Frank Lucas? The picture was loosely based on a true story. Was Frank Lucas even the real mastermind, or was it his wife, the innocent-looking Hispanic woman portrayed in the movie? They say truth is stranger than fiction, but was everyone led to believe that Frank was the head of his organization when, in reality, it was wifey? It didn't matter. Because the world told Frank's story, not his wife's.

Fancy wondered if anyone would ever tell her father's story. And then another thought crept in. Would anyone ever tell hers?

## KIM K.

She sat back and began analyzing the whole drug game. What was Nasir doing that she couldn't? Okay, he knew how to cook up crack. Well, she could learn. She would get Nasir to teach her. She was good in math, so she could certainly measure coke on a triple beam scale.

Since Nasir ruled his workers with fear, how would she be able to prove to them that she had heart and that they'd better fear her? At the moment, she didn't have an answer, so for the time being, she let her ambitions fade to the back of her mind.

# CHAPTER 15

The front stoop of Halsey was littered with people, many of whom didn't even live in the building. Loud music bumped from the speakers of trucks and cars as everyone enjoyed the late-night summer breeze. An eleven-year-old girl without supervision was vigilantly looking for action, never mind it was almost midnight, her eyes glued on the young baller in the Yukon truck.

Fancy made her way through the crowd and upstairs to her aunt's apartment, where weed smoke filled the hallways as Hugo and Solange passed their blunt. It was a regular day in the hood.

She walked in to see Shoe-Shine, and her heart skipped a beat. They made eye contact, but that was it. Neither one of them said anything to the other.

"Yo, who that?" Nasir called out from the kitchen when he heard the door slam shut.

"It's me, Fancy."

"Where the fuck you been?" he asked, his head peeking out from the kitchen.

"Excuse me?" Fancy refused to be played like a child in front of her crush.

"You heard me. We ain't heard from you all day."

She looked in his eyes and saw sincerity. He was worried. He still thought she wasn't built to survive in his neighborhood.

"My bad. I was gonna go to the museum but just decided to walk through Harlem."

"Harlem? What the fuck's out there?" Shoe-Shine asked.

Fancy wondered if he was jealous. "My business," she replied coyly. "Why you asking?"

"'Cause you could get into some trouble, and then Nasir would have to murk somethin'."

"Is that the only reason?"

He laughed. "Go 'head with that shit."

Fancy stood around in awkward silence, thinking of a reply. When she couldn't think of anything witty, she walked into the kitchen, where she saw Nasir cooking up crack, an every-week occurrence in that household. The house was saturated with the distinct fumes, and no one seemed to find it strange that dinner pots and pans were used to cook drugs too.

She started to not notice she was living in a crack house/stash house. They'd made it all seem so very casual. It was like she'd adjusted to her situation overnight.

"How much you cooking up?"

"A half a ki."

"You got buyers?"

"No doubt. All this shit will be gone tonight. Sha-Born is copping three ounces, I gotta hit off my li'l mans and them."

"The corner boys?"

"Yeah, my niggas who hug the block. That's where I make the largest profit."

Fancy thought for a moment. "How much do you net off each kilo?"

"Whatchu mean?" Nasir was still stirring the liquidized cocaine.

"After you deduct the cost from your supplier, how much do you make?"

He thought for a second. "I make two hundred off each ounce I sell, and I usually sell five ounces off each ki, so that's one large. And the remaining three ounces I cook up and put it on the blocks. I make about twenty-eight hundred off that, give or take a couple dollars if one of them knuckleheads come up short."

"How long does it take to sell through the three ounces that you put on the block?"

"About a week."

"And it takes you less than an hour to sell five ounces?"

"What are you gettin' at, shorty?"

"Just answer the question. How long does it take, and would you be able to get more customers?"

"Well, as soon as I get the coke, like I said, I have the buyers already lined up, so I unload that shit soon as I pull it off the scale. Niggas around here don't have any connects, so they come and holla at me 'cuz I got a relationship with Tone, this Colombian cat that don't trust no fuckin' body. I met dude when I did a short bid up north. And real recognize real, so he's been hitting me off for a year now."

"So, theoretically, you'd move the half ki in one night?"

"No doubt."

"So why bother with the low-level stuff? It takes you hours to cook up the coke, cut it up into the nickel vials of crack, and you wait a week to get your money, which comes in small installments and is more than likely to be short. And, most of all, look at the risk you take when one of them gets knocked. You have to have bail money and also pray like hell they don't snitch you out."

"A snitch is a snitch. They don't come with a warning tattooed on their forehead. A snitch can be at any level. Look how your parents got jammed up."

"But you know what I mean. I'd rather do time for some real shit, like building the empire my parents did, than to do life for some petty hand-to-hand crime. You still living in the hood and making peanuts but could ultimately face those same football numbers. You feel me?"

Nasir's eyes grew wide. He was feeling her. "But this is what I do. I cook coke better than any chef in the kitchen. This is my thing. People come to me sometimes just to cook up their rock 'cuz I make it come back like nobody else in this game."

"So, the coke-cooking Oscar goes to you. Now what? Like, who cares, other than your ego, that you can whip up some crack? Isn't this game all about money? Don't you want to be rich?"

Shoe-Shine walked in just in time to hear the tail end of their conversation. "Who wants to be rich?"

"We were just talking shit," Fancy replied. "But what about you? Do you want to be rich?"

"Shit, I *am* rich. I can cop any sneakers I want when I want. Take any shorty out and treat her to a good time. Smoke all the weed I want, toss it up in any club, keep the latest gear, and got my own ride. Niggas out here ain't living like me at my age."

"True that," Nasir agreed.

"That's ghetto riches. Don't you two want to be wealthy? Have that insane, fuck-you money?"

They both looked at Fancy and saw something in her eyes. She wanted more than that at the moment. Both men were content with grossing a few thousand a month, but that type of paper wasn't what she had in mind.

Nasir replied, "In due time, Fancy. We're on the come-up. In due time . . . "

Soon the house was filled with Nasir's cronies. Scooter and Lucky had joined them. They all were congregating in the living room, talking shit, cell phones ringing off the hook, music blaring in the small apartment, and blunts being passed around.

Fancy sat across the room, her eyes glued on Shoe-Shine. She watched as he inhaled the purple haze weed, the way his wet lips took a swig from his Heineken bottle, and how small his eyes appeared when he smiled. She couldn't understand the strong attraction she felt for him. He certainly wasn't the type of guy she was used to, but she figured, perhaps that was the allure—He was a bad boy who did bad things.

"Yo, Fancy, why you never told us who your father was?" Scooter asked, pulling her out of her trance.

"Excuse?"

"Your pops. My man got jammed up, and he's in MCC. He kept talking about this Colombian cat who just got knocked that made the papers. He said your father supplied at least twenty-five states with coke. His money was so long that he had the Coast Guard on his payroll."

"I told you my uncle was runnin' shit," Nasir replied, answering the question for Fancy. "And my aunt too. Y'all niggas thought I was just talking shit."

"So why you never copped from them?" Scooter asked. "You copping from Tone, and Tone was probably copping from them. You definitely coulda gotten a better number."

Fancy wanted to impress Shoe-Shine. "My father would have never done business with Nasir."

Nasir didn't like the implication that he was low-level. "What the fuck you mean by that?"

"He wouldn't. He would never have wanted you to end up where he is. He loved you too much. He talked about you all the time."

Fancy's lie made Nasir smile. Since his friends were praising his uncle, that respect was automatically transferred to him.

"I tried to tell these niggas how cool your father and I used to be. But my moms came in between that with her bullshit. I remember when I was little he came around here all the time to swoop me up after my father got murdered."

Fancy could have indulged in Nasir's delusion all night if it meant she could be around Shoe-Shine.

"Did you know my father?"

"Who, me?" Shoe-Shine asked.

"Yeah. Did you ever meet him when he came around?"

Asking Shoe-Shine such a direct question didn't sit well with Nasir. He wasn't a dumb muthafucka and knew that his little cousin was hot in her panties for his man.

"Nah, we ain't ever meet."

Nasir decided to break up their little powwow and abruptly stated, "Y'all niggas gotta get up outta here. Fancy has to go to bed."

"What? Stop playing me. I ain't a kid, Nasir."

"I ain't asking you if it's your bedtime, I'm telling you that it is. And I ain't asking these niggas to leave, I just told them to get the fuck up outta here."

That's how Nasir was, always flipping, and his friends were used to his mood swings.

But out of his whole crew, Shoe-Shine knew him best. He knew that Nasir was protecting his cousin, and rightfully so. He would fuck the shit out of Fancy and break her little young heart and never look back. She didn't know what she was getting herself into.

Shoe-Shine gave Nasir dap, and all three guys peeled out, leaving Fancy frustrated.

When they left, Nasir told Fancy, "Stop flirting wit' my man, or else." His eyes, cold and flat, focused on her in an accusatory manner.

"I could flirt with whoever I want."

"You heard what the fuck I just said!"

Nasir grabbed Fancy by her arm and pulled her in real close. He was breathing hard as her ripe nipples pressed ever so slightly up against his muscular pecs. They stared at each other for a long moment before he released her arm and stepped back.

"I'm sorry for grabbing you."

She didn't say a word.

"Listen, I'm going to check Samantha." Nasir looked down toward the floor and began adjusting his jeans.

Fancy wondered if his dick had gotten hard at their exchange.

"Do me a favor and clean up this shit. I don't want the kids seeing it in the morning."

As Fancy cleaned up all the drug residue, she wondered what had just transpired with her and her cousin. It was wrong. He was forbidden. But she couldn't deny that there was an underlying sexual tension.

# CHAPTER 16

The next night Fancy came home and noticed that her aunt wasn't home yet, nor were the twins Asia and Ava, Lisa, or Al-Saadiq. She wondered if that meant she could sleep in a real bed tonight.

She got in the hot shower, and as the water cascaded down her body, she wondered what it would feel like to have Shoe-Shine's hands touch her body. She slid her fingers between her legs and massaged her clit, while her hand groped her large breasts. She wanted to experience him so badly but wasn't sure if he felt the same way. She stayed in the shower almost an hour trying to please herself.

The gray sweatpants and spaghetti string T-shirt was her pajamas, despite the sweltering temperatures. That outfit was at the command of Nasir, who'd told her he would put his foot in her ass if she came out during bedtime in anything remotely provocative. She also took heed to not make the same mistake twice of trying to seduce Shoe-Shine in front of Nasir.

As she grabbed the blanket and pillow out of the hall closet, she could hear voices. Walking down the narrow hall into the living room, she noticed a triple beam scale, drugs, drug paraphernalia, and the distinct odor of cocaine being cooked.

"What's up, Lucky? What's up, Scooter?"

"Whaddup," they both replied, all eyes upon her.

"Nasir, is your moms coming home tonight?"

"Nah, and she said to tell you not to sleep in either room."

"Why?"

"Because it's her shit. I dunno. When she comes through, ask her."

Fancy could see that no one was going to make room on the sofa, so she took the liberty of squeezing in between Shoe-Shine and Lucky.

Nasir noticed her move. "Fancy, do me a favor."

"Anything."

"Come in here and help me cook up this crack rock. That way, we can bag this shit up quickly, and I can get these niggas up outta here, so you can get some sleep."

She wanted to tell him that she wasn't in any rush to have Shoe-Shine leave but didn't want to sound desperate.

Inside the kitchen, which was only a few feet away from the living room, Nasir gave Fancy the CliffsNotes version of how to cook crack.

"Keep this pot on high, and as the coke liquefies, I want you to keep rotating the pot. When the liquid turns a butter color, run it under cold water, and it will become solid. Got it?"

Fancy nodded.

"You sure?"

She chuckled. She'd gotten all A's in chemistry, calculus, and biology, so cooking coke shouldn't be a problem.

"Oh, by the way, make sure you use this mask. Don't want you catching a contact high and become a fiend because, fam or no fam, you steal my product, and I'll rock you to sleep."

Their eyes met, and she knew he was serious. That was Nasir's way. One moment he was showing concern; the next minute he was threatening her life. Sometimes he frightened her. More than her father ever could.

Fancy's hands almost trembled as she cooked up the drugs. She didn't want to think about how rapidly her life had changed in a matter of months. She was poor and now participating in the cocaine business. She cooked up the coke and brought the large rock to her cousin to break down into small nickel- and dime-pieces.

Inside the living room, in between cutting up the drugs, a slight disagreement had begun. All four guys, now high off weed and Heineken, were in a heated debate.

"Muthafucka, I know you ain't talkin' 'bout my shorty," Nasir said.

"Yo, pa, she ain't yours. I keep tryin' to tell you that," Scooter replied. "That bitch sucked my dick last night, and I'm going back tonight for more."

"She sucked your dick last night?" Nasir asked. "So you telling me that you violated my girl, knowing she was my girl?"

"If she is your girl, she wasn't last night."

The room erupted in laughter.

"You bullshittin'." Nasir cut his eyes toward Scooter. "Tell me you just fuckin' 'round, and we'll be square."

"Hell nah, I ain't fuckin' around. Go over there and you'll see. She won't be able to walk straight for weeks 'cause I was knee-deep up in that pussy."

"Oh, word?" Nasir stood and towered over Scooter, and suddenly the room stopped laughing, realizing he was serious.

"Yo, be easy, Nasir." Scooter was puzzled. "You ain't serious?"

"Why I ain't?"

"'Cause you know how shorty get down. I mean, you wouldn't wife nothin' like that."

No one knew it, but wife her was exactly what Nasir wanted to do. He knew that Samantha had a rep, but he'd fallen for her anyway. Foolishly, he'd thought he could turn a ho into a housewife. He'd fucked her yesterday too, and she'd promised him that she wouldn't give his pussy away, so to hear from his boy that he'd just fucked her really got under Nasir's skin.

"So you calling me a stupid muthafucka, then, right?"

"Nah, he ain't even tryin' to go there," Shoe-Shine interjected, trying to defuse the situation. "He just saying, had he known she was really your girl, he woulda—"

"He woulda what?" Nasir barked. "Let the man speak for himself. He a grown man. He put on his pants one leg at a time like the rest of us do. He don't need a mouthpiece."

"I'm just saying—"

"You just saying what?" Nasir's dark eyes looked like he was possessed. "Say what the fuck you trying to say. Ain't nobody stopping you."

Maybe it was the weed, or the Heineken that had given Scooter the courage to stand up to Nasir, but nevertheless, he didn't appreciate being barked on in front of his boys.

"Yo, who the fuck you think you talking to? You ain't got no kids up in this muthafucka. You think you the only nigga wit' a gun? Yeah, I fucked your bitch. What the fuck you gonna do about it?"

Scooter went to reach in the back of his jeans to pull out his burner, but he was too slow. Nasir already had his gat in his hand, and quicker than you could blink, he put a bullet in Scooter's head. The gun let off a low *pop!*—almost sounding like a firecracker—and Scooter's head jerked once. He took a couple steps backward and slowly sat down on the sofa. Softly, he began to sing an old Marvin Gaye song as his eyes closed and his head lolled to one side. If you weren't there to see it for yourself, you probably wouldn't believe it.

Fancy was in shock, frozen in place. *Did I just witness a murder?*

Lucky went to check on his man. He felt for a pulse and then confirmed the obvious. "Yo, this nigga dead."

*Dead? That easily?* Fancy peered at the small bullet hole in his head. It was about the size of a dime with little to no blood visible. He almost looked peaceful. *Is this what death looks like?* As she exhaled, she was almost glad she'd witnessed death. She thought it would be scarier. It almost seemed poetic. In fact, the argument between them had been more intimidating.

"Now what the fuck we gonna do?" Shoe-Shine asked.

"We gotta get him the fuck up outta here before my moms come home in the morning."

"And do what with him?"

"I know you ain't say no stupid shit like that." Nasir was about to lose it again. "What the fuck you think?"

In the midst of all the turmoil, Shoe-Shine still tried to be funny. "I don't want that dead nigga in my car. I ain't fuckin' around either. Geico has a clause in my contract that says no dead muthafuckas allowed."

"Fancy, go get me a blanket—"

She shook her head.

Nasir hollered, "Now is not the time to get shook. Do what the fuck I just told you, you stupid-ass bitch!"

"No. You wrap him in a blanket, and it seems all good, until his body is found. The first thing five-0 will do is run a DNA test on that blanket. They can pull shit off of things you never thought existed. If you need to wrap up the wound, use his T-shirt."

"Check out the brains on my li'l cousin," Nasir replied. "A'ight, she's right. I don't know what the fuck I was thinking. Shoe-Shine, go pull your ride up front, and if any of those hot-ass little girls are still out there, make them take their asses in the house. I want it to be a ghost town when we load him up. You feel me?"

Shoe-Shine nodded.

"We gonna dump his stupid ass in Howard Beach. There's this spot I know of that the mob used to use back in the day. That area is still on the low. We'll be there in twenty minutes."

After everyone had left, Fancy thought she'd be too hyped to fall asleep, but she wasn't. Her eyes slowly drifted shut on the very sofa where the murder had just been committed. Today was a big day for her. She'd cooked cocaine, witnessed a murder, and turned eighteen.

✳✳✳

At six in the morning, Nasir gently tapped Fancy on her shoulder. Groggily, she woke up. "You want the sofa?"

"Nah, you could sleep there." he said as he grabbed his inflatable bed on the floor next to her. He sat down and lovingly brushed her hair out of her face. "You know you really are beautiful."

His stare made her feel uncomfortable. And the way her pussy began to pulsate didn't help ease her anxieties. He stroked her face until she removed his hand.

"Today, you gotta take Scooter's place, hugging the block."

"What? I'm not going out there." She sat straight up. "Are you crazy?"

"This ain't a debate, it's an order. Everyone helps out in this household, and that means you too."

"Nasir, I can't—"

He silenced her with a cold, hard stare.

Fancy couldn't go back to sleep. How on earth would she be able to stand on the block and sell drugs? Finally, after thinking about it, her mind and heart warmed to the idea. But she needed to ask a question first.

"Nasir," she called.

She could hear him snoring. She turned and shook him, softly at first, and then violently, until he woke up.

"Do I get paid?"

"You woke me up for that?" he grumpily replied.

"Well, do I?"

"Yeah, damn."

Now she could go back to sleep. She would be making her own money, which was music to her ears. Hopefully, she would be able to save up just enough to buy her own half a ki of coke. And from there, the sky would be the limit. She only wondered why she hadn't thought of it sooner.

# CHAPTER 17

Fancy stood inches away from the dirty window, looking out toward the corner avenue. In a few hours she would be posted up with twenty vials of crack and twenty bags of purple haze weed. Today would mark the first day she would officially join the drug game. She was starting at entry level but hoped to work her way up.

Her Aunt Brenda had told her that all adults in the house had to make their own livings. It didn't matter that Brenda had dragged her down to the state Department of Welfare and put Fancy on the household budget. The government would give Brenda ninety dollars a month in cash and one hundred and ten dollars a month in food assistance for her niece until she was twenty-one years old, provided she was enrolled in school. Either that, or she got pregnant and had a baby. Then she could get her own assistance until the child turned eighteen.

Most young girls in the neighborhood used pregnancy as a way to independence. They thought that, once they got pregnant, they'd quickly be emancipated. Living at poverty level while pregnant, one could get government money and low-income housing. But welfare was actually the opposite—an oppressive mechanism to keep those born into poverty from striving to get out of the hood. So year in and out, the deceived received free money; kibbles and bits of what they thought was the American dream.

No, Fancy wanted more. Her aunt could receive those little pennies welfare was tossing her way, as long as it kept her off Fancy's back.

Fancy wanted to make real money. Her cousin Nasir was on the come-up, and she wanted to be a part of the ride.

"Whatchu staring at?"

Fancy turned to face Nasir, who was standing in his boxers and tube socks. She wondered if he realized that his large penis was always slightly on display. She had trained her eyes to look past his manhood and concentrate on anything above the waist.

"Just readying myself for later."

"You ain't scared, are you?"

"Nah, not at all." She shook her head. "I should be fine, right? I mean, everyone will know that I'm slinging for you, so they won't try anything, right?"

"They know better than to fuck with my workers, let alone my blood. I'd lay this whole block down."

Nasir knew how to say the right words with just enough menace and reassurance in his voice.

"That's what I thought."

"Don't worry. I'll be checking on you from time to time. I'm like a repo guy. I'll creep up on you when you least expect it."

At one o'clock, Fancy sauntered across the street and stood on her post. She'd just relieved Li'l Manny and was waiting for her first sale. She looked more like she was waiting on a date than the next customer. Her black leggings only cost ten bucks, but they hugged her curves like a glove, and her shape could entice the most faithful. Besides, the five-dollar long-sleeved T-shirt that she'd taken a pair of scissors to made a fashion statement, and her Christian Louboutin's, a staple on her feet, upgraded the outfit by at least a grand. The cropped faux fur jacket gave her an upgraded appeal.

Fancy sat perched on the stoop across from her apartment building and waited for the functioning addicts to come through or the fiends to come out for their next hit. In her small purse was her forty units of drugs with a street value of four hundred dollars. She watched as a few known addicts walked right past her. They'd cut their eyes in her direction but wouldn't make a move to come near her.

After about an hour in the steady sun without making one sale, Fancy was spent. It was an exceptionally warm day for the fall season, and the faux fur was stifling. Sweat began to trickle down her back, and small beads of perspiration formed around her hairline. She wanted to go inside the corner store to cool off and also purchase a grape juice, but she couldn't chance missing a sale.

As one hour turned into two, she knew Nasir was going to be pissed if she walked back into the apartment without selling off the product. And where was he anyway? She kept looking up at their window but saw no movement. She stood up and stretched her restless muscles.

"A closed mouth don't get fed," someone said.

She spun around to see Shoe-Shine. "Huh?"

"You can't make a sale like that, posted up here like you're a supermodel or something. I mean, you look good as hell, but that's not how you get paid, unless you selling something else," he joked.

She blushed at the insinuation. "I don't know what I'm doing wrong."

"How long you been out here?"

"Almost three hours."

He glanced down at his watch. "How much you sold?"

She shook her head. "Nothing."

"Ah, man, you bugging. Give me a sec, and I'll show you how to hustle."

Shoe-Shine did a slow jog into the corner store and came out with a Snapple for Fancy. That gesture alone made her fall deeper in lust with him. Appreciatively, she took the cold drink.

Within seconds, she heard, "Yo, what you need? What you lookin' for?"

Two young shorties were on their way past. "Shoe-Shine, whaddup, man? I'm lookin' for that haze."

Shoe-Shine nodded toward Fancy. "She got what you need, all day, every day, ya heard? Tell your friends."

"Yo, we saw shorty earlier, but we didn't know."

"Well, now you know."

The two young guys both copped a bag each of the weed. The two crisp twenty-dollar bills felt like hope in her inexperienced hands.

Shoe-Shine, a lieutenant in Nasir's organization, sat with Fancy until she'd sold off her whole package, a risk he didn't have to take. Fancy was intelligent enough to know that he only took that risk because he felt something for her, even if he was too stubborn to say it.

"Thanks, Shoe-Shine, for everything."

"I'm only doing my job."

"I don't think so. I think you went above and beyond the call of duty." Fancy looked him directly in his eyes. "And you're like the mayor of Brownsville, and yet you chilled with me."

Shoe-Shine chuckled. "*Freakin'?*" He continued to laugh. "You still got some time before suburbia is completely out of your system."

"I know a way you could help knock it out my system."

That last line made Shoe-Shine backpedal. He knew what she wanted from him, but he also knew that he couldn't give it to her. Shoe-Shine was an infamous womanizer, and the last thing he wanted to do was bang Nasir's cousin and then toss her away. He knew that it would cause dissension between him and his boy, and he didn't want to go to war with his boss. He skillfully averted the topic.

"Yo, you good, right? 'Cause I gotta jet."

Fancy exhaled. She knew he could only run from her for so long before he gave in.

# CHAPTER 18

I f Fancy thought she was going to have a fall romance, at this point, things seemed bleak. She didn't understand what the problem was. She was pretty, smart, sexy, and available. Each night her hormones were blazing when she went to bed. She did everything to seduce Shoe-Shine, but he would always freeze up. She knew that Nasir had a big problem with them hooking up but felt that Shoe-Shine was his own man. Although he was second in command to Nasir, she didn't really see him fearing Nasir as the others did. They were equals in her eyes, so why didn't he push up?

Day in and out, Shoe-Shine came around to handle business with her cousin. Sometimes he would linger and watch her, occasionally chatting her up and giving her compliments. "You know you're gorgeous, don't you, Fancy?" he would say. Other times he would pretend she wasn't even in the room, sending her on an emotional roller coaster with his mixed signals.

Today she dressed in her best outfit and waited for him to come through. As usual she didn't have anything to do. She hadn't made any new girlfriends since her parents were arrested. Her new friends were Nasir's crew. She began sitting in on their weekly meetings and giving input. Her cousin had pulled her from the block almost as quickly as he put her there. He'd recruited a new shorty, a kid named Nicholas. He was a rough-looking teen with battle scars and an alcohol problem, but he showed up on time, and so far he hadn't shorted Nasir's paper.

Fancy was back to being broke, and she didn't like being on that island. She was back to relying on Nasir to clothe and feed her, which he didn't seem to mind doing.

She watched as Nasir counted and recounted eight thousand dollars and placed the stacks of paper into rubber bands. It was the wholesale price for the half ki he needed to purchase.

"Y'all headed uptown?" Fancy asked.

Nasir nodded, still concentrating on the task at hand.

Fancy looked around and saw a couple pistols on the coffee table and could see the gun imprint in everyone's waistbands.

"I wanna go too," she said.

Nasir stopped counting. "For what?"

"Just to go, for whatever."

Shoe-Shine said, "Nah, shorty, you can't ride wit' us. This trip ain't for kids."

Nasir cut his eyes and looked at Shoe-Shine sideways. "Since when you runnin' shit?"

Shoe-Shine was a little shocked. He thought that Nasir would never permit Fancy to ride along for a couple reasons. First, he didn't think Nasir would allow her in his presence for that long, and second, they were going to do grown men business with real thugs. Anything could jump off.

"I just thought—"

"She a'ight. She could come. Ain't shit gonna happen to her. Not on my watch."

Nasir looked at Fancy, and she almost blushed. The two stared at each other for a long moment, making others in the room feel slightly uncomfortable.

The ride uptown was a tense one. Fancy sat in the back in between Lucky and Nicholas, while Shoe-Shine drove and Nasir rode shotgun. For the entire ride, Shoe-Shine glared at Fancy through the rearview mirror.

At first she felt intimidated. And then soon she began rolling her eyes and smirking.

Nicholas noticed the gestures and became confused. He decided not to get into grown folks' business. He was just coming along for the ride too, and to make sure his bosses were okay if shit jumped off.

The five jumped out of the Tahoe jeep and stretched their cramped limbs.

Nasir looked to Lucky and Nicholas. "Y'all niggas stay here. He don't like a lot of muthafuckas in his crib. But be alert. If you see anything suspicious, lay a nigga down and rock them to sleep. Shoot first and don't give a fuck 'bout asking any questions."

Both guys nodded.

Fancy stood hopeful in her form-fitting dress and stilettos, hoping she could go and watch firsthand how a drug deal of this magnitude really went down.

Nasir must have read her mind. "You can come with us."

Inside Tone's stash house up on 127th Street sat him and two goons. When Fancy walked in, her eyes began to scan each room. She saw several money counters, an expensive camera system, machine guns, paraphernalia, and one big-ass pit bull. Immediately she took several steps back, until she was flush against the wall, her heart beating rapidly.

Everyone broke out into laughter just as Tone came from out back. He stopped and stared at Fancy, and his eyes scanned her body from toe to head. He turned to face Nasir.

"You brought wifey?"

"Nah, that's my cousin Fancy."

"Oh, you Fancy, huh?" he sang, like the rap song.

She smiled.

Tone looked toward one of his goons. "Yo, go put Big Pun in the back. Can't you see we in the presence of a lady?"

His worker nodded, grabbed the dog by the collar, and headed toward the back.

Everyone took seats on the sofa and chairs inside the small living room. Tone had the obligatory amenities of any drug hideout spot—flat-screen TV, leather furniture, and hi-tech computer and sound systems. If he thought Fancy would be impressed, he was mistaken.

"You want something to drink?"

Fancy shrugged. "Okay. I don't want to put you to any trouble."

"Pedro." Tone stood up. "In fact, I want to get it myself. What you drinkin' on, ma?"

Everyone was shocked at the attention Fancy was garnering from Tone, who everyone in the room knew had a lady he was crazy about. Not to mention, they were there for business. It was supposed to be an in-and-out transaction.

Fancy was loving the attention. She cut her eyes toward Shoe-Shine. His jawbone was clenched so tightly, she thought he'd shatter all his teeth in his mouth.

She was now in full flirt mode. "You choose something for me."

"You trust me like that?"

"I do."

Tone ran into his kitchen, took a few minutes, and then came back with a champagne glass. "It's a mimosa. I mean, I didn't squeeze the orange juice myself, but I hope you like it anyways."

"I'm sure it'll be the best I ever had."

"Yo, could we get down to business?" Shoe-Shine interrupted. "We got a long drive back to BK."

Tone looked toward Nasir and smirked.

"That nigga been buggin' all day. Don't pay him no mind. He think females are only supposed to be in the kitchen and bedroom, so he ain't feeling my cuz right now."

Tone knew there was more to it than that. He knew Shoe-Shine wanted to hit that, as he did.

Fancy watched as the men conducted the business. Money was exchanged, and a half a ki of coke was purchased. She knew she should mind her own business, but she liked expensive things, and since Nasir was her only source of income, he needed expansion.

"What about consignment?"

The room went silent. Everyone looked at Fancy like she had two heads.

"I don't do consignment," Nasir replied. "And, Fancy, stay in your lane."

The mimosa had Fancy feeling nice. "And why not? You'll sell this shit off tonight and you'll be coming back tomorrow? Taking all that risk driving up and down the highway dirty? Isn't that what dealers call hustling backwards?"

The room erupted in laughter, mostly because she still had that suburban twang.

But Fancy wasn't going to let a little laughter silence her. "Why y'all laughing? I have it all figured out."

Tone's interest was piqued. He loved a hustler, male or female, and he was feeling her. She looked out of place and sounded out of place, and the combination was alluring.

"Sit down, love. Tell me what's on your mind."

Fancy walked back to the sofa and sat down. She had Tone's undivided attention.

"Well, I was thinking you could front my cousin a ki of cocaine and give him some time to move it. Maybe a week should be good." She looked toward Nasir, who stood silent. "He has customers lined up to purchase the powder, but he feels he makes the most profit from the crack rock. And that's true. But time equals money, and when you run the numbers, providing that you give us the ki at a good number, he could move more weight in a shorter period of time and come out ahead. If he could grow to moving eight to ten ki's a week, he could be set."

That last line made Tone snicker at her innocence. "Nasir, how do you feel about this?"

"We've been politicking about this for a minute now, but I ain't make a decision yet."

"Seem like shorty made it for you," Tone said. "Pedro, go in the back and get Nasir two ki's."

Pedro immediately went toward the back.

Tone continued, "I ain't fuck wit' consignment since the late nineties. You know how many niggas got their lights put out over that shit?"

"I feel you," Nasir said. "But I ain't the average nigga. Whatever I walk outta here with today I'm good for."

Shoe-Shine said, "Nasir, this ain't even you, man. How many times you warned me about that consignment shit? It's too much of a risk. Fancy is bugging, yo. I know she blood, but she don't know this game."

"She grew up around the best that ever did it," Nasir replied. "She know something. She probably know shit she don't even know she knows."

Before they left, the handsome bossman asked Fancy if he could have her telephone number, and she obliged, forgetting all about Shoe-Shine for the moment.

# CHAPTER 19

The next two weeks passed swiftly, with Nasir and his crew moving more weight than ever, and Fancy and Tone's relationship moving at the same swift speed. Tone had managed to sweep Fancy off her feet. Now every morning when she woke up, she felt like she was walking on air. She was no longer sweating Shoe-Shine, who she considered to be nothing more than a low-level bum driving around in his secondhand jeep. She decided to only fuck with the boss.

Tone would come around on her block, switching it up with different luxury cars. From his midnight blue Benz to his powder-white Range, he turned heads. And not only was he handsome, with his low Caesar haircut, six-pack abs, and golden brown skin, he also wasn't cheap.

On their second date he took Fancy shopping in Roosevelt Field Mall and let her tear it up as he sat back and watched her try on outfit after outfit, and shoe after shoe. She thought, actually hoped, that he would take her back to his place and fuck the shit out of her, but he didn't. He took her to eat and then dropped her back off home at a reasonable time. Although she was grateful that he took her shopping, she was turned off that he didn't try to get in her panties. And she was also annoyed that they never hung out in Harlem where he was from. He always kept her in Brooklyn or Queens or on Long Island. She knew he had a woman, and that made her crazy, but she wasn't a dummy. She knew to keep quiet, and hopefully she would move into the number one position.

Fancy couldn't get to her cell phone quick enough. She knew it had to be Tone. Only, it wasn't. It was a private caller. Reluctantly, she picked up, hoping it wasn't her mother.

"Hello."

"Hey, baby girl."

She smiled. "Hi, Pop-Pop."

"How are things? Are you well?"

"Of course. Did you get the money order?"

"Yeah. How are things at The Gap? They must be giving you more hours, if you can afford to send me a thousand dollars."

Fancy wasn't working at no damn Gap. And at this very moment she knew her father knew the same.

"I'm working two jobs now," she said, embellishing her lie. "Nonstop hours until I start my school semester."

"Is that so?" he asked, his pitch elevated. "I need you to come and see me. Tomorrow. And you better not have me looking for you."

She knew she was busted. "Sure, no problem. I'll be there."

Fancy knew that even if the sky fell tomorrow, she had still better carry her ass to see her father. She was off the phone for only a moment before it rang again. A huge grin appeared on her face. It was Tone.

"Hey, sexy," he began. "You wanna see me tonight?"

"You know I do."

"Okay, I'll come through around eight. Make sure you wear something sexy for me."

She wondered if he could feel her smiling through the phone.

"And tell your aunt you're staying the night out."

"Seriously?" Fancy couldn't contain her excitement.

"When have you known me to bullshit?"

"Okay, babe. I'll tell her. Not that she cares, but whatever. I can't wait to see you."

"Keep it wet for me."

Wet was indeed going on down there. He turned her on so much, she couldn't wait to fuck him. She wanted to suck his dick so good tonight. The mere thought put a Kool-Aid smile on her face. After they hung up, she began running around the house in preparation.

"What are you smiling about?" Nasir asked, noticing the silly grin.

"Huh?"

"The stupid-ass expression on your face." He shook his head. "You must be going with that nigga later."

"Yeah, he's coming through."

"You fuck him yet?"

She blushed. "Nasir! That's none of your business."

"Like I give a fuck. I'm just telling you to put your work in and take him from that Harlem broad he fuckin' with. You get in good with him, and he will come down on his numbers. I got an organization to build. One day I want to be like your pops."

"I'm not fuckin' and suckin' dick for you to get a *G* knocked off each ki." She rolled her eyes. "Who knows . . . I might be fuckin' and suckin' dick to get my own ki's."

Nasir stared at Fancy for a long moment. He wondered why she would say something like that if she didn't mean it. Suddenly he felt a shift inside his soul that at the moment he couldn't shake. He didn't ask her to elaborate on her plans. He merely walked away.

Fancy gave less than a fuck that Nasir was mad with her. Her new boo was on his way, and she had things to do. She hopped in the shower and douched out her vagina. She washed her hair and left conditioner on it while she ran around in the living room looking for the perfect outfit. Of course, she would wear one of the new outfits Tone had bought her.

She decided on a pair of silver-and-navy blue leather booty shorts with a cropped blazer. Her thick thighs would be on display. She would wear the navy blue six-inch Louboutin's, shimmery navy blue tights and a clutch purse. Once her outfit was pulled, she ran back into the shower to wash out the conditioner, and then she blow dried her long, silky hair before hitting it with the hot flat iron.

She still had a couple hours before Tone came, so she ran to the nail salon and got a fresh manicure and pedicure, making it back just in time. She had roughly thirty minutes before she knew he would pull up. She pulled her outfit on and looked in the mirror once, twice, and then a third time, until she felt right.

If Tone was anything, he turned out to always be on time. She came downstairs and slid into his sleek Maserati and leaned over to give him a kiss on his full lips. His cologne turned her on. He always looked and smelled like money. He was the first man to remind her of her father. They had the same type of swagger. Looking back, she wondered why she never picked up that Alexandro wasn't an ordinary businessman.

"You look good enough to eat."

"That can be arranged." She smiled coyly. "Where are we going tonight?"

"You hungry?"

"Yeah, sure."

Tone peeled out and headed toward the Belt Parkway going into Queens.

"I thought we could have dinner in the city tonight, do something different. I've never gone to Cipriani's. Have you?"

"Ma, I'm tired. And I want you so badly. I've booked us a room at the Marriott. We could order room service and relax for the night."

Fancy knew she was being played like a hoochie. Before the shit had hit the fan, she had men at her beck and call. They would take her to the hot spots like Philippe Chow's, Nobo, The Waverly, and other great eateries. She didn't appreciate being taken to a hotel to get slayed and eat bullshit room service, but she said nothing. She decided that she would give him the best, wettest pussy he'd ever experienced and suck his dick better than he could ever imagine.

She ordered the lobster. He had the soft shell crab. The champagne was on ice, and the dessert was what would take place in between the sheets. Fancy moved in on Tone with the grace of a panther. She was dark, sexy, and exotic, and her passionate kisses were driving him crazy. They undressed quickly. In fact, he barely took time out to admire the sexy lingerie she'd worn for his benefit.

Fancy had played out this night over and over in her head. She thought she would seductively strip for him, allowing him to stand back and take in her every curve right before he would make soft, passionate love to her. Instead, he pushed her down on the bed, practically ripped off her clothes, flipped her over, and entered her roughly from the back.

Tone was big, but not too big. It wasn't his size or girth that snatched her breath, but the way he was pounding into her vaginal walls had her wincing in pain. He was a maniac in bed, tossing Fancy's fragile body all over the hotel room. They tried every position imaginable. He was pulling and stretching her legs, until they felt like they would snap. He would go from deep strokes to pumping in short, quick succession. And they both collapsed on top of each other, breathing and sweating heavily.

"You like to have sex in the mornings?" he asked, after catching his breath.

She had never really thought about it, nor had anyone ever asked that before. "I guess . . . ."

With that, he turned over and quickly drifted off into a peaceful sleep.

✳✳✳

The morning started pretty much the way the night ended. Fancy was awakened by a stiff dick pounding into her dry pussy. For a second she felt violated. He hadn't even tapped her on the shoulder before he took her body. But once he started hitting her G-spot, all traces of anger began to dissipate as she screamed his name and ran her nails down his wide back.

After the two lovers had showered and dressed, Tone pulled out a wad of cash and tossed Fancy three stacks.

"What's this for?"

"Go get you an apartment somewhere in Queens. I'm not fuckin' with that Brooklyn shit for too much longer." He leaned down and tied the laces on his vintage Adidas sneakers. "Make sure it's on a quiet residential block, somewhere on the low and safe."

Fancy wanted to ask so many questions. Like, how does she apply for an apartment? How does she begin looking? And, most importantly, will he pay not only the rent but the bills too?

"Could I get some money to go shopping?"

He tossed her another stack. She was worth it to him. He was used to dealing with women who had expectations and liked to look good. "And, Fancy . . . "

"Yes."

"Make arrangements for me to see your father. Tell him I'm your man and I want to politick. He should know what's up."

# CHAPTER 20

The exhilaration Fancy felt when Tone said he was her man couldn't be kept under wraps. She couldn't wait to tell anyone who would listen.

"Listen, I need you to help me find an apartment," she said to Nasir. "My man wants me up outta here." She pulled out her four bundles and put the crisp money on display.

"Word," Nasir replied, unimpressed. He was too focused on a shooting that had taken place late last night in Brevoort Projects that involved one of his soldiers.

"Yeah, he needs a safe place to lay his head at night, and he doesn't want it to be in Brooklyn."

"So go uptown." Nasir wanted to fuck with Fancy, who he noticed was prancing around like her shit didn't stink. Right now she thought she was too cute. "Oh, yeah, you can't, 'cuz his real girl lives there."

Fancy was furious. "He don't fuck with that bitch no more."

"He told you that?"

"He didn't have to say it. He showed me last night what was really good."

Nasir burst into laughter right in Fancy's face. He laughed a good minute or two before watching as she angrily stormed out of the room.

"Aunt Bee, you got a second?"

Brenda rolled her eyes but remembered Alex's threat. "Yeah. What you want? Make it quick. I'm watching my stories."

Fancy peeled off a hundred-dollar bill and tossed it toward her aunt.

"What's this for?" she asked, stuffing it into her bra.

"When you have time this week, could you help me find an apartment for me and Tone?"

"Tone?" she asked, surprised. She had no idea who her niece was running with. "The Colombian connect from uptown?"

"Yeah, him."

"Y'all fuckin' around like that?" she asked, impressed.

"That's my man now."

Brenda chuckled. "You work fast, don't you?" There was something about a woman locking down a wealthy guy that made her peers respect her.

"Oh, for sure. He's going hard for me."

Suddenly, Brenda didn't want anyone playing her niece except her. "So he's moving in with you and will be paying all the bills, right?"

Fancy pulled out her same four stacks and flaunted the money to her aunt. "He gave me this, and there's more where that came from."

"Well, tell him you need a car. Shit, he could certainly afford to buy you one."

Nasir appeared in the doorway of his mother's room. "Ma, I know you ain't buying into Fancy's bullshit fantasyland. That nigga selling her the Brooklyn Bridge."

Fancy wanted to wipe the smug smile off his cute face. "You don't know shit, Nasir. We're official. And he wants to meet my father. That's how serious he is about me."

Nasir's face distorted with rage. "What the fuck you just say?" He didn't wait for an answer before hemming her up by the collar. "Why that nigga wanna see Uncle Alex?"

"Get the fuck off me!" Fancy screamed and shook loose. "Stupid muthafucka!"

Fancy refused to be abused by anyone, especially those who weren't dropping serious bank on her.

"Why the fuck he pushing up to see Alex? That nigga tryna be funny?"

Fancy couldn't buy a clue with all the money in the world; she was lost as to what Nasir was so enraged about.

Nasir was always thinking. In fact, sometimes he would miss out on good opportunities because he needed to fully assess certain situations. He had wanted to go up and visit his uncle to try and get his connect. He wanted to blow up, but he wanted to do it smartly. If he took one misstep, he would certainly end up dead or behind bars. So while he was weighing his options, a smart nigga like Tone was moving forward full steam. And that infuriated Nasir, who felt like he was an heir to the throne.

"Nasir, what's going on, baby?" his mother asked. All the commotion had piqued her interest. This drama was better than any story the TV could produce at this moment. "Tone trying to play you or something? Is this bitch helping him?"

Fancy couldn't believe they were tag-teaming her. And what had she actually done? "What are you talking about? Helping him, what?"

"You all stuck on stupid on this nigga, and he don't give a fuck about you. Tonight he gonna be up in the spot with his real bitch, while your stupid ass is about to give him a connect that will make him untouchable."

"Calm down, Nasir," Brenda said once she understood what was going on. "Trust, when I tell you this. Alex ain't letting go his connect to no fuckin' body, whether he fuckin' Fancy or not. He ain't dumb. He probably won't even give it to ya ass."

"If Fancy tell him to do it, I bet he will." Nasir was seething. He had been trying to pace himself, gather enough customers, and then he would push up on his uncle to give up his supplier. Now, it seemed Tone had the same idea.

"I want in," Fancy finally said. "Make me a partner, and I'll go to my father for you and deal with the connect on my own."

Nasir literally wanted to slap the black off of her for even thinking she could come in and stand toe to toe with him. He'd been hustling since he was knee-high and had never been shot or played by any fucking body.

"I don't have partners; I have sons. And from what I can see, you don't got what it takes between your legs to qualify." And on that note, he stormed out.

Fancy was almost too amped to stop her day and go and see her father. But she knew it was the only way to get him off of her back. She sat at the visiting table a new woman. Long gone were the tears from the seventeen-year-old Fancy. She'd turned eighteen, had a new man, and new beginnings. Her hands were touching more paper in a week from Tone than the past few months. She looked good, felt good, and wanted more of the good life. What she was experiencing now couldn't compare to her former life, but she was grateful that the veil was lifted. Her former life was a lie. She didn't even know she was a character in a life that her parents had orchestrated. Now, she had her freedom and was able to make her own decisions.

"Don't you look gorgeous, sweetheart?"

"Thanks, Pop-Pop. You look good too!"

Alexandro smiled. "You lie."

"Never," she replied, and chuckled.

The first hour of the visit was filled with idle chitchat. Hardly the reason he demanded she come and see him. Suddenly, the conversation turned a corner.

"Who you fucking with?" The question was short and to the point.

"What are you talking about?"

"You're coming up here in new clothing, you're sending large bundles of money to me and your mother when just a few weeks ago you didn't have two nickels to rub together. Who is he? I want a name."

"What are you talking about?"

"Name?"

"Nasir sent you the—"

"Name." Alexandro leaned in close so she could feel the tension emanating from his body. "And I am not going to ask you again."

Fancy wondered if her father would have her man murdered. Although Tone told her to tell him about them, now, looking in her father's eyes, she wasn't so sure that was a good idea.

"I'm not seeing anyone. I swear."

"Who is he, and what does he do?"

There wasn't any way she could come right out and say he pushed weight. Not to her father. It was easier to say it in a roundabout way. "He said to tell you that he wants to meet you . . . to politick."

"That little nigga thinks he could use my daughter to get at me?" Alexandro gritted his teeth in frustration. "That he's even earned the right to sit at a table with me and fuckin' politick?"

"Why are you so upset? He's only trying to make a living so he can take care of us."

Alexandro ignored her last remark. "What's his fuckin' name, and where's he from, Fancy?"

"Why?" Fancy's voice was shaky.

"You don't question me! Who the fuck do you think you are?"

"Please don't have him killed, Pop-Pop," she blurted out. Her heart was palpitating and the love high she was floating on earlier had dissipated. Tone was the gravy train that she wanted to ride until the wheels fell off. "He's a good man, and I love him."

"You're too young to love anyone."

"I am not!" she countered. "Because you're my father I understand why you feel that way, but I am no longer a little girl. I'm grown and I do grown things."

Alexandro could only imagine what things she was referring too. It made his stomach slightly uncomfortable but felt it was Belen's job to speak with their daughter about boys. It was his job to protect her from wolves. He planned to get at this unknown predator one way or another, just have someone tap on his shoulder and give him a warning, which would go like this: *If you break Fancy's heart, you're dead.*

She watched as her father sat in deep thought. She didn't like the silence. "Why are you so quiet? What are you thinking?"

"I'm thinking that I don't like the road you're traveling on. I'm thinking that you better take your ass to college this semester and leave these li'l corner boys alone."

"But he's not . . . he's bigger than that." She leaned in close and whispered, "You have to believe me. He's doing big things out here, but we need your help. He needs your connect—"

"Get out of my face with that ignorant shit you're talking!" Alexandro roared and the whole visiting room was silenced. "And don't come back to see me until you have the sense that your mother and I thought we instilled in you!"

Alexandro got up and left the visiting room leaving Fancy embarrassed and temporarily stupefied.

✳✳✳

It didn't take Fancy—with help from her Aunt Brenda and a realtor— long to find her an apartment in a quaint little area in Queens. The tree lined block was quiet, just as Tone had requested, and the neighbors were mixed races: Caucasian, Indian, Asian, and German. Tone showed up once to approve the apartment and also to give her another five stacks to shop for household items, like linens and kitchenware. He'd arranged for furniture to be delivered, and she was all set up, but then he disappeared.

Days turned into weeks and he flat out didn't return her calls. At first she was worried, she thought he'd either gotten murdered or was incarcerated. But when Nasir told her that Tone was still hitting him off with coke; Fancy was hurt. She knew he was with his main chick, and each day he didn't come to see her she would get clowned by Nasir.

She wondered if his distance from her had anything to do with the fact that Alexandro refused to meet with him and give up his connect. Or was it that his Harlem chick had found out about her and had put an end to their affair? Either way, she needed answers. And was determined to get them. One way or another.

# CHAPTER 21

Fancy's heart was pumping ice water through her veins. If what Nasir had said was true, tonight she would see Tone and his Harlem bitch up in the club. And her mission was to make him choose right then and there in front of all his homeboys who he wanted to be with. And from the way she looked and felt, she knew it would be her.

The line outside Club Reign curled down the block. Fancy handed the gypsy cabdriver his thirty-dollar fare and even managed a small tip. As she and her Aunt Brenda strutted toward the venue, both women instantly caught the attention of the partygoers. Eyes scanned their thick, sexy legs and their sexy outfits. Hoodlums and thugs made catcalls at them, and the women tossed their eyes toward the sky in envy.

Fancy smiled. She was feeling wickedly sexy and dangerously horny tonight. The thought of challenging Tone was a complete turn-on.

She led the way past all the losers who stood obediently in line, and sidled up to the stocky, muscular head bouncer with a wrestler's build. She leaned in close and said, "I'm not on the list, but I'm Fancy Lane. You may know my father."

The bouncer gave her a look of recognition and then smiled. He nodded and opened up the ropes. "Tell Alex, Bubba said hello." And then he added, "Let him know I took care of you."

Fancy was slowly getting used to her life of ghetto fabulousness. Sure, just mere months ago she was living with a platinum spoon in her mouth, which was great, but in the underworld, she got props too. People respected her and even feared her because of who her father was. His rep was still telling his story. She reveled in her newfound respect and intended to use it to her advantage, finally understanding what it meant to be Alexandro's daughter.

It didn't take them long to spot Nasir, Shoe-Shine, and the rest of the crew inside the club.

"Damn, Fancy! Why you bring my moms?" Nasir sucked his teeth in disgust.

"Just in case that Harlem bitch try some shit wit' my niece," Brenda replied.

"And whatchu gonna fuckin' do?" Nasir was thoroughly disgusted. Cutting up coke and all that shit behind doors with his moms was acceptable, but in a nightclub where the median age was twenty-two, it was just ghetto. He had to draw the line somewhere. "You should take ya ass home!"

"Don't get cute, Nasir." Brenda stared him down viciously. "I'm still your mother, and I've already earned my respect. Now, buy me a Henny on ice, so I can drop it like it's hot." She dropped down to the floor and popped back up like she was Beyoncé. "Owwwwww!" She burst into laughter. "An old bitch still got it."

Nasir just stormed off, embarrassed by his mother's behavior.

Meanwhile, Fancy was too preoccupied scanning the room, looking for Tone.

"He ain't here yet," Shoe-Shine said, stating the obvious.

"Mind your business."

"I'm just trying to look out for you."

"I don't need your help."

"You need something." He leaned in close. "'Cuz right now you playing your cards all wrong. You don't chase a nigga, you let a nigga chase you, ma. We love a challenge. Right now you too easy."

His words infuriated Fancy. She cut her eyes and tried to tune him out. Any second she would hopefully see Tone and his soon-to-be ex-chick. Or bitch. Or whatever.

The club was popping off like it was a New Year's Eve celebration. The hoodlums, ballers, sexy chicks, and stickup kids were all in attendance. "Marvin's Room" by Drake blared throughout the club, and everyone was getting their sexy on.

Fancy began dancing to the track—She loved Drake—and grinding her hips in a circular motion on the floor, reciting the lyrics like he was her man. She looked up and could see Drake in the crowd, surrounded by his entourage. He had on a Brooklyn Nets fitted cap, probably in support of Jay-Z, and was surrounded by bottles of champagne, Cîroc, and Voss water bottles. He was so sexy to her. She would give anything just to have him eat her pussy out.

She almost ran up to the VIP area he was hosting but decided against that. How would it look if she was dick-riding Drake when Tone walked in? Could she really ask him to choose between her and his girl if she was swinging from some rapper's nut sack?

"I need a drink," Brenda said, after realizing Nasir wasn't coming back.

Fancy agreed. She looked in the VIP area, where Nasir and his crew were doing it big. She wondered if they should crash their circle, and then wondered about Tone. Would it be better to be all tight with Nasir and his peeps, or be dolo with her aunt? *Which is a better look?* she thought.

Fancy couldn't take two steps toward the bar without some random dude trying to pull her on the dance floor, so she decided it was safer to go and hang out with her cousin.

As the night moved forward, the music seemed to get better. Fancy's drink was definitely going to her head. DJ Kid Capri was murdering the tracks. He was mixing vintage Biggie with Lil Wayne and then would add

Mary J. Blige and blend in Jay-Z.

Fancy and Brenda were in the VIP area, gyrating their hips and putting on a show like they were in a strip club. And the men didn't have a problem giving them the attention, copping cheap feels and grinding behind Fancy in her form-fitting dress.

✳✳✳

Tone, flanked by his henchmen, stood in another section of the VIP booth unbeknownst to Fancy, his jewels shining heavily. He was watching his side chick show out and parade herself in the club like a slut.

His slanted eyes narrowed in on Fancy, her short dress inching up her curvy thighs, just barely covering the panties she had on. He snorted his disgust as the men surrounded her like it was a free cheese line in Harlem.

He placed the champagne glass on the table and suddenly headed toward the VIP section that Nasir was hosting. He pushed past a thick crowd of partygoers, and no one dared to argue with him, except one sassy chick, who did it to see if he would stop to give her the time of day.

He zeroed in on Fancy dancing with a young kid named B-Real from Harlem, her ass and titties shaking like Jell-O, as B-Real's hands gripped her tiny waist. B-Real was making faces like he was in a porno movie.

✳✳✳

Fancy took a large gulp from the champagne in her hand and swallowed the expensive, bubbly liquid.

Brenda wasn't too far from her getting her swerve on. She was hoping the young dude she was grinding on wanted to go back to her place and get his fuck on. His body was lean, tight, and full of youth, just the way she liked them. She backed her ass up into the young man's crotch and felt his hard dick pressing firmly against her butt.

Tone approached Fancy and didn't say one word. He just glared, allowing his presence to be felt.

Suddenly B-Real saw Tone out of his peripheral vision and stopped dead in his tracks. He was trying to reconcile why Tone was looking at him in such an unsavory manner. He knew he hadn't done shit. Well, he hoped he hadn't. Could it be Fancy? B-Real had seen Tone only hours earlier toasting and doing it big with his wifey.

Fancy realized that B-Real had stopped grinding on her and looked to see why. That's when she noticed Tone. A sly grin crept across her face. *So he did show up.* Next, her eyes looked to the left and right. Where was his woman?

As Tone loomed closer, B-Real threw his hands up in surrender and began backpedaling. He didn't want any parts of a beef with Tone.

Fancy screamed, "Where the fuck have you been? You just fuckin'—"

Tone yanked her arm with immense force, lifting her stilettos slightly off the ground like she was a ragdoll, and Fancy was momentarily stunned.

The club's patrons began to spread out, just in case the crazy guy pulled a gun. Nasir and his crew noticed the commotion, but they fell back. They knew one way or another it would go down tonight with Fancy. They were just surprised that it was between Fancy and Tone and not mistress and wifey.

"This is how you represent me?" he screamed. "All up in the fuckin' club getting finger-fucked by some lame muthafucka?"

She looked and saw jealousy and rage, a combination she loved. It meant that he was really feeling her, despite what Nasir kept saying.

"Don't try to change the subject! Where have you been?"

Tone hated to be challenged, and he also didn't like that she kept sassing him. He grabbed her by the back of her hair and began dragging her out of the club. Not one person—no bouncer, no aunt, cousin, bystander—did anything to stop the assault. Fancy screamed for dear life, but it was to no avail. Tone continued this behavior until he tossed her into the passenger's seat of his Cayenne truck.

"You've been with that Harlem bitch, and now you want to scream on me?"

Tone remained silent as he maneuvered his luxury car through the streets of Manhattan, over the Brooklyn Bridge, to the Belt Parkway, and into Queens.

The whole ride Fancy continued to call him all type of names and accuse him of cheating on her. Inside the apartment was where she received the first slap.

"Don't you ever disrespect me in public again! You hear me, bitch?"

She picked up an ashtray and logged it at him, just barely missing his head.

He lunged forward, grabbed her arm, and began to twist it. Mercilessly. Her knees buckled, and she collapsed to the ground. Next, he began to smack her around their apartment, while she begged him to stop.

"You were never my main chick. You understand me, bitch?"

"Fuck you!"

"You're not worthy enough to walk in my girl's shoes."

"So why are you here? Go be with that bitch if she's so fuckin' great!"

He continued to verbally and physically assault her, stopping short of hitting her with a closed fist. He wasn't that *loco*. When he was tired of abusing her and she was tired of being abused, they both fell into a deep sleep.

# CHAPTER 22

Nasir stood in the doorway watching the two lovers devour each other like their lives depended upon it. He looked on as the male buried his head in the female's pussy until he brought her to a climax, and she continued to moan her pleasure and scream out his name. When he entered her, Nasir watched as she gasped and then took her manicured fingers and lightly scratched his back, her soft skin, ripe breasts, and curvy thighs glistening in the early morning sunlight.

"You're my heart, Fancy," he said, breathing heavily. "I adore you."

Nasir couldn't take his eyes off the lovers, but he knew he had to. Slowly, he backed out of the Queens apartment and drove back into Brooklyn. He was filled with so much confusion. Anger and rage flowed through his veins, along with lust and desire.

He reached home at just barely eight o'clock in the morning. He was like a time bomb just waiting for the countdown to explosion.

After they made love, Tone left without giving Fancy any promises or guarantees. She didn't know when he would come back, or if he would, for that matter. Her whole body hurt from the lovemaking and the beating the night before. Now, with her broken heart, she was an absolute wreck. Feeling empty and alone, she was only able to lay in bed and cry her eyes out. How could he treat her so brutally the night before and then wake her up and make sweet love to her and then turn dark again? She was on an emotional roller coaster and didn't know how to get off the ride from hell.

✳✳✳

She knew she shouldn't be alone with him. The action alone could cost both of them their lives. If Tone found out that she was standing toe to toe in their bedroom with Shoe-Shine, he would make them pay. But she couldn't resist him. His lips looked so soft and full, all she thought about was kissing them. Sucking his bottom lip and exploring his mouth was something she didn't want to do but needed to do. He knew he made her nervous. All he had to do was ask her, and she was ready. For anything.

"You want something to drink?" she asked. They were inches apart, and she could smell peppermint on his breath.

"Whatchu got?"

His deep voice made her weak.

"I have rum and coke, just what you like."

"I hope not that cheap rum." He had every intention of making this slightly difficult.

She smiled coyly. "You could drink your spit, for all I care."

He grinned. "You lie."

"Sometimes."

He followed her into the kitchen, and she pulled out Captain Morgan's Original Spiced Rum. The good shit. Exactly what he liked. She poured him a rum and coke and felt confident while doing it, but she had to wonder when she went to the liquor store with her Aunt Brenda a couple weeks back, why did she actually pick it up? It wasn't Tone's drink of choice, and it certainly wasn't her preference.

"I knew you would have my shit."

"You knew no such thing."

"You're a man-pleaser, Fancy." He looked her in her eyes. "You do it not to actually please the dude, but for the praise and adulation you get from them after you've given them what they want."

Fancy didn't understand his psychobabble, but she knew it didn't sound like a compliment. She walked back into her living room and sat down.

"So, tell me what was so urgent?"

A couple hours after Tone had left, Shoe-Shine called, saying he needed to politick, but she had to give him her word that whatever they discussed would be kept between them. Fancy wasn't up to any company, since she was still reeling from her morning of uncertainty. Reluctantly she agreed, and now, in the early afternoon sunlight, stood Shoe-Shine.

"Yo, we need to talk business."

"We?"

"Yea," he said, his voice high-pitched. "'Cuz you don't see what I see."

Her interest was piqued. "And what exactly is that?"

"I see that you could take this whole drug game to the next level, pick up where your father left off."

Her eyes popped open wide like saucers. "That's exactly what I've been wanting."

"That's why I'm here. I know both them niggas don't see you the way I do."

"Did Nasir tell you that I had a talk with him?"

"Nah, he ain't tell me shit. He just keep saying that a bitch need to stay in her lane, ya feel me?"

"That sounds like something you would say."

"And I do say shit like that, but now I see things differently. I see you differently." Shoe-Shine took a gulp and downed his drink. "You got what it takes to be boss lady. Only, them niggas will block. Trust."

Fancy thought for a moment. She had been asking Nasir and Tone to let her come on board so she could make her own money, but neither of them wanted to fully entertain the idea. They'd rather have her kissing ass, fucking, or sucking dick to get a come-up.

"So what are you suggesting?"

"I'm suggesting that you go and talk with your—"

"He won't see you."

"I don't want to see him. See, that's where I'm different than those niggas. I want to be the man behind you, not the other way around. They both wanted to use you for your connect, and once they get it, you'll be back to living day by day with uncertainty. If you let me ride on your team, I promise you protection. Won't no nigga get at you, not on my watch. I put that on my life."

"Tone would never allow it."

"You ain't gonna hear from that nigga for a long time, baby girl. I promise you that."

Her greatest fear came upon her when he said those words. She would never admit it to Shoe-Shine or Nasir, but she was jealous of Tone's girl. What did she have that Fancy didn't have? "What? He just left here. He'll be back."

"You think so? Call me in January when rent time comes around and tell me if the nigga came through."

"What is it that you know, Shoe-Shine? Fuckin' tell me!" Fancy was furious. Shoe-Shine spoke so matter-of-factly, it was driving her crazy. "Did he get married?"

Shoe-Shine smirked. "I don't know if that nigga married."

"Well, is he dead?"

"Nah, but he's lucky to still be breathing. I heard he jetted out of town and will most likely be there for a while. He claims he had business, but I heard some niggas tried to get at his bitch ass today, and now he's ghost." Shoe-Shine deliberately left out the fact that it was him and Nasir who'd tried to get at Tone.

***

Nasir had come banging on Shoe-Shine's door earlier that afternoon, talking about how Tone had violated his cousin and he had to go.

"I'm tired of that fuckin' pretty boy disrespecting my blood," Nasir spat.

"Yo, but that's her man, though."

"And she's my fuckin' cousin!" Nasir paced around Shoe-Shine's apartment with a crazed look in his eyes. "If Uncle Alex was out here, this shit wouldn't be going down . . . him pulling on her and shit all up in the club. He still fuckin' parading that Harlem broad all around town like she's made out of diamonds, and my fuckin' cousin is stashed away in some Queens breadbox of an apartment, like he 'shamed of her."

Shoe-Shine listened carefully but knew that there was more to the story. Since when did Nasir give a fuck about how other niggas treated their chicks? Shit wasn't adding up, but Shoe-Shine went along for the ride.

They drove in their man's black Pontiac, a car unknown to Tone. As they turned on the block, Tone was just peeling out, which pissed Nasir off. They followed him for a couple blocks before Shoe-Shine pulled alongside the unsuspecting Tone, who was on his cell phone, apparently arguing with someone.

Nasir leaned out the window and opened fire. Miraculously, Tone wasn't hit. His glass shattered, and he hit the accelerator hard. Shoe-Shine would have given chase, but that whole neighborhood was a cop's playground. So they jumped back on the highway and headed home.

Two hours later, Tone called Nasir's phone, telling him he had to bounce OT on some business shit. Nasir knew better. He knew Tone was shook. The murder attempt ensured two things: Tone wasn't ever going to lay his head down at Fancy's again; and, secondly, he was skipping town, leaving the streets of New York wide open to be taken over, if only momentarily.

✳✳✳

Fancy stood up and walked toward her small window. She didn't know what part of Shoe-Shine's story was true, or if any of it was, but she did recognize the feeling in her stomach. She felt despair, and she'd been there before.

Now how would she live? Nasir certainly wouldn't be able to afford to take care of her and his family as well.

Shoe-Shine noticed how tense she was. "You fixed me a drink. Seems like I should return the favor. You want me to get you a drink?" He stood behind her and barely let his body touch hers.

"No," she sputtered. "I mean, yes."

"Which is it?" he asked, amused.

"It's yes." She took a couple steps back. "I could use something to drink. I've had a long day."

"Is that all it is? 'Cuz, if you ask me, you look a little nervous."

"I am not!" she spewed defensively.

"Be easy, gangsta. I'm just making an observation."

Shoe-Shine walked over to the bar and thought for a second. He didn't bother to ask her what she preferred to drink. He just took the initiative, which Fancy liked. He poured her Baileys on the rocks and fixed himself another rum and coke. And they both sat down, they were two people with one solitary thought—fucking.

Well, Shoe-Shine wanted to fuck, but Fancy envisioned a long lovemaking session.

He stared at her intently. His eyes gazed over her curvy body, until the alcohol began to take effect. He saw her shoulders relax. He fixed her another drink.

Three drinks in, and they still sat in silence, staring at each other. It was highly erotic for both of them.

Fancy wondered if he would ever touch her, which was driving her crazy.

"Stand up."

"What?"

"Stand up and take off your shirt."

Briefly Fancy wondered if she should object.

"Now."

Slowly she rose to her feet and unbuttoned her blouse, which she let cascade to the floor. Her cinnamon skin glistened from the sparkly Christian Dior lotion she'd applied, and the gold specks almost made her glow.

"Step out of those jeans and then put your heels back on."

The top button on her skintight jeans opened easily enough, but pulling them down while trying to look sexy was turning out to be a feat. She slipped off her five-inch heels and stood barefoot for a brief moment before putting them back on. She stood in front of him with only her bra and panties on.

"Aren't you going to join me?"

Lustfully, he continued to stare. "Dance for me."

Fancy wanted to dance on his dick, not alone. She was slightly turned off and highly intimidated. She knew she could move, but she'd never danced for a man in her life. But she was tipsy and up for the challenge.

She began to move her hips, slowly at first, in a figure eight. There wasn't any music playing, so she had to rely solely on her imagination and ingenuity. She began to grind down to the floor and work her way back up. She could see his eyes lowered and his dick bulging. This encouraged her as she fought back thoughts of Tone. If he could see her now only hours after they'd fucked.

Fancy started to feel empowered. She tapped her pussy. "If you want it, come and get it."

Shoe-Shine stood slowly and approached her deliberately. His massive hands cupped her breasts, and he leaned over and devoured her nipples. He licked then sucked and then blew softly, and Fancy encouraged him by softly moaning.

Shoe-Shine pulled his T-shirt above his head and tossed it, exposing a chiseled, masculine chest. Fancy walked over and unbuttoned his jeans. She slid her hand into his boxers and gripped his fully aroused dick. She couldn't help but compare his penis to Tone's. Tone had length and girth, and his dick was light colored, like the French vanilla latte she drank almost every morning. Although Shoe-Shine was taller, his dick wasn't weighty. His length was a little above average, but it was slim, and his deep cinnamon complexion extended to his dick.

Fancy was a little disappointed but was still curious enough to see what he could do with his member. As she began to massage his balls, they passionately kissed. His kisses were rushed and aggressive. She felt like he was raping her mouth.

She pulled back and murmured in his ear, "Be easy, baby. We have all night."

Shoe-Shine nodded. He was so excited, and he realized he was rushing it. He fully undressed and walked her into her bedroom. Fancy climbed back onto her bed, and he climbed in between her legs. Her clean-shaven pussy was so intoxicating. He knew he was a beast at eating pussy. If he seemed too eager a moment ago, he knew he was about to change her mind.

He took his hands and spread her legs wide then took two fingers and opened her pussy lips and concentrated on her clit. Slowly and methodically, he began to suck and gently bite on her clit, applying just the right amount of pressure. And he wouldn't let up, no matter how hard Fancy begged him to enter her.

"Please, ohhhh, please, I can't take it. Just enter me."

He continued to ignore her, and soon her knees began to tremble from pleasure. Her pussy began to pulsate, and her moans deepened.

"Oh God!" she cried out. "Shoe-Shine!"

Shoe-Shine nodded his head. He knew he was driving her crazy. "You want me to stop?" he asked.

"No, no. Please don't stop," she begged, her words breathy. She was at his mercy.

Before long, Fancy was climaxing all over her and Tone's king-sized bed, gripping the bed sheets and moaning her pleasure.

Shoe-Shine was fully aroused by what he had done to her body. It was an ego booster. He grabbed a condom from out of his jeans and wrapped up his dick. Fancy was nice and wet and full of lust, so his dick eased into her without any maneuvering. He placed a pillow under her butt to angle her in the right position, allowing for deep penetration and to hit her G-spot easily.

He pumped slowly but assertively as they tried to find their rhythm. The constant friction was driving her crazy. The whole time he was either kissing her or keeping his lips so close to her face. It was very erotic to her in a different way.

There wasn't a whole lot of switching positions, just traditional, yet it was fulfilling. And once again, she came.

Shoe-Shine didn't pull out of her quickly. Instead, he stared into her eyes and then began planting soft kisses on her face, showing a tender side of himself, and from that, she felt more emotionally attached to him than she had to Tone.

"I've waited so long for this. Was it good for you?"

Fancy blushed. So much was going through her mind. Did she really just fuck Shoe-Shine? In her man's bed? What would Nasir say if he found out? And what about Tone? He could walk in at any moment, and yet Shoe-Shine didn't show any fear. Would he protect her? And what about his faith in her? He'd told her that he would hold her down and wouldn't let anyone touch her.

"What now?"

"Whatchu mean?"

"We can't undo what's been done."

"You still sweet on that nigga?" Shoe-Shine got upset quickly.

"No, not like that. I wanted this to happen. What I mean is, are we really going to move forward together in front of everyone? Even Nasir?" Fancy turned to face him. "Am I yours? In public? Or only in the recesses of the night?"

"You mines." Shoe-Shine jumped to his feet and towered over Fancy butt naked. "And I'd kill a nigga if he tried to say differently. Fuck Tone! And fuck Nasir, if he has a problem with it! I ain't nobody's son, you feel me?"

Fancy was actually flattered and loved being the center of attention. "So you would go up against them both? For me?"

Shoe-Shine looked directly into her eyes. "Only if you let me."

"I'll let you do whatever you want to do for me and to me. But first we gotta get our shit straight."

"I feel you, ma."

"Do you? 'Cuz I'm talking about paper, not this relationship."

Shoe-Shine liked her style. He'd finally met a broad who was about making paper over dick. He knew that, deep down inside, Fancy could help take him to another level. She wanted to come up so badly because it was written in her DNA, and if no one else saw that, he did.

"What's on ya mind?"

"Look, I've had money, and then I was dead broke. It doesn't take a rocket scientist to know which side of the fence I like most." She ran her hands through her hair. "With Tone, it was short-lived, but he gave me a taste. Now I want it all. Not kibbles and bits that a nigga could give me only if I swallow enough of his seeds. I want my own."

"You could get that with me. Right now I don't have much to offer you, ma. Shit, I ain't even got that much dick, ya feel me?" Shoe-Shine said, clowning his own penis.

"So what are you saying?"

"What I've *been* saying—Let's get this money together."

"But why roll with me, and not Nasir?"

Shoe-Shine knew but would never admit, if Nasir got the connect from Fancy, he was doomed forever to stay as an employee and not a boss. But if somehow he knocked Nasir out the way and got the connect through Fancy, then the world would be his. But he had to do everything the right way.

"Why did your pops roll with your moms and not a right-hand man? Because women are easily underestimated in this game, and they can see shit ignorant niggas just can't."

Shoe-Shine had Fancy's full attention.

He told her, "I got a way we could come up off some real bread, but I might have to use you as bait."

"Bait?"

"If you trust me, you won't get hurt. But before I tell you more, you gotta promise to keep this between you and me. If we make this score, we'll have enough money to cop big time from your father's connect and shut the whole tri-state down." He looked Fancy squarely in her eyes. "It involves these Haitian cats who came up off a lot of work."

The two discussed their dreams, which was interrupted by the incessant ringing of their cell phones. They eventually checked to see that Nasir was blowing them both up, which they chose to ignore.

Shoe-Shine and Fancy talked for hours and made love twice more before he headed back to Brooklyn around nine in the evening.

The moment Shoe-Shine left, Fancy tried calling Tone, but her calls continued to go to voice mail. After leaving several messages, she began to rethink about all of Shoe-Shine's promises. Making love with him was different, but nonetheless, it was satisfying. Fancy knew she needed a soldier if she wanted to break into the drug game, and he seemed thorough enough and was a willing participant.

By eleven o'clock, she was exhausted. She'd taken a long, hot bath after a full day of lovemaking. Her vagina was sore, and so was almost every muscle in her body. As she lay in bed, she drifted into a light sleep almost immediately.

✳✳✳

Fancy was awakened by a presence that frightened her. She opened her eyes, and there stood Nasir, hovering over her body with bloodshot eyes and reeking of alcohol.

She gasped. "You scared me," she said, once her eyes focused on the shadowy figure. "How did you get in here?"

Fancy had no idea that Nasir had secretly made a copy of her keys months ago and would come and go as he pleased.

"Why haven't you answered any of my calls?" he demanded.

She sat up straight and tried her best to cover her nakedness. "Did you hear me? How the fuck you get in here?" She clicked on the light and glared at him. She was tired of him thinking he could rule her life.

Then he saw something through his peripheral vision and turned to fully focus on the item. A pair of Ray-Ban shades that his man never left home without.

"You had that nigga up in here!" His voice sounded loud, raspy, and intimidating, like a lunatic's.

Before Fancy could respond, he added, "You fucked him, didn't you? I told you to stay away from my man!"

Nasir wished he could control his anger, but he was too far-gone.

Visions of Shoe-Shine fucking Fancy so soon after he saw her making love to Tone was too much to take.

He leaped on the bed and pinned her down with his body. His large hand went over her mouth while the other pulled down his jeans. His large manhood was pressing up against her already sore opening.

Fancy tried to struggle free, but he was much too strong. When she realized what he wanted, she managed to spit out, "Nasir, no. Don't . . . please."

Nasir pulled back the covers to expose her full nakedness. His lust for her, coupled with the alcohol, had impaired his thinking. All he knew was, he wanted her. Badly. The sight of her curvy thighs, flat stomach, and full, heavy breasts were like spinach to Popeye.

As he kicked off his jeans and sneakers, she realized she could have screamed, but she did not. Forcefully, he pushed into her resisting pussy until she was fully open.

Fancy gasped as his big dick tore through her vagina, his thrusts long and deep. He was rough and angry as he pulled her hair and called her names. His angry assault on her was laced with passion and remorse.

She looked in his eyes and saw pain. He knew what he was doing was wrong. As did she. But, soon, her body began to respond, and she became wetter and wetter as she moved her hips to his rhythm.

"I can't resist you," he crooned. "Your pussy is sooo good."

In the very deep recesses of her brain, she knew she should tell him to stop. She tried to muster up the strength but could not. His lovemaking was exquisite and sensual.

"Make love to me," escaped her lips, and she drifted into complete and utter pleasure.

Nasir pulled out and buried his head in her pussy. Softly he nibbled and sucked her clit as his long tongue explored her. Fancy rocked her thick hips and ran her hands through his soft hair. As her breathing increased, he applied more pressure. Soon strong waves of pleasure came cascading through her body. She shuddered and climaxed.

Nasir inched down and grabbed her small foot into his massive hands and Fancy realized he wasn't anywhere near done making love to her. As he sucked her tiny toes, her pussy began to pulsate. The thrill and sensation was exquisite; highly erotic to her. They looked eye to eye and his were searing with deep passion.

"Please forgive me . . ." he murmured.

Nasir mounted her again, this time gently easing his dick inside of her. "I don't want to hurt you," he breathed. "Ever again."

He began making love to her with deep, slow strokes and she was swept away. His kisses were so good, so passionate, that she didn't want to face reality.

"Look at me," he pleaded.

She shook her head vigorously. She knew that if she opened her eyes again that she would fall in love. Fancy kept her eyes closed tight to not look at who was making her feel this good. And his erection seemed to last all night.

After she climaxed for the third time, she was spent. Her eyelids were heavy, and every portion of her body, from lip to lip, was sore.

Nasir dressed in silence. Neither one of them had much to say with words, their bodies expressing their indiscretion. When he reached the doorway of her bedroom, he turned to face her. He wanted to tell her how much he loved her, although he knew it was wrong. How he couldn't stand to see her with another man. How he'd never made love to anyone as he had just made love to her.

He opened his mouth, but no words came out. He was ashamed. He knew that, come sunlight, they both would be filled with regrets.

After Nasir left, Fancy's head was totally fucked up from making love to three men in one day. But what brought her over the edge was, one of the men was her cousin. She wanted to think it was rape, and that was certainly how it started off. But it ended with them making sweet, passionate, incestuous love. How could she ever get past that? How could she erase such a sweet moment from her memory? She felt slutty, whorish, ashamed, embarrassed, yet sexually fulfilled.

By morning, she felt nothing but contempt and hatred toward her cousin.

# CHAPTER 23

Over the next couple weeks a few things happened. Nasir avoided Fancy by any means necessary, and Shoe-Shine and Fancy continued to sneak around. Lastly, Fancy continued to try to reach Tone, whose cell phone was turned off twenty-four/seven and was no longer able to receive messages.

And Shoe-Shine was right. Come rent time, Tone never did show up.

Shoe-Shine dug deep into his pockets and gave her the $1500 she needed, plus a couple hundred for utilities. But Fancy knew he wasn't flush like Tone. He didn't even have what Nasir was working with because he wasn't his own boss. He was just an Indian with aspirations to be chief. She knew that next month, when rent was due, she was going to need a new sponsor, since Shoe-Shine didn't seem to have more where these dollars came from.

**\*\*\***

Nasir navigated his new Lexus through the congested streets of Queens. He had just copped it from a used car dealership on Northern Boulevard, dropping thirty stacks cash on his whip. These were the kind of profits he'd been seeing since Fancy had convinced him to stop selling hand to hand and step it up.

It was late in the afternoon, and the sun would be going down shortly. He knew he should go home, but he couldn't get her out of his mind—the way her pussy tasted on his lips, her soft caramel-colored skin brushing up against his, and the way she ground her hips on his dick. He wanted to possess her totally. And when the guilt became too overwhelming, he hated her.

Nasir pulled hard on his Newport as he sat reclined in his ride, J. Cole's smooth vocals playing in his ear. He was reminiscing about how he had made love to Fancy. He couldn't admit it publicly, but he loved her from the first moment he'd laid eyes on her.

He found parking on the cluttered block and stepped out of his car looking like a thug. When he got to her front door, he put his ear to it and heard faint movement inside. He knew Shoe-Shine was on a business run for him, and Tone was still OT. He stuck his key in the lock, turned the knob, and entered the premises.

Fancy turned around, slightly startled. Nasir thought he saw a faint smile. Alicia Keys was playing, and he could smell something cooking.

Nasir drank in Fancy's outfit. Her tight leggings outlined her thick, curvy hips and legs, and her skimpy T-shirt exposed her flat abs. She was so voluptuous up top. Her dark brown hair with blonde highlights flowed down past her shoulders effortlessly, and her eyes were hypnotizing. Fancy's body was to die for, and he never got tired of looking at her from head to toe.

"What are you doing here?" she said, placing her hands on her hips.

"You ain't glad to see me?"

"Look at my face. Do I look glad?"

"Actually, you do," he replied smugly.

"You're dumber than I thought, if you see glee written all over me," she remarked dryly.

Nasir chuckled. "I guess not changing the lock makes a nigga feel wanted."

Fancy was seething. "I didn't change the lock because I have a nigga that actually lives here."

Nasir thought Fancy's outburst was over the top, and he didn't come there to fight.

"Yo, be honest. Why do you think I'm here? And don't bullshit me, Fancy. It's just you and me right now."

"The truth? Well," she began, "I've got the wettest pussy you've ever had. Blew your mind and you can't get enough of it. Only thing, you've got a problem."

"Kick it."

"My shit never was and could never be yours to keep."

"What if I don't want to keep it? What if I just want to borrow it from time to time?"

Fancy smirked.

Nasir walked farther into her apartment and began to admire the decor for the first time. It was very modern and had a Puerto Rican flair with an oversized peach leather sofa set and lime-green and peach-colored area rugs, floral silk flower arrangements, along with the obligatory hustler amenities—flat-screen TVs, high-tech stereo system, Xbox, and a treasure trove of gangster DVDs.

"Who the fuck picked out his wack shit?"

"This furniture, right?" Fancy grinned.

"That Spanish muthafucka don't got no flavor."

"Except in his women."

"Yeah, that Harlem bitch is bad as shit," Nasir joked.

Fancy shot him a deadly glare. "You thirsty?"

"I'll take a drink."

Fancy sauntered over to her fully stocked bar and began pouring Nasir a shot of Patrón. She was around him long enough to know it was his favorite. Nasir's eyes lingered on her round ass that fit snugly in her leggings. He had a strong craving for her that ate away at him like a cancer.

She handed him his drink.

"So, what you gonna do for money?" Nasir shot at her. "'Cuz the way I see it, you don't have many options."

"Which are?"

"You can either get a job, a real job, 'cuz fuckin' niggas ain't exactly working out for you."

"Don't you ever have anything good to say about me?" she screamed, her temper flaring up once again. "If I'm so dumb as you and my parents keep saying, then why are they locked the fuck up? And let's not forget— You would still be selling nickel vials of crack if it wasn't for my dumb ass."

"You really need to go to anger management," he said, trying to lighten the mood. He didn't know why he always felt a need to belittle her, but he thought it had to do with his confused feelings for her. She was forbidden, like the apple in Eden, yet he needed a taste.

"Just please . . . stop pushing my buttons."

Fancy was spent. All she wanted to do was get nice off the liquor she was drinking and hopefully get a couple dollars out of her cousin before he left.

"Stop being such a baby. The second option is that you could set it up that I get with your father's connect. I need that shit like I need air to breathe. I done ran out of the work I got from Tone, and getting quality shit ain't that easy in these hard economic times, ya feel me?"

"And how does that help me if I get you the connect? Are you going to make me a partner?"

"We already discussed that, Fancy. As long as I'm straight, you'll be straight."

Fancy wasn't trying to hear the song Nasir was singing, since he had his own plans to rise to the top and be an American gangster just as her father. The conflict was, she had the same plan. She wanted to know as much about Nasir's operation as possible, so she lied. "Okay, I'll talk to my father and see what's up."

"But you also gotta set it up that I can speak with Uncle Alex too. There are questions that I need to ask that I want to hear firsthand."

"Oh, that's not a problem," she said, continuing to tell him what he wanted to hear. "But once you get the connect, what are your plans? And what about Shoe-Shine, Lucky and Nicholas? What positions would they hold, if any?"

"My niggas are thorough and about their business. I need them on my team, especially Shoe-Shine. That nigga would take a bullet for me. He and I've been through some grimy shit together, and he's always been loyal." Nasir pulled out a pre-rolled blunt and sparked it. "The only problem I see is, he thinks we're equals, you feel me?"

"Equals? You mean, in rank?"

"Yea, yea, that nigga be buggin' sometimes. Like he wanna walk in my shoes. Sometimes I get the feeling that he wants his own organization, but he ain't built for it."

"He ain't built to sell drugs?" Fancy laughed in his face. She realized that drug dealers really thought they were running Fortune 500 companies.

The inflection in Fancy's voice irritated Nasir. "He ain't built to be me, a'ight?"

"A'ight." Fancy waited a moment before adding, "But that's a long shot, right? Him walking in your shoes? How could he expect to pull that off? I mean, everyone respects you as boss—the connects, customers, soldiers."

"If there's one thing you need to know, it's that there isn't much loyalty in this game. That's why you keep the niggas that love you close. Everyone else is liable to flip. You think my customers won't buy work from another muthafucka? Or my bottom-level soldiers won't switch sides?"

He took a long drag from his blunt, inhaling the drug in his lungs as long as he could before releasing the smoke into the clean air Fancy was breathing. She wrinkled her small nose and kept listening.

"That's why I need this connect. Once I flood these streets with that potent shit, everyone will pay allegiance to me. And, finally, Shoe-Shine will respect the god."

One thing Fancy got out of Nasir's sermon was how much he felt like he needed Shoe-Shine. Whether it was because he truly loved him and was quite possibly the only person he trusted, or because Shoe-Shine had a quality that he found valuable in the drug game, she couldn't decipher at the moment. But she knew that in due time Shoe-Shine would indeed flip . . . right over to her side.

As the evening moved forward, Nasir got the urge to spread her legs and finger-fuck her.

"You lookin' sexy right now, Fancy."

"Ain't I always?"

"Yeah, but you lookin' good enough to eat." He inched closer, wondering if she would push him away.

"You wanna fuck?" Fancy was intoxicated after downing shots of Patrón and inhaling his secondhand weed smoke. "You tryin' to really go there again?"

Nasir took Fancy by her waist and pulled her into his strong arms, desire showing in his eyes. He wrapped his arms tightly around her sensuous curves and took in her sweet, intoxicating fragrance, Omnia Crystalline by Bvlgari.

Fancy wanted to purr in his grasp. Nasir seemed to hypnotize her and make her forget about reality. "You miss it?" she whispered in his ear.

"You know I do."

Slowly, Nasir bent her over the dining room table and rolled down her leggings to her ankles. Fancy was pantiless, and her shaved pussy was on display. He inserted his index finger into her wet cave, and her warm juices seeped out.

Nasir unbuckled his jeans and dropped them to the floor. He cupped Fancy's breasts and neared his dick to her goodies. He tried to ease his dick into her resisting pussy but had to apply some pressure. Fancy let out a pleasing moan, and she began to respond accordingly, and their bodies became one as he fucked her from the back.

Fancy, curved over the dining room table with her legs spread apart, moaned louder as Nasir placed both hands around her slender neck and gently squeezed. The feeling of her air tunnel being slightly constricted was highly erotic.

"Fuck me, baby," she cried out. "Harder!"

Nasir aimed to please. He began to pound harder with deep, long strokes.

"Is that as hard as you can go?"

Nasir pulled out of her and slammed her up against the wall and entered her roughly, and she squealed delightfully and then moaned.

Soon, they moved into the bedroom, where Nasir had her contorted into several positions, doing things to her body that had never been done.

After they both climaxed for the third and fourth time, they stayed in each other's arms. Nasir wondered what people would think. His mother, his aunt, and uncle would probably put a hit out on him. It was evident on Nasir's face and in his actions that he was truly in love with her.

Fancy raised her head from Nasir's perspiring chest and reached for the pack of Newports Shoe-Shine had left only days earlier. She lit a cigarette and took a deep pull.

The two were silent.

Nasir closed his eyes for a moment and took in the tranquility in her room.

Fancy took a few more pulls from the cigarette and then turned her head slightly to catch a glimpse of him, his muscular upper body gleaming with sweat. He looked relaxed.

"You know I came over here only to show you my new ride."

"And instead you just fucked the shit out of me."

He chuckled. "Something like that."

"Well, correct me where I'm wrong."

"I like to think what we do ain't just fuckin'."

Fancy looked up and could see he was serious. She knew they were making love, but why admit it to the smug Nasir? Instead she put up a cantankerous front. "Well, we aren't making love, are we?"

Nasir didn't answer her. Instead, he just buried her fingers in her hair and began to massage her scalp. *What are we doing? This can't lead anywhere,* he thought.

Changing the subject, she asked, "How much did you pay for it?"

"Thirty grand."

She nodded. "And what do you have left?"

"What do you mean?"

"You understand the question—How much money do you have in your stash?" Not waiting for a response, she added, "You live in the heart of the ghetto, in a godforsaken hellhole, with your momma, might I add, and you just dropped your last money on a car."

Nas was still feeling weak from the fuck session and really didn't want to argue. He knew what she was saying was right, but in the drug game, no one ever thought that there wouldn't be more money.

Calmly, he replied, "Look at you preaching, when you spend your last money on clothes and shoes before food and rent."

Fancy was in no mood to examine her own flaws. Naked and hovering at the end of the bed, she had the look of a person with something important to say. She sighed. "You know Shoe-Shine is ready to come up in the game. He has serious plans. Big plans. But while he's thinking on how to expand an empire, you're out dropping serious cash on a whip. He's ready to take his from some Haitians, but you won't let him make moves. You won't give him a chance."

Fancy didn't know why she spilled the beans about the Haitians. It could've had something to do with the good fuck her cousin had given her, the fact that she never knew how to keep a secret, or perhaps her need to make a point of kicking Nasir off his pedestal by pointing out his stupidity. Whatever it was, the toothpaste was out, and she couldn't put it back in the tube.

"Shoe-Shine? When you saw him?"

"I ran into him last week when I came to check your moms."

Hearing Fancy speak about his lieutenant on the come-up had him vexed. He knew, if given the chance, Shoe-Shine could hustle and also put a nigga six feet under like the best of them. And although Nasir always knew he was ambitious, it was disturbing coming from Fancy. She continued to praise Shoe-Shine like he was God Almighty.

Nasir shouted, "Why you keep ridin' this nigga dick so hard? He fuckin' you better than me?"

Fancy smirked. She leaned over and put her cigarette out in the ashtray. Finally she locked eyes with him. "All I was saying is that you should get smart. And if that means making me your partner, then you should do it. Before it's too late. I'm only telling you this because I love you. You're my blood. But if you keep doing that ghetto shit, then you never will get to my father's status. You have to be like an ant, storing up your profits for a rainy day. I don't know about you, but I don't want to live in a fuckin' tenement building for the rest of my life. Not when bitches are flying around in Learjets."

Nasir remained silent. It was time to bounce.

# CHAPTER 24

Fancy sat in the loud, crowded waiting room with a new vigor. After his last outburst, she had written to her father and he immediately accepted her apology. Sadly, she realized her parents weren't ever going to be released. Even if both of them were delusional. A small part of her felt it was her fault for fucking up the money. But she rationalized that the money would have only gone to serve her purpose. They could back up the Brinks truck on the courthouse steps, and still her parents wouldn't be set free.

Alexandro, as handsome as ever, came walking out the back. He scanned the room for his baby girl. His eyes gleamed when he spotted her. He hated that she didn't come more often, but he was also wise enough to know that she had to lead her own life and that weekly visits weren't something on an eighteen-year-old girl's agenda. Still, he welcomed her with open arms whenever she came.

They embraced. He kissed the side of her face and grasped her hands. "You look gorgeous, sweetheart. How are you?"

"I'm doing okay, Pop-Pop." She leaned in and gave him another kiss. "And you?"

"I've been reading a lot, getting my exercise in, you know, keeping my mind busy."

She nodded.

Fancy half-listened as her father spoke about the latest novels he'd read. He also told her that he had signed up for his GED and would soon be able to take college courses, something he'd always wanted to do but didn't have the time between drug deals. He also spoke about the impending trial and how it was being alleged by his attorney that Belen was going to turn state's evidence against him.

"Did you hear me? I asked, have you spoken to your mother? Did she mention testifying against me?"

She blinked once. And then again. "Pop-Pop, I spoke with Mommy at length about this subject. She isn't a rat. She's not going to snitch on anyone, and that includes you. I don't know why your attorney would say something like that. In fact, I am so tired of the 'snitch' word being thrown around in the same sentence as Lane. And of all people, I'm looking at you sideways. I thought you said we don't break." Fancy was upset.

Alexandro shrugged. "We don't."

"So why would you think that the government broke your wife?"

"Calm down, Fancy. I was just asking a question. In here all alone your mind begins to wander, that's all, and my gut keeps telling me something ain't right and there's some merit to what my lawyer is saying."

"You really have a strong feeling?"

"I do." Alexandro exhaled.

How could her mother go against Alexandro and cut a deal? Alexandro was a legend. How would it look if his wife snitched him out? How would that affect all the respect Fancy got in the streets? She'd never be trusted. Especially not while she had hopes and dreams of building her own empire. "How could she really do this to us?"

"Shhhhh. Calm down. I don't know this to be true. That's why I asked you. There's a sealed indictment with only Jane and John Doe witnesses after the state's last witness was murdered. If you could, if you have time, go and see Belen and ask her what's what. Could you do that for me?"

"Of course."

Fancy had so many things swirling around in her head. She'd gone through so much in such a short time. She didn't feel eighteen. She felt like a fully-fledged adult and wanted so badly for her father to see her that way as well.

"I need to ask you a huge favor, but I want you to fully assess it before you tell me no," she began slowly. "And please don't flip out and go berserk. I hate it when you're angry with me and we don't speak. It drives me crazy. You're my rock, and I need you in my life, but you need to understand that I'm maturing. I am older than you were when you started your empire. And I hope that you realize that it could not only help me but you as well. I'd be able to hire you a real attorney and get some of these charges knocked down and perhaps even dismissed."

"Each charge holds a life sentence, so we'd need to hire a helluva attorney." He smiled warmly, as if resigned to his fate. Alexandro knew what she wanted to ask. Fancy was stubborn and spoiled, and an outburst from Daddy wasn't going to change much. "Go ahead. Ask me anything without the strawberries and whipped cream on top. Keep it one hundred."

She leaned in close and looked him squarely in his eyes. "I need you to put *me* in touch with your connect, not my man."

If she thought her father would slap her down, scold her, or even try to speak to her like she was a child, she was wrong. This time things were different.

"That's a valuable resource," he admitted. His voice was level and confident.

"So I'm told."

"Does this have to do with this new kid Tone you're messing with?" Alexandro stared at his daughter to see if she'd flinch. "You know he has a woman, don't you?"

Fancy was shocked. She'd never mentioned Tone's name to her father. "How do you know about him?"

"When you started dropping C-notes into my commissary, I began to ask around. I know most of what you do from in here within a twenty-four-hour turnaround. We get our info federal expressed in here."

Fancy was impressed. "Well, as you said, he has someone that's obviously more special to him than I am." She looked off, thinking about the last time they'd been together. "So this isn't for him."

Alexandro clasped his hands together. "Then what are your thoughts?"

"I need the connect for me, Pop-Pop. Honestly." Fancy braced herself for impact. "And before you say anything, I can do this."

"Tell me, what do you think qualifies you to handle this game?"

Fancy thought about his question. She had gone over this meeting a million times in her head. She thought she had all the answers. Truthfully, she actually thought all she would need to do was bat her long eyelashes and her father would be putty in her hands.

"I've learned from the best. And I've put together a crew that will hold me down."

Alexandro shook his head. "Your mother and I have put you in a precarious situation. I know you want to do whatever you have to, to get back on top, but this ain't the way."

"So it's only the way if you give the connect to my man?"

"I'm not giving the connect to anyone, whether or not they're holding down my daughter."

"But why?" she whined.

"Because you and these li'l niggas ain't built for this level of distribution. Those five-and-dime block huggers would be signing their death certificates."

"How hard could this be, Pop-Pop?" Fancy wasn't giving up. "I know, with your help and guidance, I could do this. I could take this game to the top. Get us back where we used to be."

"Fancy, I want a different life for you. I want you back in school."

"That's not happening, at least no time soon." She closed her eyes tight. When she opened them, she opened her heart. "I don't know why I don't long to be the studious girl I was only last year, but things changed. I have this calling that I can't shake. It's like when I'm around it, you know, the life, I feel like I belong."

"You don't know what you're asking."

"But I do. I really, really do."

"My connect is a descendant of Escobar. He supplies tons of cocaine by the hour to the North, South, Midwest, and Western regions. Very few get to meet him personally. I am one of the few. But that introduction doesn't come without guarantees."

"Guarantees?"

He nodded. "You have to guarantee a relative, someone you hold dear to your heart, in order to get to that level."

Fancy was confused. "What do you mean, guarantee a relative?"

"Are you sure you want to hear this?"

"I told you that I want to know who my parents are—really are."

Alexandro felt it necessary to tell Fancy the truth, to show her how the drug game turned even the most level-headed people, the people who are supposed to love and cherish you, into monsters.

"Your mother and I were making a come-up. We were moving ki's. It wasn't low-level, but we wasn't making fuck-you money." He paused, recounting the good old days. "Our names started ringing out in the streets, and I began rubbing shoulders with some major players. When we were introduced to the connect, we sat down at the round table as businessmen and discussed how we could both expand our organizations. We hashed out the terms, and then he hit me with something from left field."

Alexandro gritted his teeth as his body tensed up. "Casually, he asked, 'Who do you love most in this world, your wife or your daughter?' Naturally, I said that I loved you both."

"But you do, Pop-Pop. What was wrong with his question?"

Alexandro exhaled. "Then he said, 'Do you believe in a higher power?' I told him I did. The next question was, 'If your God said you could save one person on this earth from Armageddon, who would it be, your wife or your daughter?'" He appeared to choke up. "I said my daughter. I'd save my daughter."

As a lone tear slid down Alexandro's face, Fancy jumped up and embraced him. "I love you just as much." She kissed him on the cheek. "Why are you sad?"

"Sit down, Fancy."

Fancy was startled, but she did as she was told.

"I didn't know what I had walked into. Usually, in this game, when a dealer fucks up, they take the dealer out. But the connect and his cartel are different. They don't take the dealer out, they take out the one he loves most. Which is you."

Fancy blinked a couple times.

"You have a bounty on your head. It took us by surprise, Fancy. We didn't plan it this way."

"Please stop talking."

"You need to hear this." Alexandro leaned in close. "As long as we don't talk, you're safe. But if your mother is cooperating with the federal government, she knows that you're as good as dead."

Fancy imploded. She wanted to gouge her father's eyes out. Who was she? Who were her parents? How could they claim to love her and have her walking around the streets of New York with a tag on her toe? And how the fuck would she know if her mother was cooperating? All Belen ever talked about was getting free.

Fancy wondered if she was expendable to a mother who was facing the death penalty. And there always was the probability that the connect could send them an early message, if he thought her parents were cooperating.

Fancy needed money, and she needed it now. Her new plan would be to make enough money to blow town. Get lost in one of the many states and never, ever see her parents again. She needed to speak with Nasir and tell him everything. She was sure he could help her in some way. But then she realized, if word got out that she didn't have access to the connect, she would no longer be the goose who laid the golden egg.

"I think this has gone far enough without any action from you, Pop-Pop. Aren't you supposed to be the patriarch of the family? How could you have me walking around here while my life is in some godforsaken drug lord's hands while he decides if he should or shouldn't kill me? These snitch rumors have been whirling around for months! You, yourself, are even paranoid that your wife is selling you out. What if the connect starts itching and wants to scratch?"

"Fancy, calm down. Getting anxious about this isn't helping the situation."

"Calm down?" she replied, sarcastically. "Really? Really, Pop-Pop? That's the best you could say after all you've just told me?"

"I also told you I would handle this."

"When!" For the first time Fancy looked at her father with disgust. "How could you allow your wife to sit in a dirty jail cell, even for one second, and claim to love her? You should have copped out and taken the weight from day one. That's what real men do! You're a spineless, weak man. They've pulled down your pants, and I see panties!"

Fancy stormed away from the visiting room with her father calling after her. Alexandro went back to his 8 x 6 foot jail cell, defeated. He didn't know where he went wrong with his only child.

# CHAPTER 25

As days passed, things got bleak for Nasir and Shoe-Shine. With the attempt on Tone's life, Nasir no longer was able to buy work from him because he was ghost. There was another Harlem cat, Tone's rival, but he wouldn't fuck with Nasir because he was from Brooklyn. Now Nasir had to buy work from Devon, but his shit was stepped on too many times, and everyone was complaining.

It was close to rent time when Fancy went to Brooklyn to search for Shoe-Shine, who had suddenly stopped coming to Queens. She found him in Nasir's living room in a heated debate.

"You know you fucked us up with that move last month," she heard Shoe-Shine say.

"What move?" she asked, walking in and placing her purse on the counter.

"What the fuck you doing here?" Nasir said angrily.

Fancy saw in his eyes that his words belied his true feelings. "I was coming to check you."

He smiled. "Really?"

"Yeah, really." She looked over at her man, or lover, not knowing which he was. "Hey, Shoe-Shine."

"Wassup?" He took a swig of his Heineken.

"What's going on with you two?"

Nasir answered, "We just politicking 'bout business."

Shoe-Shine added, "You know, men shit."

Fancy glared at Shoe-Shine. "Nasir, I need to talk to you about something."

"Go 'head."

"Alone."

"Oh, now, you two actin' like you ain't tight? What? Y'all estranged?" Nasir chuckled at his own joke. "Y'all think a muthafucka dumb?"

"We ain't a couple." Fancy rolled her eyes. "And I came here to discuss Tone."

That name made both men uneasy.

"What about him?"

"Well, he's been MIA," she began. "And before you can say some smart shit, you were right—He played me for his Harlem bitch and left me dead broke. Bottom line, I need rent money."

Nasir felt a little guilty because he knew he'd cut off her meal ticket, Tone. Fancy was used to living better. He dug into his pocket and counted out nine hundred dollars. "How much you need?"

"The minimum, fifteen hundred, but I need money for utilities and also just to live, you know, cab money, food money, hair and nail money."

"Yo, sounds like you need a man."

"Tell me something I don't know."

Shoe-Shine reached into his pocket and counted out nearly six hundred dollars, and they handed the money to Fancy.

Fancy sighed. "This isn't enough."

"Shit is tight around here, Fancy. You know I would look out if I could."

She heard the sincerity in Nasir's voice but couldn't understand why he didn't have any cash. "What's going on? Where's your money?"

"We put all our money in some bad work. Now we can't move it. It's garbage," Shoe-Shine explained.

"Oh, you had to find another connect once Tone left?"

Nasir nodded.

"You didn't test the shit before you bought it?"

"The first two ki's were potent shit, and then we got hit wit' this weak shit."

"Well, get your money back."

Both Shoe-Shine and Nas laughed.

Nas said, "It don't go like that, baby girl. My new connect, Devon, is stuck with at least twenty ki's of bullshit. And those Colombians ain't giving him a refund, and he sure as hell ain't doing returns. But that nigga ain't sweating it, 'cuz his paper is long. And we can't sweat it either. We gotta charge it to the game. It'll move . . . eventually. Just gotta wait it out."

"So, in the meantime, what do we do for money?"

Nas shrugged. "Go on a caper."

"Go on a heist," she suggested.

Nasir remarked dryly, "I wonder where that idea came from."

# CHAPTER 26

It was early afternoon when Fancy stepped out of the black Benz in Queens within walking distance of St. John's University. Dressed like a scholarly college student with her nerdy Ray-Ban glasses propped squarely over her small nose, she sported a small Louis Vuitton knapsack, skinny jeans, and flat Tory Burch shoes. The noise from the city buses and cars was bustling. The fall months were gradually fading into winter, and the brisk breezes were replaced with cold winds.

She noticed her mark's car coming out of his building's underground parking garage, just as Nasir said she would. He got to the corner and hesitated for a second. She pretended to drop her things. Then he and Fancy made quick eye contact before he peeled out. Fancy started to gather her books, thinking she'd missed the opportunity.

Seconds later his cocaine-colored Range Rover made a U-turn. He rolled down his window and continued to coast slowly, as she walked.

"Excuse me, beautiful. Do you go to school here?"

Fancy glanced up shyly. She smiled and slightly nodded.

"You don't talk?" he said, already losing patience.

She stopped walking. "Not to men who choose to ride while I walk."

His interest was piqued. "Oh, my bad." He placed his foot on his brake. "You want a ride to school? Hop in, ma. I could give you door-to-door service."

"I'd rather walk." She turned toward him, as if examining his face to make sure he was interested. "But you could walk me."

He thought about his options. He really just wanted to grab her digits and keep it moving. He had to go and meet his man and take care of business, but there was something classy about her. And he liked her voice and how she demanded respect.

He hopped out of his car, as she waited patiently on the sidewalk. "My name's Chris. And your name is?"

Fancy thought for a second. Her mark's name was supposed to be Devon, but then she realized he was probably using a fake name, as she was instructed to do. "Jacqueline, like in Kennedy-Onassis."

"Did your mother name you after her?"

"My parents did."

He loved that—both her parents in her life. He scanned her up and down and loved her attire. She was well-spoken, obviously a daddy's girl, and going to one of the top universities in New York. He couldn't wait to fuck the shit out of her and make her call him daddy.

"Are your parents still together?"

"Married twenty-four years."

"How old are you?"

"Eighteen. And you?"

He chuckled. "I'm a little older than eighteen."

She looked up at him again. He was extremely tall and fit, graying around his goatee and sideburns, and his eyes looked worn.

"You look aged." Before he could take it as an insult, she added, "Like a fine wine."

A huge grin spread across his face.

*So he's a sucker for a compliment*, Fancy thought.

"So, ma, when could we get up? Let me take you out and show you a good time."

His vernacular was appalling to Fancy. He was too old to be calling her ma and asking if they could get up, but what did she care? She had a job to do.

"Honestly, you seem like a nice person, but my father won't let me go out with you," she said, her voice laced with innocence.

"Do you have a boyfriend? Is that the real reason?"

Fancy shook her head vigorously. "No, sir."

*Sir?* He couldn't believe she was so inexperienced. Oh, he was definitely going to fuck her raw. His dick was getting hard just looking at her shapely body. "Then he doesn't have to know about me."

"Every hour of my day is accounted for. I come to school, and then I go to practice. I made the twenty-twelve Olympic track team."

At first Devon only wanted to bang her out. But hearing how disciplined she was and that she was an accomplished athlete, he suddenly wanted to possess her. He wanted her so badly, he wasn't going to take no for an answer. He knew that her father would be a problem, but he also knew that if he got too much in the way, he'd have one of his little men take him out.

"Listen, gorgeous. Don't break my heart. Just give me your number, and I promise we will figure something out. I've never met someone like you before. For me, it's almost love at first sight."

Fancy feigned bashfulness, and then, reluctantly, gave him the digits to her prepaid telephone, just as planned.

✳✳✳

The first date made Fancy's skin crawl. She pretended to cut class, and he took her to a quaint restaurant on the outskirts of Long Island. Fancy didn't know who was hiding from whom, but she definitely couldn't chance running into anyone, and apparently neither could he.

Once they got back to his apartment building, which was also his stash house, he invited her upstairs. She had to go to get the layout and report it back to Nasir and Shoe-Shine.

As soon as they got upstairs, she noticed that he made her walk in front of him. When she turned around, she could see that he had his hand resting near the buckle of his jeans, which undoubtedly was his burner. Secondly, he handed her a key and told her to unlock the door. After he shut off his alarm system, he turned it right back on, only, without the motion detector. That meant they could roam around the apartment safely, but if a window cracked or the front door opened without deactivating the system, the alarm would go off.

Then he called someone on the telephone and said, "Give me a question." He paused, then said, "Oh, that's easy. Metropolis." Then he hung up his phone.

"Who was that?" Fancy knew it was all a part of a routine—a routine of safety. What she didn't know was how to penetrate his defense.

"Don't concern yourself with such things," he said.

"You have someone in your life?"

"Excuse me?"

Fancy feigned jealousy. "You're acting strangely and making strange phone calls. My parents told me that's the number one sign that a man is either married or has someone very special to them. And if that's the case, I want to leave."

He exhaled. "Do you see any ring on my finger?"

She looked at his bare hand. "Please don't lie to me."

The frailty in Fancy's voice was a new phenomenon for Devon. He was used to dealing with young, sassy chicks who had been around the block a few times in their young lives but still pliable enough to mold. He was saying things like "metropolis," and she thought he was talking to wifey.

*Her parents sure as hell aren't doing her any justice by keeping her so sheltered,* he thought.

175

Against his better judgment, he decided to tell her just enough to keep her jealousy at bay. "Baby girl, that's my man. I pay him to look out for me. He lives in the building. When I'm on my way up, I call him, and when I get safely inside, I call him again."

"So why Metropolis? I don't get what Superman has to do with your safety."

"Nah, we ain't even on no Superman shit. He always asks a question that I would know. If I answer incorrectly, he knows it's about to go down, that my safety is at stake."

Fancy looked at all the locks, and he followed her eyes. "What are you into? Something illegal?" She hugged her shoulders and pretended to be frightened.

"I have to tell you something that I've never shared with anyone. Can you keep a secret?"

She stepped closer to him and opened her eyes wide. "Yes, I promise."

"I'm CIA."

Fancy did everything in her power to not burst out into laughter. *Men are hilarious at what they will do to get some pussy.* She placed her hand over her mouth. "Like Jason Bourne?"

With a straight face, he nodded. "So, you see, my safety is a top priority. You see these cameras? They're hooked up not only directly to my superior, but also my cleanup man. He's only a couple floors away."

Once he felt that he had her intrigued, he ushered her farther inside his stash house/fuck pad. Moments later, he was all over her.

"Chris, please, you're rushing me."

"It's okay, baby," he crooned, pulling at the zipper of her jeans. "I'll make you feel good, I promise."

Finally, she blurted out, "I'm a virgin, okay?" Instantly, she burst into tears, deflating his hard-on.

"Why are you crying?"

"Because I'm ashamed."

He hadn't had a virgin in two decades and wasn't really interested in having one now. He wanted someone who knew how to suck him off and ride good dick. With Jacqueline, he didn't know if he had the patience to teach her. But the flip side to that was, no one had had her before, and that seemed to outweigh the cons.

He reached out and cuddled her. "Shhhh, don't cry. There ain't nothing to be 'shamed of. And don't let none of your fast-ass girlfriends tell you otherwise. From now on tell them that your man loves that you saved yourself for him."

She whispered, "Are you my man?"

"Hells yeah, I'm your man."

Fancy wanted to throw up at the weak game he was laying down. *Does this shit actually work on dumb-ass broads?* "So you'll be gentle with me when you make love to me?"

His dick began to stir. He leaned over and gave her another sloppy kiss. "I'd never hurt you, Jacqueline. I'ma grown-ass man. I know what I'm doing."

She leaned on his chest. "Okay, but I'm not ready yet. We just met, and, you know, I want my first time to be special."

Devon kissed her forehead. He knew what he had to do to get her to relax and trust him. He also knew that it wouldn't be today.

"Listen, let me walk you back to your car. I don't want to get you into trouble."

"Yes, you're right. I should be heading home."

"And make sure you make up the work you missed at school today. I don't want you thinking I'm a bad influence."

After they arrived at her car, just up the street near the university, Devon gave her a tender goodnight kiss. When he turned to walk back home, Fancy peeled off his block, checking her rearview mirrors.

She exhaled when she saw Nasir driving behind her with Shoe-Shine riding shotgun. They drove back into Brooklyn to discuss what she'd learned.

"That nigga is creepy. His old ass!"

"Did he try and fuck you?" Nasir asked.

"What you think?"

"But that shit ain't happening," Shoe-Shine said. "We gonna lullaby his ass before he can even get his dick out."

"No doubt. Think we could run up in there the next time y'all meet?"

Fancy thought for a moment. "He's no dumb-ass hustler. That apartment is set up like Fort Knox. He has at least nine deadbolt locks on his door and locks them all. How would I be able to sneak away from him and unlock them all? It would take too long and make too much noise."

"We could get around that, I'm sure. Just gotta put our heads together."

"Actually, that's the least of our worries. He has an alarm system."

"We make that nigga give up that code. Put the burner to his head, and a muthafucka will fold. Trust."

"But what if he doesn't?"

"Then splatter his brains all over that front door."

"Okay. But after that, you better be ready for war," Fancy warned.

"With who? Don't nobody know we planning on juxing that nigga. And don't nobody know about you, right? You ain't talking, are you?"

"I'm talking about the war that will come when he doesn't make his follow-up phone call."

"Stop talking in riddles," Nasir said. "Tell us what the fuck we up against."

"I'm fucking trying, but y'all keep interrupting a bitch." Fancy hated that they were always speaking to her so disrespectfully. Especially when without her there would be no robbery. They needed her. It wasn't the other way around.

"He has a triggerman who lives in the building. He calls him when he gets to his building, and whoever this person is, they ask him a question that he would know the answer to. And then I guess they time how long it would take to get upstairs. At that point, he calls again, and the mysterious stranger asks another question. If we got him hemmed up and force him to place the call, how would we know if he's going to answer the question correctly? Which we both know he won't."

This last bit of information silenced both Nasir and Shoe-Shine.

Finally, Shoe-Shine said, "That's that *O-G* shit. This muthafucka ain't fuckin' around."

Shoe-Shine understood, even if Nasir didn't.

"Fuck that! Anybody could get got!" Nasir began pacing around the tiny apartment, biting his bottom lip. With this fucking mark on some cloak-and-dagger shit, making it more difficult to do their home invasion, his pressure was steadily rising.

Finally, a thought occurred to Nasir. He snapped his fingers repeatedly. "Yo, Fancy, you ain't gonna like this one bit, but you might have to fuck that nigga."

Fancy glared at him with nothing but hatred and contempt. "What did you just say?"

"You fuckin' heard me. You gotta do that nigga to at least make him comfortable enough to get the alarm code. And then maybe we could go up in his crib when he ain't there, and perhaps not have to murk your boo."

"You know his lame ass ain't my boo!" she screamed. "And I ain't fuckin' that old bag of dirt!"

"Why?" Nasir asked. "You fuckin' everybody else."

Shoe-Shine asked, "Who she fuckin'?"

Nasir rolled his eyes and took a pull from his purple haze. "Fancy, tell Shoe-Shine who else you done fucked."

The question left her hot under her collar. Did he actually want people to know that they'd slept together? She wanted to charge at him and scratch his eyelids out. Instead, she stored up her disdain for him in a place where she would never forget it. Her mind. Her heart would allow her to forgive her cousin for all his transgressions, but her mind was much stronger than that.

"Don't worry about who I sling my pussy on. But it won't be his way."

Just as Fancy said those words, visions of the times she and Nasir made love infiltrated her thoughts. She closed her eyes and shuddered. How could she? What disturbed her most was that she actually felt herself get moist.

She looked at him, his cinnamon-complexioned soft skin so soft and smooth. His baby-soft hair cut low and his masculine physique was more than she could handle. She got hot and began to fan herself as she took a couple steps back.

"What's wrong with you?" Shoe-Shine couldn't understand her beef. She'd told him that she'd do anything for that paper. In his mind, sex was sex, as long as she only gave him her body and not her mind.

Shoe-Shine thought like an old-school pimp. He truly had little to no respect for most women. As a child growing up, he watched men beat on his mother, and seconds later, he'd hear them in the other room fucking their brains out. As each moan echoed throughout the house, he lost more and more respect for her. And as he watched his aunts and girl cousins repeat the same behavior, he began to lose respect for all women. No woman had actually captured his heart. They were too weak for a nigga. He learned that a woman's mind could be altered—molded into whatever a man wanted it to be, especially if he was laying the pipe correctly.

"Didn't you just hear Nasir?" she barked. "He really wants me to fuck dude."

"Calm down, Little Orphan Annie." Nasir rubbed his chin. "I think I just thought of a way we could bypass all that red tape and you could keep your wide legs closed, at least for another twenty-four hours." He chuckled, amusing only himself.

# CHAPTER 27

The mood of the room was tense. The entire team, Nasir, Shoe-Shine, Lucky, Nicholas, and Fancy, convened in Nasir's living room on the morning of the heist, carrying automatic pistols and dressed in black.

"There ain't no coming back from what we about to do today," Nasir began. "If anyone of y'all muthafuckas don't have the heart, bow the fuck out now. Walk away like a man, and I could respect that. But don't get there and bitch out, 'cuz that won't be acceptable."

Nasir took the time to look each one of his people in the eye and, when he was satisfied, told them they could bounce.

**✳✳✳**

Everyone had a specific job to do but probably not as important as Fancy thought hers was. Dressed in a snug-fitting black dress with black heels with the red bottoms, she set out on her mission, driving the black Benz into Queens and arriving on time for her date with Devon. She knew her plan was hit or miss.

Devon hopped out of his Range with a pep in his step. He was about to get some eighteen-year-old virgin pussy, and his eagerness was evident.

Fancy rolled down her window, and he leaned in and gave her a juicy kiss. "Leave your car parked here," he stated, and opened her car door.

When Fancy got out the car, she noticed he was gawking.

"You wearing that dress."

She smiled, feigning innocence. "You like it?"

"Do I?" He chuckled. "Ma, you don't even know what you're working with."

Fancy got inside of his truck, and they entered his garage. He did his usual protocol and called the anonymous person on the telephone to let them know he was going to his apartment.

When they stepped off the elevator, there stood Joyce, Devon's baby momma, and to Fancy's dismay, she'd brought their son, Devon Jr.

"I caught ya bitch ass!" Joyce screamed, looking Fancy up and down. "And with this bum-ass skank bitch!"

"What the fuck you talkin' 'bout?" Devon started inching away from Fancy. "I ain't wit' this bitch!"

"You a fuckin' lie!" she screamed.

Fancy had called Joyce only an hour earlier pretending to be the gay lover of the female Devon was fucking. The fake dyke and Joyce planned to bust both their lovers in the act. Joyce didn't want to take along little Devon, but under such short notice, she didn't have a choice.

Devon was unaware that Nasir, Shoe-Shine, Lucky, and Nicholas had all slid out of the stairway and were about to surround him. He saw the expression on Joyce's face, her eyes popped open wide, her mouth open.

Before Devon could react, he had a gun to his left temple. In a desperate attempt, he still tried to go for his piece, but Nasir slammed him in the head with the butt of a gun.

"Make the call," Nasir demanded.

"Whatchu talkin' 'bout, man?"

Nasir hit him again.

"Make the fuckin' call. Don't make me ask you again, or your li'l man right here gets it."

Joyce was shell-shocked, frozen with fear, even as Shoe-Shine hemmed up her son with a pistol to his ear.

Finally, she screamed, "Do something!"

Fancy's eyes kept darting back and forth. She thought at any second there would be a full-fledged shootout in the tiny hallway. That would be sure to take several lives. But they were so close to getting enough money to put their lives back on track.

Devon slowly reached into his pocket and pulled out his cell phone. In a million years he never figured it could actually go down like this. He thought he was a thinker, an Einstein in his own right. He'd gone over a million scenarios, and never once did he think his setup was penetrable. He tried to think. Should he chance it with the password? How would they know whether or not he'd answered correctly? In a heartbeat, his soldiers would come flying down to his apartment with guns blazing.

"And before you get any ideas, you better say the right fuckin' answer, 'cuz if I even think that heat is comin' off that elevator or out that staircase, your li'l man gets it," Shoe-Shine, said, his voice gruff and menacing.

Devon turned to face Fancy. Finally realizing that she'd set him up, he didn't have to speak his contempt for her. His eyes spoke volumes.

"Don't hate her ass now!" Joyce began. "She set your dumb—"

Everyone screamed simultaneously, "Shut the fuck up!"

Finally, there was silence. And the only movement was that of Devon dialing his enforcer. So many thoughts went through his mind, but ultimately he just couldn't chance them doing anything to harm his son.

He noticed that each man was wearing all black with red bandannas tied around their face. That was a good indicator that they would allow him to live. They hid their faces, so he couldn't recognize them and exact revenge. Which, if he lived another day, was exactly what he'd do because, bandanna or no bandanna, he knew the ringleader was none other than Nasir from Brooklyn. He'd done business with Nasir on a few occasions and not only was his voice distinctive, but his complexion and physique fit the mold.

When the enforcer picked up, you could hear his voice through the quiet of the hallway. "Yo, I was just about to come and get ya ass!"

"Nah," Devon replied coolly. "I told you 'bout shorty."

There was a long pause.

"So?"

"So, she had a nigga delayed, in my front seat."

Another long pause.

"Yo, what the fuck happened back in ninety-three at the B'more basketball game?"

"Damn. You digging way back, nigga."

Nasir pressed the gun more forcefully into Devon's temple.

"We watched as Wayne sent his man to murk Domencio. That shit was crazy. Everyone scattered like roaches!"

"Whew! Nigga, you had me worried for a minute. I thought the wolves had you cornered."

"In what world? These niggas know my fuckin' name."

Devon ended the call and was instructed to open his door and deactivate his security system.

Once inside, Joyce and Devon Jr. were taken into the bedroom, placed face down, and restricted with duct tape. Devon, too, was restricted, but they kept him in the front room.

"Where the stash at?" Nasir asked.

"I got fifteen grand in a Nike shoebox in the bottom of the closet," Devon replied.

"Damn, yo! We did all of this for fifteen *Gs*?" Nicholas said out loud. He was hoping to get car money out of this deal.

Nasir glared at him. He then ripped off his bandanna so Devon could see him, man to man. He lifted his gun and struck it down upon Devon's head, and he toppled over in pain.

"That dumb-ass move done cost you your life."

Nasir cracked his knuckles before kicking Devon several times in his rib cage. "You got two seconds to make a choice. If I go in the room and let your baby momma and your son see me, then they gotta die too. So either you give up the stash, or you all go out in body bags!"

Devon knew he'd fucked up by playing with these grimy stickup niggas from Brooklyn. He should have just given up the stash and lived to fight another day. Now that Nasir had revealed himself, he knew he'd signed his own death certificate. The only question was, would he sign Joyce's and Devon Jr.'s? The thought of turning over so much money and weight over to these derelicts had him vexed. But he also knew he had to charge it to the game. And what he loved more than money was his little seed.

With blood spewing from out of his mouth, he answered, "Nah, man. Take all I got. Just put your mask back on. Don't hurt my family. They don't have anything to do with this life. It's me you want . . . just take me."

"Where's the shit?" Shoe-Shine barked, thinking that they'd already been in there far too long.

"Please, Nasir, just promise me!"

Devon was virtually crying real tears, which tugged at Fancy's heart. She was positioned in an area where she could see Devon and into his bedroom with his baby momma and his son.

"Your two seconds are up, nigga. Make a choice."

"Nasir, please, man!"

*Click-clack!*

Nas began to walk toward the bedroom.

Devon cried out, "Okay, okay! Here . . . come back here, and I'll tell you." He gathered his composure. He nodded toward a late-edition, floor-model television. "It's in there. It's all in there."

Nas motioned for Lucky and Nicholas to go and check it out.

Within seconds they unscrewed the back and saw that the inside of the TV was removed. They found thirty ki's of cocaine and $255,000.

185

"Yo, this nigga loaded," Nicholas remarked. "All I see are big faces and that Christmas snow that will make anyone happy."

"Shut ya stupid li'l ass up!" Shoe Shine barked. He hated that he had to ride with ignorant muthafuckas to have a crew. He tossed them the black duffel bags, and they began to pack.

In the meantime, Devon continued to beg for his life. "You ain't gotta do this, Nasir," he pleaded. "I'm worth more alive than dead, man. We could be partners. We could take over this whole city."

"I don't do partners, partner."

Fancy saw the smirk on Shoe-Shine's face. Still, she remained silent. This was the first time she'd ever done anything remotely this morbid, yet somehow she kept wondering why she didn't have more remorse.

"But we could—"

"Shut the fuck up," Nasir remarked. Devon was trying his patience. He felt that they all knew the consequences of being in the drug game, and getting murked was one of them. "Tie this nigga's mouth up."

Fancy snapped to attention. As she grabbed the duct tape and wrapped up his mouth, she couldn't help but allow her breasts to rub up against his head in a sexual manner. Just one last gesture, which was a reflection of her depravity.

Nasir, who was watching her like a hawk, instantly noticed her move. He didn't say anything; he just glared.

Nasir kicked Devon in the back, and he fell face first on his plush carpet, with his hands tightly fastened and his feet bound. Nasir then clicked on the stereo and turned the volume up.

Immediately Devon began to squirm and move around, in a desperate attempt to prolong his life.

When Nasir grabbed the pillow and placed it over his head, Fancy wondered if she would look away. But she didn't.

Poot! Poot!

Devon stopped squirming.

Nasir looked at Fancy. "It's your turn."

Fancy's heart dropped, and she took a step closer toward Shoe-Shine. "You not gonna kill me, are you?" Her voice was rushed and laced with fear.

Nasir stared at her fiercely. "I'm surrounded by some ignorant muthafuckas!"

She asked, "So what are you talking about?"

"You got your burner, right?"

She nodded.

"Well, Bonnie, get your Clyde on!"

"Come on now, Nasir," Shoe-Shine said. "Let's just end this shit and bounce."

"Am I fuckin' talkin' to you?" The last thing Nasir wanted was for Shoe-Shine to defend Fancy. If he was only bluffing with what he wanted to ask of her, now he wasn't. "Fancy, you didn't come along just for the ride. We coulda got at this nigga without you."

"So why didn't you?" Fancy wasn't about to be played like she didn't do her part.

"Fuck all that! Go in there and send li'l man to meet his father."

"What?" Her eyes popped opened so wide, she thought they would snap out. "Nasir, I can't."

"Yo, Nasir, I'll do it. Let me do it for her." Shoe-Shine could see Fancy trembling from a distance. "Let me do it, man. I'm telling you, don't do this to her."

Nasir ignored their pleas. He pulled out his pistol and pointed it toward her head. "Either you go in there and put shorty to sleep, or I'ma put *you* to sleep. It's your call."

He inched closer, never taking his eyes off her, yet keeping Shoe-Shine in his peripheral vision. Lucky and Nicholas also had Nasir's back. He was their boss and the reason they were about to come up off of all this cash.

"This bitch keep suggesting that she could do what I do, so do what the fuck I do. I just played God in this bitch. Show me you could do the same, and maybe you could earn my respect . . . 'cuz all you are is a piece of pussy. And fuckin' a nigga don't get you thirty ki's and a quarter of a mill within fifteen minutes. If you could walk in my shoes, prove it."

Shoe-Shine didn't know how to handle the situation. It was fucked up what Nasir was asking her to do. He wanted to intervene, but he was outnumbered. And although he cared for her, he wasn't ready to die for her. There was a dead nigga at his feet who'd just gotten two holes in his head over this same broad. Shoe-Shine was sure, if Devon had to do it all over again, he would have chosen differently.

Fancy glared at her cousin. Nasir wouldn't have ever raised a gun to her if her father were around. Slowly, she pulled out her pistol and weighed the heavy object in her hands. How could she go in there and take a life? The life of a child, to boot.

Her knees felt like jelly as she tried to move, each step wobbly. She turned around and looked Shoe-Shine directly in the eyes, perhaps one last plea to see if he would intervene, but his face was stoic. She then looked to Lucky and Nicholas. No one said a word. They even looked slightly impatient, she thought. Last, she looked at Nasir, and his face was stone.

Fancy could hear Joyce and her son whimpering through the duct tape. Then she remembered the story her mother had told her about the hit being put out on their lives when she was just a child. Her father had protected her. Why couldn't Devon have protected his family better? Visions of her former life tried to flood back, but she pushed them away. She was no longer the girl in the dark who vacationed in Europe while her parents ran a drug empire. She was a black woman trying to survive with the hand they'd dealt her.

For a split second she wondered if Nasir would kill her if she didn't do it. Not after the way he made love to her. Would he? But then she thought about all the guilt attached to that act and thought that maybe, just maybe, he would. It would be a way to get rid of her, and their dirty little secret.

Fancy looked at the little body lying in front of her. He was scared, but surely he didn't know what was in store. She walked into the room, pistol drawn, and Joyce inched over and put her body, as best as she could, over her son's. Her movements were restricted, but you could feel her hysteria. It was sad. Really sad.

But Fancy told herself that there wasn't any way the little boy was leaving that apartment alive. The plan was for both his parents to be killed. No one factored in that Joyce would bring him along to bust his father having an affair. Maybe it was better that they all died together. As a family. Maybe . . .

"Hurry the fuck up!" Nasir yelled, knocking her out of her daydream.

Fancy said nothing. She wanted to keep the world tuned out.

She grabbed the pillow from off the bed, just as she'd seen her cousin do only minutes earlier, and tried to drop it over Devon Jr.'s head.

Only, his mother was still fighting. She'd managed to turn on her back and kick Fancy, lifting her off her feet as if a strong wind had tossed her.

Fancy quickly recovered. This action had everyone's full attention, all squeezed into the tiny room, beads of sweat trickling down their cheeks.

She was taking too long. This whole jux was taking too long. What if the enforcer got suspicious and came to check on his man?

Nasir walked over to Joyce and without hesitation put a bullet squarely between her eyes, killing her instantly. He turned to Fancy. "You got one fuckin' second to make it happen, captain."

Fancy stood over Devon Jr., closed her eyes, and tried to amp herself up. She counted to three and then pulled the trigger once.

*Poot!*

Her arm jerked.

And then again. *Poot!*

And then she exhaled. With her eyes still closed, she turned around and tried to walk, and then collapsed into Shoe-Shine's arms. He pulled her out of the room, while Nasir grabbed the fifteen *Gs* in the Nike shoebox, the video surveillance tape, and then ordered Lucky to take Joyce's jewelry.

Joyce was wearing a pricey Rolex watch and a huge engagement ring. She knew she was going to confront Devon with some random chick, so she'd put on her best jewels.

The crew walked calmly out of Devon's apartment, stepping over his dead body. They were happy with the take they got, but unaware of the nearly three million dollars he had stashed in the makeshift refrigerator, toilet bowl, and sewn into his mattress. The only other person who knew all the stash spots was Joyce. And she was dead.

# CHAPTER 28

Nasir and Fancy jumped into the Benz, while Shoe-Shine, Lucky, and Nicholas drove away in the Yukon. The air was chilly for a late September afternoon, and an afternoon thunderstorm was brewing. As the dark cumulonimbus clouds began forming in the sky and the rain burst through, so did Fancy's heart.

She buried her face into her hands and cried out her grief. "We can't tell anyone what I did," she pleaded. "That wasn't me up there."

As Nasir gripped the steering wheel, a few thoughts went through his mind. Although he saw her crying, he couldn't help but come to terms with the fact that she'd just murdered a six-year-old child. Most niggas would have bitched up, yet she'd done it. She had to know in her heart that he wasn't gonna do shit to her up in that apartment. Let alone murder her. Didn't she know how he felt about her? He loved her, deeply. All he wanted her to do was openly admit that she wasn't built to do what he did. He was a man's man—an alpha dog—and only wanted her respect.

He cut his eyes toward her. Who was she really? Was her former proper speaking voice and I-didn't-know-what-my-parents-were-into gimmick just a cover?

"Ain't nobody gonna ever find out. Niggas in our crew don't snitch. If someone starts runnin' their mouth, then we all get knocked."

They pulled up on the block in Brooklyn and ran into the building full speed. The rain was still heavy. Fancy was pissed that her flat-ironed hair had gotten wet. They jogged up the three flights of steps to her aunt's apartment to wait on the rest of the crew to arrive.

The house was filthy, loud, and stuffy. Fancy opened up the window to allow some fresh air to come in. She looked at Asia and Ava walking around with dirty diapers, while their mother sat perched on her bed watching soap operas. Al-Saadiq was intensely engrossed in the Xbox game, while Lisa was talking on the phone to one of her friends.

"Yo." Nasir tapped Al-Saadiq on his shoulder. "Y'all get the fuck up and go in the room."

No one moved.

"Yo," he said, more bass in his voice. "What the fuck I just said? My peoples be here any second, and we got business to discuss."

Grudgingly, Al-Saadiq and Lisa both walked into their crowded room, where they instantly began bickering. You could hear Brenda scolding them from her room.

The noise gave Fancy an immediate headache. She weighed her options. Did she really want to sit near Nasir after what he'd pulled earlier?

Grabbing up both twins, Fancy took them into the bathroom and decided to give them a much-needed bath. The tub had a thick ring of dirt on its dingy porcelain surface that took way too long to clean. Sweaty, her black dress damp with cleaning products, she looked at the two twins, their fat cheeks full of hope, and thought, *Why not?*

After they were washed and put in clean clothes, she brought them into their mother's room.

"What's goin' on?" Brenda looked up like they weren't her kids.

"We're having a meeting in the living room. They need to be out of the way."

Brenda thought to say something slick like, my kids can go wherever the fuck they want, but she was too grateful that Fancy had given them a bath.

"What made you clean them up?"

Fancy shrugged. "They needed it."

"Isn't this mighty white of you?"

Fancy wanted to believe she did it to avoid Nasir, but deep down inside she knew better. She wanted to prove to herself that she could have compassion and that she loved children.

✱✱✱

Two hours later, Shoe-Shine and the crew still wasn't there. Nasir continually kept blowing up his phone, thinking that something had happened.

"Yo, I should ride back out that way and see what's up."

"Are you crazy?" Fancy asked him. "Police might be crawling all around there."

"So what?" he barked. "They can't fuck wit' me if I didn't do nothing."

Fancy looked at him like he just got released from the G Building. "You did do something." She lowered her voice. "You just participated in a triple homicide, ass wipe!"

"You know what the fuck I mean. If I just drive through the block wit' a legit car and license they can't fuck wit' me. I just need to see what's up."

"You're black. Dummy!"

✱✱✱

An hour later, Shoe-Shine and the goons came storming into the apartment.

"Yo, we had a shootout wit' them niggas!" Shoe-Shine said, hyped, his clothes damp from the rain and his knuckles scraped.

"What niggas?" Nasir leapt to his feet.

Shoe-Shine went ballistic. "Who the fuck you think?"

Shoe-Shine began pacing up and down the living room and pounding

193

his fist into the palm of his hand. Fancy had never seen him lose his cool in this way. Yes, he was always menacing, but it was always controlled. Now, as he ran down the details, it looked like he was on the brink of doing something crazy.

His outburst caused Brenda to come running out of her bedroom to check on her oldest son. She didn't know if someone was trying to hurt Nasir. "Baby, you okay?" she said, her face frozen in fear.

"Yeah, I'm all right, Ma. Just go back in the room."

"You sure?"

"Yeah. Damn! Please, just go."

Brenda could have laid down the law and begun bitching, but she knew her son. He would come and tell her what happened when he was ready to talk. She had been giving him advice all his life, and nothing was going to change that. She retreated back to her bedroom without incident.

Fancy was confused. "But how did they find you?"

Shoe-Shine never looked her way. He turned to face Nasir. "Yo, we were trailing behind you and Fancy until we got on the Belt."

"True. I saw y'all," Nasir said.

Shoe-Shine nodded. "And then I said to Nic that it seemed like we were being followed. I didn't know if it was an undercover DT or the goons. When we hit the Belt and it was crawling, the last thing I wanted was for a muthafucka to get the drop on us while we're caged in like animals. So, right, check it," he said, continuing to pace. "I didn't want them to get on to you and Fancy, so I peeled off, and three jeeps pulled off too. So we amped right now."

"We all got our burners in our hands ready for whatever," Lucky added.

"So I'm driving down Jamaica Avenue, and all of a sudden, I see flashing lights on the truck behind me."

"Five-0?" Nasir asked. "Get the fuck outta here!"

"That's what I'm thinking," Shoe-Shine said. "But, yo, I gotta pull over 'cuz I know we can't outrun these muthafuckas. So I pass my burner to Lucky to tuck away, and I'm thinking, if they try that pop-open-the-trunk shit, then we just gonna blast our way outta there."

Shoe-Shine continued, "They on some your-vehicle-fits-the-description-of-one-used-in-a-robbery-let-me-have-your-license-and-registration type shit."

Lucky takes over the story. "So Shine hands over his shit, and it comes back clean, and we think we just dodged a bullet. Then they ask, could they search the jeep, and we like, hell nah, you ain't searching shit. The officer is like, 'Shut down your ignition while we wait for backup.'"

"What probable cause did he have to try and detain y'all?" Fancy asked.

"That's exactly what I said." Shoe-Shine was shaking his head wildly. "I'm like, partner, you ain't got probable cause to search my shit 'cuz I ain't break no law and we ain't rob shit."

Nicholas said, "I look out the back window, and he got two other trucks pulled off to the side. What more backup did these muthafuckas need? I told Shoe-Shine that shit wasn't right and to get us the fuck up outta here."

"Yo, I hit the gas and got my Mario Andretti on!" Shoe-Shine began demonstrating how he was maneuvering his truck. "And before I know it, I hear, *Boc, Boc, Boc, Boc, Boc,* like eight or nine shots ring out."

"Say word?" Nasir stated.

"Word." Shoe-Shine nodded. "Those muthafuckas were playing for keeps, so I give word and tell Lucky and Nicholas to light the niggas up."

By now all three guys were animated, reenacting the scene of how they almost just got murdered.

"Now we're in a gun battle and being chased through city streets by po-po. I drive up on the sidewalk to avoid hitting a crowd of pedestrians and lose control of my whip. I swerve and skid a couple yards before hitting several parked cars. We all bail out of my truck and take flight. I'm running, ass out, 'cuz Lucky got my burner."

"But I had ya back, though. I put you in front and turned both my pistols on the faggots and backed them up off you!"

"True dat," Shoe-Shine agreed.

Suddenly it dawned on Fancy. "Where's the money?"

Shoe-Shine blurted. "Bitch, is you stupid?"

"Wait, wait, hold up. Who you calling a bitch?" Nasir stepped up in Shoe-Shine's space. "Don't you ever disrespect my cuz like that, ya heard?"

Shoe-Shine acquiesced. "Oh, no doubt. My bad . . . I'm just amped, that's all. I'm buggin', yo. Pardon me, Fancy."

Fancy rolled her eyes.

"But I just told you we nearly got our domes splattered open, and you asking 'bout some paper?"

The room fell quiet.

Nicholas said, "I went back to the scene on some bystander shit and watched as they emptied the truck and then peeled out."

"So we lost everything? The cops took all the heist money?" Nasir didn't want to believe it until he heard it from Shoe-Shine's mouth.

"See, that's just it. They weren't cops. And if they weren't cops, then who were they?" He looked angrily toward Nasir and Fancy.

"Why aren't they cops?" she asked.

"They took the money and fuckin' drugs and tried to murder us! Jeez! Like a four-year-old kid!" Shoe-Shine peeled off his wet T-shirt, exposing his muscular physique.

"You think it was Devon's goons?" Fancy asked. She couldn't disguise the disappointment in her voice. She needed that score. She wanted a better life for herself, and if that meant taking a life here or there, then she was down for that.

"Hell, nah, it wasn't his goons. They would have caught us on the premises. And, besides, why would they pose as five-0?" Once again, he glared at Fancy and Nasir. "We were set up. Somebody knew we were coming up off some real paper, and all they had to do was lay on us."

"But who would know about this heist?" Fancy asked.

Shoe-Shine scrunched his face up. "That's what I wanna know. I nearly got rocked to sleep, and somebody in this room set us up."

Nasir exploded. "How the fuck we know you ain't set this shit up! Fuck you lookin' over here sideways for?"

Everyone exploded at once as the accusations flew.

For hours, each crewmember had to do his best to convince Nasir that he wasn't a snitch. Finally, when they realized that they all were broke again, and nothing was resolved, Nasir offered Shoe-Shine to take Fancy home because he was mentally spent. He'd spent days masterminding what he thought was the perfect jux, and for them all to end back up at ground zero had him vexed.

✳✳✳

"How could he have done this to me? I'm his fuckin' blood, for Christ's sake!" Fancy began ranting as soon as she got in the passenger's seat.

"I keep telling you that nigga don't care 'bout nobody but himself. You heard him up there, talking 'bout how he don't do partners. I'm tired of that nigga taking me for granted."

Fancy wondered how Shoe-Shine turned the conversation around and made it about him. She was the one who'd murdered a child. "I'm going to be haunted for the rest of my life by the look in his little eyes," she cried, her eyes puffy and her face covered in tears. "I fuckin' hate him!"

"I hate his ass too!" Shoe-Shine looked nervously through his rearview mirror.

"He's ruined my life. His black ass is a fuckin' monster! He's gonna recognize one of these days, I ain't his little flunky like the rest of y'all."

Shoe-Shine knew she was trying to hit below the belt. "Well, at least you're still among the living."

"What did you just say?" she roared.

Unfazed, he said, "You keep making this about you, but you had a choice up there. You're bitching about how he fucked up your life, but you are alive. And shorty's dead. By your hand. And that's fucked up. You killed a kid. I ain't never done no shit like that in my life. And guess what? Nasir ain't even killed a kid either. We all gonna be looking at your ass like a grimy bitch."

Fancy felt faint. Like she needed to check out. She couldn't believe what she was hearing, how he was speaking to her. What was it with the men in her life, always disappointing her? First her father. Then Tone. Nasir. And now Shoe-Shine. It was all incredulous.

"Keep it one hundred, Fancy. This me you talkin' to. I been inside you."

"What does that have to do with anything?" She hated the day she'd fucked Shoe-Shine. This whole day was laced with only regret.

"All I'm saying is, Nasir might be right. You ain't built for this here life. You're too emotional, and you can't recognize when you're being tested. And that's dangerous."

"What the fuck are you talking about? Stop talking in fuckin' riddles!"

The rain was beating down hard on the windshield. Shoe-Shine had to slow down the Benz as traffic began to slow to a crawl. He'd gotten on the Belt Parkway East, heading to Queens.

"There wasn't any way Nasir was going to kill shorty. He was six, Fancy. Do you think we're monsters?" He dug into his pocket and pulled out a Newport.

Fancy waited impatiently for him to light it.

"All he wanted to do was put fear in your heart. Have you admit, in front of everyone, that you can't do what he's done, that he's some sort of king and shit, and hopefully get out of your head for good that you could be some sort of gangsta. It wasn't real. The kid ain't see none of our faces, didn't know any names, and was too young to seek revenge. But when you pulled the trigger the first time, I saw the shock in Nasir's face. But the cat was already out of the bag. The kid already had a bullet in the back of his head."

"But he saw *my* face!" she countered, trying to justify her actions.

"You sound dumb as shit if you think a six-year-old could give a description to the cops and there'd be this massive manhunt for Fancy Lane. You must be crazy! Bottom line, what you did was out of order. Face it."

His words numbed the young Fancy. Was he telling the truth? Had it all been just a test? Did she actually take a life that was supposed to be spared? And if what he'd said was true, then he was in on the test as well. He was up there pretending like he would ride for her.

"But he pointed the gun right at my head," she said, her voice barely a whisper. "You were right there. You saw him."

"Like he would have murked you." He chuckled. "And have your father on his ass? Fancy, be smart."

There it was again. Another person questioning her intelligence.

"That's why I keep telling you that you need me." He clicked on the radio to Hot 97 and turned it down low enough so he could still politick. "If only you would trust me and go to your father and get with the connect, we could blow up. Once that's done, we could let the world know that I'm your man. No more sneaking around."

"What does that have to do with what happened today?"

"As your man I could school you to shit like this. I could have protected you in there."

Shoe-Shine was a bag of noise as far as Fancy was concerned. She didn't know if she should believe him or not regarding Nasir and the little boy. What she did know was, what went down in that apartment felt real. And that was all that mattered.

"I guess the fear I saw in your eyes when Nasir barked on you was all an act as well. That wasn't real, eh?"

"I don't fear no man."

"Please." Fancy wondered if he was trying to convince her or himself.

Shoe-Shine thought he was being invited up to get some ass, but she wasn't having it. Nasir and Shoe-Shine had put a bad taste in her mouth, and she was reeling from the day's events.

# CHAPTER 29

It didn't take long for the landlord to attach a Notice to Dispossess on Fancy's door for nonpayment of rent. She knew the inevitable was coming. It was the first week in March, so she never gave up looking for and calling Tone. She kept thinking he would swoop in and save her from Brooklyn, but he was ghost.

And so was Nasir. After the botched robbery, he'd moved in with some chick he was fucking with up in Harlem. He didn't let anyone know her address, which vexed Shoe-Shine. He still came around to run his crew, but he didn't lay his head at his mother's.

That left Brenda lonely.

So when Fancy asked if she could move back in, her aunt was more than eager. Plus, the fact that Fancy was coming with all her furniture made it all the merrier. They recruited a few teens from off the block to throw out all of Brenda's dated, dilapidated furniture to make room for the pricier stuff.

Fancy still had to sleep in the living room, but now she had a leather pull-out sofa and a 60-inch flat-screen. Her aunt kept her bedroom set, and they even bought a few gallons of paint and had the superintendent of the building put some color on the walls. In no time, the apartment was brought into this millennium.

The act of kindness that Fancy displayed had warmed her Aunt Brenda's heart. She began treating her more like a daughter than a stranger off the street.

Fancy wondered, with all the money that had passed through Nasir's hands, why he never did anything to fix the place up, instead leaving his mother and siblings living in squalor. She thought that fixing up the crib was the second thing drug dealers did after purchasing a whip.

**✳✳✳**

The days of sexing Nasir and Shoe-Shine had ended. Nowadays, Fancy was back to being broke and alone, yet always looking out for the next baller or come-up. So, it was a complete shock when her cousin came through with a job offer.

"Yo, if you wit' it, I need you to take this work for me OT."

"How much work? And what's my cut?"

Nasir sat down and looked at what the two women had done to the apartment and couldn't explain his pangs of envy. His younger siblings were actually in clean clothes, and his mother was in the kitchen preparing dinner. Fancy had a part-time job at the local Wal-Mart Supercenter. It didn't pay much, but she was able to boost food and cosmetics, which helped out tremendously. And since she didn't have to pay her aunt rent, she used the cash to keep her hair and nails done.

"It's two bricks. I usually give five hundred, but since you fam, I'll double that."

"Oh, you'd do that for me?"

"I just said you fam, didn't I?"

Fancy extended her middle finger. "Eat a dick."

"What?"

"Who the fuck you think you talking to?" She began brushing her long hair to wrap it. "You think I'm risking my freedom for one stack? In what world? If you can find a bitch that will take weight outta town in this day and age for five hundred, then I suggest you wife her. 'Cuz either she on your dick or she wants to be."

Nasir thought there was something different about Fancy. She now possessed a certain cynicism that you only get from years in the hood. She seemed wiser and not as desperate to be a part of his world. He realized that she'd been through a lot. And perhaps he was the catalyst that had changed her. The incident with the kid had to be something she could never completely reckon with. He wasn't sure, but he felt that had to be the answer.

"So how much you want?"

"Ten percent."

"I paid thirteen point five apiece," he lied. "So you telling me you want twenty-seven hundred?"

"Ten percent of the *gross*, plus expenses."

Nasir was selling both bricks for twenty large, so Fancy was looking to make four grand for a couple hours work. "You must be outta your fuckin' mind."

She shrugged and kept brushing her hair, infuriating Nasir. He wanted to choke her up, but he needed her. His best customer needed the work first thing in the morning, and his usual mule was in Florida attending a funeral. He tried to play it casual and not press the issue.

He walked into the kitchen to see what was up with his moms. He gave her a big squeeze but didn't get the love back.

"Whatchu cooking?"

"Some food for the kids."

"I can see that. What is it?"

"Meatloaf."

"Oh, that's my favorite. Maybe I should stay for dinner."

"There's really not enough for you, Nasir. These kids gotta eat. They're in school now, and with Fancy tutoring Al-Saadiq and Lisa, they getting good grades. I don't want them in class tomorrow on a half-empty stomach."

"So you gonna deprive your oldest child food?"

Brenda turned to face her son. He had on an expensive watch. She didn't know what the brand was, but it was flooded with diamonds. He was also adorned in a long, 18-karat rose gold and diamond chain with the letter *N*. The diamonds in the *N* were so large, she felt she could sell one and live off the profit for a year. His clothing was brand-new, from his sneakers to his jeans. His fresh haircut was lined professionally, and he looked and smelled like wealth. And in the months that he'd been away, he hadn't as much as dropped off a coin to help out his family.

Brenda's loyalty went where the money was. And, at the moment, Fancy was the one making sure food was kept in everyone's mouth.

Nasir could feel the shade. He just walked back out of the kitchen, and his mother didn't stop him.

"A'ight, yo, four grand. That's my final offer. Be ready tomorrow morning at eight." He stormed out of the apartment with a major attitude.

Fancy walked over to the window and caught a glimpse of his ride. He hopped in a gleaming silver Mercedes SLK 55 AMG with deep bucket seats and leather interior. She could see some light-skin chick sitting shotgun. A bitch who obviously thought she was too good to come upstairs and meet his family. Pangs of jealousy shot through her body. *How the fuck did he get so flush?*

Fancy wanted to renege on the deal. She was ready to tell him to let his bitch risk her freedom taking his work from state to state. But she realized she did need the money. Christmas was just around the corner, and she wanted to get the kids a few things to keep them happy.

Brenda came out of the kitchen. "What did he want?" She knew Nasir certainly didn't come there to check on her.

"He wants me to move some weight for him in the morning."

"You gonna do it?"

"I'm thinking about it. I mean, we could use the money."

"I wouldn't do shit for his tired ass."

Fancy was shocked. Brenda would have died for her son, but when he'd walked out that front door, cut off all communication, and began taking care of his new girlfriend, and from what they heard, her moms too, it broke her heart. Fancy understood. That's how she felt as well.

"It won't really be for him. It'll be for me. For us. For the kids."

Her remark almost brought tears to Brenda's eyes. All these years she'd hated Fancy because she hated her mother. When Fancy had first arrived, Brenda thought she was just like her sister. All her hatred toward Belen was transferred to her daughter. But Brenda wasn't as ruthless as Belen. She had her ways, but her sister was spineless.

"I tried to hate you, Fancy, but I just can't."

"I know." Fancy smiled. She tied her silk scarf around her head. "I guess I grew on you, huh?"

"I guess so." Brenda went back into the kitchen and began preparing plates when Fancy came up behind her.

"Aunt Brenda?"

"Uh-huh."

"Tell me the real story of why you and my mother fell out."

"Did you ask your mother?"

"I said tell me the real story." Fancy laughed. "It seems nothing that comes out of my parents' mouth is the truth."

"If you want to hear it, I'll tell you later, after the kids are in bed. But, remember, you asked. And what you hear you might not like. You may not even believe. But it will be the truth."

✳✳✳

Fancy had eaten, showered, and was in bed when Brenda came back into the living room. She thought she had changed her mind, so she didn't want to push.

Brenda sat on the edge of the sofa bed and exhaled. You could see that what she was about to say was tough. She was going to dredge up memories that had been buried for decades.

"Your mother and I grew up poor. I mean, we were worse off than I am now. Our mother was an on-again, off-again prostitute addicted to crack in the early eighties. We would spend days at a time hungry and surviving off neighbors' scraps. By the time I was nine and your mother was seven, we learned how to find food in the garbage cans. We walked around with bare feet in the winter months and layers of scrap clothing so thin, a paper towel probably would have given us more warmth.

"When I reached twelve, I fell in with a group of hustlers. They weren't much older than I was, and they knew how to boost. It was either boost or go hooking with your grandmother. And, believe me, my mother could have cared less which profession I got into, just as long as I could take care of myself. Well, I ended up taking care of not only me but your mother as well. Anything she wanted, I got it for her. I didn't know it, but I turned her into who she is. She wants what she wants when she wants it, and she doesn't care about the consequences.

"As my name started ringing out on the streets, 'cuz now I'm the flyest bitch around, I caught the eye of a few made men. Dealers decades older than I was wanted a piece, and I gave it to them for the right price. If they took care of me, *and* my sister, they could have all the pussy they desired. Up until that point I'd never fallen in love. Not until I met Alexandro."

"You met my father first?"

"He was the love of my life, Fancy. And everyone, especially your mother, knew that."

Brenda looked off as if reliving her past. Then she added, "We were going strong every day, inseparable. He was a young li'l nigga, but he had the heart of a lion. But most of all he was loyal to those he loved." She shook her head like she was trying to knock a painful memory out.

206

"Around this time everyone in the crack game was blowing up, making money hand over fist. That boosting shit became petty to me. It could keep clothing on my back but couldn't really lace my pockets. I tell you, Fancy, back then I had big dreams. I wanted to own businesses and be my own legitimate business boss lady. And I shared these dreams with the two people I loved most, who were Alexandro and Belen.

"By nineteen eighty-seven, I was stacking paper hand over fist. I saved nearly every penny; I was that anal. I didn't have any addictions like drugs or alcohol, but I did have a vice. I was a party girl, so almost every night you'd see me on a dance floor letting loose. I spent most nights in Studio 54 or at Limelight working up a sweat to club music." She chuckled. "Well, while I'm dancing the night away, my quiet lover is making love to my sister."

"Noooo," Fancy stated, wondering how her mother could be so grimy.

"The betrayal must have gone on for months, enough to establish a bond between the two that Alexandro and I didn't have. When I found out about the affair, I was six months pregnant with his first child. I was planning on buying a strip mall out on Long Island, and I was on a first-name basis with Bernardo Martinez, the most ruthless and feared drug distributor at that time."

"Is he still my father's connect?"

She shook her head. "No, he was long since murdered. No one knows who the new connect is."

Fancy exhaled. At least she tried.

"I came in one night only to find your father and Belen making love in my house and in my bed. I tried to take your mother's head off, but I was limited, due to my pregnancy, and also Alexandro stopped me. Immediately, I kicked your mother out. For days she tried to convince Alexandro to leave me, but he wouldn't, not with me carrying his seed. He didn't have family or know his father and always said that he wanted to be different.

"I was eight months pregnant when your mother begged to come and get some of her belongings. She had been staying with a cousin of ours. I finally agreed. I allowed her to come and get her things because it was the right thing to do, but truthfully I missed her. After all she had done, she was still my sister, and I loved her very much.

"On that day it was raining something awful. The thunder was so loud and intimidating. I remember standing at the window of my house hoping your mother was okay, driving under such conditions. She called and said she was delayed a few and for me to leave the back door unlocked. At first, I hesitated, but she said she was just down the road."

Brenda had to fight back tears. "It all happened so fast. One moment I was in the kitchen making tea, and the next I was being jumped upon by several masked assailants. They beat the baby out of me and also robbed me for every dime that I had saved. I was in ICU for five months before I was well enough to be released. In the meantime the bank had repossessed my house and my car, Alexandro walked out of my life and into hers, and my drug empire had collapsed. I was never whole again after that incident. Of course, she claimed it was just a coincidence and that she didn't have anything to do with it. And, sadly, the only person who ever believed her was your father.

"They broke me, Fancy. Took everything I had. They took my baby. My happiness. My connect. She stole my life and never looked back. It took me years to rebound. When I met Nasir's father, things began to make sense again. I began to smile and live a little. It was nineteen-ninety, and everything started changing. Music, our style of dress, our people as a whole seemed to be coming out of the bleak eighties. He was doing his thang in the drug game, and I was schooling him on what I knew. He'd just bought me a candy-apple red BMW 535i, and the news spread quicker than a virus. I came prancing out of my building and hit the alarm and noticed your mother stuntin' in the same car. We hadn't seen each other in years.

"I said things like she always wanted to be me, and how she only got my leftovers, you know, shit you say to get a bitch's pressure up. I told her, which I will regret until the day I die, that my new man was going to knock her and Alexandro off the throne. Less than twenty-four hours later, he was shot up in our hallway. Again, no proof. But I know Belen, the real Belen . . . and she's dangerous, Fancy. She's more Satan's sister than mine."

"How do you know that it was my mother who orchestrated both events and not my father?"

"Of course when I flat out asked her, and then accused her, she denied it. Her exact words were, 'I could never do something so grimy? That would make me a *monster.*' But I saw the look in her eyes. And if you haven't ever seen that look, the day you do, you will wish you hadn't."

# CHAPTER 30

In the morning Nasir came through with a 2002 Honda Accord that had a stash box built in. The previous day he went to the mechanic and made sure it was in excellent driving condition. The gas tank was on full, and all tires were checked and rechecked for air. He showed Fancy how to unlock the hideaway compartment, gave her traveling money, and also her destination.

"Remember, count that paper before you leave," he told her. "I'ma tell ya ass now—If the bread come up short, it's comin' out your cut!"

"You're paying me to make an exchange. I drop off a package and pick one up. If you want an accountant, I suggest you hire one."

Nasir stared at her, baffled. "What the fuck is ya problem?"

"Look, I ain't stopping to count shit. So either you tell your man that his money better be correct, or you take the risk. Either way, I'm still walking away with my four grand."

Nasir lunged at Fancy to slap the shit out of her, but she was too quick. She reached for a large steak knife sitting on the small, round table and put it just a millimeter from his carotid artery. He froze in his tracks. The wild, crazed look in her eyes gave him pause.

Sounding like an insane asylum patient, she whispered, "Go ahead. I dare you. Hit me. Hit me, bad boy."

Backing away, he lied, "Wasn't nobody gonna hit ya crazy ass! Look, it's already late. You need to hit the road."

Fancy knew at that point that they had a new understanding.

The drug mule hopped into the Honda Accord to meet with an infamous drug dealer. She was headed to Maryland, roughly three hours from New York. Nasir told her not to take 95 South through the New Jersey Turnpike. Instead he instructed her to take the back streets, 78 West through New Jersey through Pennsylvania through the outskirts of Maryland. It added about forty-five minutes to her drive, but she didn't care. What else did she have to do? And it was better to be safe than defiant. She had her CDs with driving music: Drake, Trey Songz, Melanie Fiona, and vintage Notorious B.I.G.

She tried her best to maintain the speed, only sometimes going slightly above the limit. Throughout the ride, the highway was littered with highway patrol, and every hour or so she'd see someone pulled off to the side.

On the drive there, she thought about all the people who'd made plenty of promises. Her father had always promised to take care of her. That promise ended the day the feds kicked open their front door. Tone had said he adored her and promised that he was her man and would take care of her. That promise ended months ago after they made love and he never looked back. Nasir and Shoe-Shine, dogs cut from the same cloth, both entered her, made promises, and then threw her away like trash.

Despite her young age, she wanted to take over this drug game like no one had ever seen. At first she couldn't understand why she wanted it so badly. As she rode down highways and byways, she told herself that she wanted that life so ferociously because everyone said she wasn't built for it. They all felt she should be something boring and girly. They didn't get that she was changing.

Fancy pulled the car over to the address that she had programmed into her GPS system via her iPhone. She called Iquan's cell phone and was told, "Bring the shit inside, shorty."

She walked coolly, with nerves of steel, up the concrete steps leading to a modest house. The area was quiet. She deduced that it was because it was noon on a weekday. She could tell that the block got a lot of action. With two kilos of cocaine in her purse, she kept telling herself that she was born into this lifestyle. Carrying a deadpan expression and moving like a model in a music video, she put a little switch in her hips.

Although she had traveled the world, Fancy had never been to Maryland, most importantly, Baltimore. Baltimore was an odd city to her. The tenement buildings looked historic and not in a good way. All she kept thinking about was the HBO series, *The Wire*, which her father loved. Would she be kidnapped and duct-taped in some strange basement with a dyke chick taunting her before blowing her brains out? But Nasir guaranteed that no harm would come her way. He claimed that he was so feared OT, and that he had a ruthless reputation for that work he put in on the streets of New York. But just in case they didn't give a fuck about reps, she took her own precautionary measures. A .380 fit snugly on her left thigh beneath her sexy dress.

Iquan, the dealer she was supposed to meet, was supposed to be a black man with cornrows and in his early thirties. The guy who came to the door had a low Caesar cut and looked twenty-five, max.

"I'm here to meet Iquan," she stated when the door flung open.

"This me, ma."

Fancy looked confused and immediately felt like it was a setup. She took two steps back and looked from left to right. At any second she could feel the heat coming around the corner. She was prepared to at least get off a shot or two.

Noticing the frightened look in her eyes, he laughed. "Yo, shorty, you all good. Ain't shit gonna happen to you." He lifted up his shirt to prove he wasn't holding a Glock.

"Where's Iquan?" she wanted to know.

"Damn! I am Iquan." And then he remembered. "Oh, you looking for Iquan with braids, true?"

"And over thirty." Fancy placed her hands on her hips where it wasn't too far from her gat.

"Ma, I just cut my braids yesterday. I was getting too old for that shit. Once you start seeing gray hair, you gotta let that shit go."

Fancy still wasn't convinced. Not too long ago she'd participated in an ambush. She'd walked someone into a trap and didn't know if what goes around really does come right back around. She pulled out her cell phone and called Nasir. He picked up on the first ring.

"What's up? You a'ight?"

She could hear concern in his voice. "I need you to confirm that this is Iquan. He looks nothing like you described." She handed the phone to him.

"Yo, shorty buggin', yo. Where you get her from?"

Nasir laughed. "Nigga, what she talkin' 'bout? Whatchu workin' wit'?"

"I told shorty I cut my shit off." He chuckled. "But she fine as hell, though. And sassy . . ."

"Oh, that's what's up. A'ight, lemme holla at her."

Iquan passed the phone back to Fancy.

"Everything is good, love. You can hit him off."

*Love?* Fancy was thoroughly disgusted. Nasir and his many mood swings were giving her whiplash.

It was supposed to be a quick transaction. They would meet, exchange the two ki's for money, and she would head back up North. But Iquan was a handsome thug, six-two and well built.

He opened his front door wide, and she walked through his threshold. Instantly she knew this was a stash house. There wasn't any way a baller lived in this half-furnished dump.

Fancy looked around. "You must tell me, who's your decorator?"

He chuckled. "Oh, you got jokes."

"A li'l somethin'-somethin'."

"Have a seat in my parlor," he said, playing along. "Let me go grab that."

Fancy took a seat in his living room and began to thumb through the latest *Vibe* magazine with Lil Wayne on the cover. In no time, Iquan came back with a brown paper bag filled with money.

Fancy took it and stood to leave.

"You not gonna count it?"

"Only my share."

"You gangsta."

"I'm getting there."

"But check it—That's not how we do things."

"Look, I'm a businesswoman, and my time is money. I get paid to do a job, and my job is nearly done. If it's not all there, that's between you and Nasir."

"It's all there."

"So why are you bitching up?"

"You too pretty to have such a foul mouth." Iquan stared at Fancy and wondered what her story was. But before he got too personal, he needed to know if she was fucking Nasir. "You Nasir's girl or something? Is that why you so self-assured?"

"A man could never tell me who I am. I used to think that a man in my life defined me."

"Your man?"

"No. My father. Now I realize that I am who I am, and can't nobody make me but me."

Usually, Iquan didn't mix business with pleasure, but there was something mysterious about her. "You want to go and get something to eat?"

She laughed. "In the middle of a drug deal?"

"The drugs are safe, and you could leave the paper here. It'll be safe too. Ain't nobody gonna run up in here."

Fancy thought about it. He was cute, but he wasn't that cute. "Nah, I need to head back. Nasir is waiting for me. He has something planned for this money."

"He ain't sweating that little bit of paper."

Fancy smirked. This was probably more paper than Nasir saw in a long time. "I doubt that."

"Shit, as many ki's as that nigga been pushing through B-more these last couple months?"

"He's been moving a lot of weight?" she asked, her interest piqued.

Iquan wondered if he was running his mouth like a bitch, but she was so damn sexy, he couldn't help himself. "Hells yeah, he been flooding our town with work."

"Is his product potent?"

"I don't fuck wit' anything less, ma."

# CHAPTER 31

Fancy had a few hours to think about what had transpired. She wasn't really sure there was something to it, but she had a nagging suspicion that she was being double-crossed, and she didn't know who was involved. She thought there wasn't anyone she could confide in except her father, and she wasn't sure he would accept her visit after her last disrespectful outburst, but she knew she had to try, First, though, she needed to get this paper back to its rightful owner.

Late that evening around ten, Fancy was back in New York with $36,000 in her purse for Nasir, and four grand in her titties for herself. She trusted no one. She moved through the FDR drive with ease.

When she saw his gleaming Benz idling outside his chick's crib, a large smile appeared on her face. *This muthafucka up here stuntin'.* She quickly tapped her horn twice to get his attention.

He hopped out of his sedan, all dramatic, his heavy chain swinging. "Hey, cousin!"

She didn't want to give off her suspicions, so she played along. She smiled widely and then handed him the two bundles of cash.

Nasir smiled. "It's all there?"

"Minus my cut, of course."

"Of course." Fancy noticed that he was all smiles. She could smell the purple haze from a mile away. She didn't even have to look at his slanted eyes to know what was up. "You did a nigga good, Fancy. I'm glad you came through for me. I owe you one."

"Glad you like my work."

He whispered, slightly paranoid from the weed, "I want you to make another run for me."

"Where?"

"VA. I got peoples down there. It'll be in and out, just like today."

Fancy nodded.

"Did I ever tell you you're my favorite cousin?"

Fancy gave him the finger and pushed back off to Brooklyn in his Honda.

✳✳✳

The visiting room was plagued with sour faces and bad attitudes. She was sure Alexandro wasn't going to be much different. Her father walked through the doors, and Fancy couldn't read him. It had been so long since she'd last come to visit. Briefly, she remembered being daddy's little girl. Now nineteen, and having endured what she had, she felt she wasn't anybody's little anything.

Alexandro's dull eyes brightened when he saw his daughter. "You look well," he said, leaning in for an embrace. She smelled of jasmine. He inhaled the light-scented perfume heartily. "It's been a while."

"I know. But I don't want to get into that. I came here to see you, not get scolded."

"So see me."

She could tell that she'd already gotten under her father's skin, a feat that usually took longer. If Alexandro was anything, it was always composed. It took a lot for him to show his anger, which didn't necessarily mean he wasn't angry. He just knew how to keep it under wraps.

"How's your case going?"

He shrugged. "It's going."

Fancy didn't have time to coddle her father and kiss ass. If he wanted to behave like a brat, then she'd just move forward with the real reason she came.

"I have a dilemma that I need your advice with."

"Kick it."

"You're not going to like it, but I gotta keep it one hundred." Fancy could see her father clench his jaws. "There was this kid Devon. He was moving weight—"

"He was moving a lot of weight throughout the tri-state, South, and West Coast. He got himself murdered a couple months back, along with an innocent kid."

Fancy lowered her eyes at her father's glare.

"Were you fucking with him?"

"No, Pop-Pop."

"Not that I'd believe you. Nothing that comes out of your mouth lately is ever the truth."

*Ain't this the pot calling the kettle black?*

Her whole life was a lie, and he had the nerve to point fingers.

"As I was saying, Devon got himself murdered." She looked around and then lowered her voice. "And me and Nasir were there."

Alexandro's eyes turned beady. He could have burned a hole right through her. He held his composure because he needed to hear the rest. "Go ahead."

"Well, we, um, Nasir came up off of two hundred and fifty thousand and thirty ki's."

"Punk money," her father spat.

"Not quite sure how that's punk money, considering you're broke." She glared right back. No one was ever going to make her feel less than adequate again in her life. If they could dish it out, then they should be able to take it. "In any event, we walked away with all that money and coke, but not an hour later Nasir's right-hand man, Shoe-Shine claimed to have gotten into a shootout with some unknown assailants. He claimed it was like the O.K. Corral on the streets of New York."

"And the drugs and money got confiscated."

Fancy blinked. "Well, yes."

Alexandro thought for a second about how to respond. "You can't miss what you never had."

The heat began at her toes and continued to rise. She was so hot under her collar, she could blow steam out of her ears. Perhaps he didn't understand what she was getting at.

"Well, the thing is, I don't think we got robbed. In fact, I think the opposite. Nasir made a large leap to how he was living before Devon. And if it wasn't for me, he wouldn't have a penny of that money."

"I don't know how many ways to say it, but stay the fuck out of this game. You don't know what you've gotten yourself into. The people that Devon worked for aren't to be fucked with. And if they even suspect that you had anything to do with his murder, they will cut you up into little pieces and bury you all over New York."

"But what about Nasir?" Fancy was furious. "He's just gonna get away with this?"

Alexandro stood to go. "If I weren't a wise man I would tell you to change your life, get married, go to college, I would say all those things that a father would say. But I've said those things and you've chosen to ignore me. So here's a piece of advice. Keep looking for trouble, and it will find you."

He turned his back on his only child and went back to his cell. Deep down, he felt that she was doomed. That she'd already signed her fate when she'd participated in the assassination of Devon and his whole family. Devon's connect Shaheem had put a bounty on the head of anyone and everyone involved. Alexandro knew that things could get ugly. He also knew there wasn't much he could do from behind bars. He couldn't ever mention his daughter's name. Not even to try to strike a deal for her safety.

And if he gave up Nasir, he was sure Nasir would give up Fancy. When the goons have you in a locked room with more torture devices than a kid has toys in his toy chest, you begin to say things you never thought you would.

Alexandro had to admit that he was scared for Fancy. But he knew that he and Belen were at risk as well. People would think that they'd sanctioned the hit on Devon, or possibly had a hand in it.

Alexandro didn't have any answers. He wanted to communicate with Belen, but it wasn't safe. Although he was the mouthpiece, Belen was the brains. He went back to his cell and hung his head. The drama just kept coming.

***

Fancy had just enough time to make the visit with her mother. She had to sign in before noon and she'd made it. It was just a hunch, but she wanted to know if her mother would feel as her father did. Should she just walk away?

Belen came out looking more masculine than Fancy had ever remembered. She knew not to make a comment on her mother's increasingly changing persona. They embraced.

"Hey, Mommy," she said, without any enthusiasm.

Her mother returned the lackluster response. "Hey."

The two engaged in idle chitchat for a few minutes until Belen looked bored. She could have more fun back in her dorm playing poker or blackjack with the girls.

"I'm glad to see you all right, but I gotta jump."

"Wait." Fancy gushed. "I came here for a reason. I need to talk."

Belen was impatient. "I know you think that all I have is time, but my time is accounted for. I got shit to do in the back. If you need to talk, talk."

Fancy rolled her eyes. "I need you to sit back down. What I'm about to say ain't sweet."

Belen wanted to laugh in her daughter's face, but she played along.

"Your nephew and I went on a caper."

"Who?"

*Whoa!* Fancy thought. Her mother cut right to the chase. No long sermon about how could she, what about school, what kind of caper.

"Devon."

"That was you?"

Fancy nodded. She could see so many things in her mother's eyes.

"That's a tall drink to swallow."

"Well, not that tall," Fancy joked. "But here's the situation. We came up off two hundred and fifty thousand and thirty ki's."

"Not bad."

"It would have been all good had I seen a dime of that money."

Belen smirked. "Who played you?"

"I think, Nasir."

"He definitely has it in him. What gives you that impression though?"

"Well, Shoe-Shine claimed to have gotten into a gun battle and the assailants ran off with our whole score."

"Get the fuck outta here! In what world?"

"So, you're thinking like I am?"

"No doubt, but you said Nasir in the beginning. Who's Shoe-Shine? And how is he involved?"

"He's Nasir's lieutenant and the one driving the car with the duffle bags full of cash and coke."

"Oh, I think I heard 'bout that li'l nigga. Those niggas woulda died over that kind of bread. Everyone in that crew has been looking for a come-up all their lives." Belen inched closer. This was the most excitement she'd had in a while. "Did this shootout make the news?"

"No."

"Did he take a bullet?"

"No."

"He stuck dick to you, Fancy, and that shit burns me the fuck up." Belen was heated. She felt that Nasir had to sanction the setup to cut Fancy out of the deal. Nasir was the boss, and his underlings wouldn't make that move unless they were *ordered* to make that move. And because Nasir was her sister's seed, she thought they were trying to take advantage of her daughter now that she wasn't around. "You know Brenda had her hand in this too."

It was Fancy's turn to get heated. "Everything doesn't end and begin with Brenda!"

"What are you talkin' about?"

"She ain't had nothing to do with what her son did to me. He left her fucked up just like me. If it wasn't for my Wal-Mart money, she would barely have food to eat. He up in Harlem with some bitch. Meanwhile, he's been selling his birds state to state."

Belen wasn't convinced that Brenda wasn't involved, but she respected that her daughter felt certain enough and could vouch for her.

"Who else knows about this jux?"

"Just all those involved—Me, Nasir, Shoe-Shine, Lucky, and Nicholas."

"That's four people too many."

"What do you mean?"

"I mean that there's a bounty put on the head of anyone who had a hand in killing that little boy. I hate to be the one to tell you this, but there's a million dollars on your head."

Fancy swallowed hard. "That's only if they find out about me."

"With four other loose ends, baby, it's only a matter of time."

"None of them guys will talk." Even Fancy noticed that her voice quivered. "Right?"

"You trusted Nasir, your blood, and he beat you in your head. You honestly think there's honor amongst thieves?"

"Well I don't have proof that Nasir was involved. He was riding with me when they said they got ambushed. And it might not have only been Shoe-Shine. Now that you mention it, he couldn't have pulled it off if Nicholas and Lucky didn't back him up. Which leaves the boss. I can't see them not cutting him in on the deal."

"You have to believe they all were involved."

"But how do I prove it? I guess that's my question. Should I go around asking questions? Run up on his girl? What? I'm so fuckin' furious right now!"

"In this game you don't need proof."

"Huh?"

"You don't need proof. In this game we go on gut instinct, and instinct alone. It will save your life, if you let it. What does your gut tell you about that paper?"

Fancy searched her soul and then said, "It tells me that I got beat and they all were in on it."

"So what are you gonna do about it?"

Fancy felt so betrayed. She'd lost her apartment, had to work crazy hours in Wal-Mart, and had even murdered a child, and they didn't give her one coin for her troubles. She wanted to confide in her mother that not only did they do her dirty, but she had fucked Shoe-Shine and Nasir as well. And still they left her out on the streets to starve.

"I just want to know, how could they do this to me?"

"Because you're a female, Fancy. You gotta fight your way into this game, and even then it's an uphill battle. Men will always try you, because they'll think you're weak."

Fancy shook her head. She was still stuck. "I think it's because they wanted the connect and Pop-Pop wouldn't give it to me."

Belen laughed crudely. "Your father didn't give you the connect because it's not his to give."

The revelation hit Fancy like a lightning bolt. What her father and Aunt Brenda had said about her mother was all true. She was the head of the Lane cartel. The queenpin. Fancy wondered why her mother played the back and pretended that her father was something he never was.

"So, you have access to the connect? You've seen him?"

"His name is Jesus, and he is a descendant of Pablo Escobar. His bloodline is that of a thoroughbred when it comes to our line of work. He's old school and follows a strict code. The only person who could vouch for a new ally is me—not Alexandro."

The two talked until visiting hours were over. Mother and daughter connected more in three hours than they had over the course of Fancy's nineteen years. Belen gave Fancy strict instructions on how to move forward, and this time, Fancy listened.

"It'll take me some time to put this together. In the meantime, hold your head, and don't show your hand. To anyone. Keep your cards close to your chest," Belen instructed.

"Ma."

"What?"

"Why didn't you tell me you were the head bitch in charge?"

✳✳✳

Two days later, Fancy was on I-78 heading South on I-81 to Virginia with four bricks in her oversized purse and instructions about where to meet with the buyer, a big-timer named J-hood, who had Portsmouth and Chesapeake Bay, VA locked down with his violent crew. He wasn't as attractive as her last drop-off, but nevertheless, he too tried to get with her. When her parents had first got knocked, Fancy would have fucked an invalid if it meant he would take care of her. Things changed. Now she liked having her own money.

Once she turned down J-hood, he didn't want her in his presence for much longer. He obviously was used to having his way. He paid, took his weight, and they parted ways.

After VA, it was DC, and then Philadelphia. Nasir was quickly becoming a major supplier. Fancy heard that he had a string of mules to transport the drugs for him, not just her. So if she was picking up at least a hundred grand a week, it didn't take Einstein to realize he was making long paper. Pounds and pounds of cocaine were being trafficked from city to city, either on I-78 or I-95.

✳✳✳

By the time Christmas rolled around, Fancy had gone through most of the money she had earned with Nasir. But it was the holiday season, and she wanted to be festive. She'd just pulled up in a cab coming from one of her many shopping sprees in the city, where she tore up Saks Fifth Avenue and Marc Jacobs.

"I ain't never seen anything like this in my life," the cab driver commented. "You think they shooting a movie?"

Fancy saw four Maserati sports cars in the colors of black, midnight blue, canary yellow, and cloud white all parked in front of her aunt's house. She paid the driver and jetted upstairs, where she caught the tail end of the conversation.

Nasir had handed Brenda two thousand dollars to buy his siblings Christmas gifts. She looked at Lucky, Shoe-Shine, Nicholas, and Nasir. They all had on full-length mink coats, platinum jewels, and expensive cologne, and everyone looked and smelled like wealth.

Fancy knew to control her anger. "Nice cars," she commented, as she walked fully into the living room.

"That's how we do," Nicholas said.

Fancy noticed that none of them had taken a seat. They all stood around like they were too good for the old apartment. She remembered feeling the same way not too long ago.

"Word, you should have seen the dealer's face when we walked in with a briefcase full of Benjamins. He took us in the back and cracked open vintage Dom *P* two thousand two." Lucky's grin was irritating.

"Well, I'm glad you boys are doing it up, but what about Fancy?" Brenda asked. "Nasir, you gonna let her still make drops for you?"

Nasir hadn't used Fancy as a mule in almost three weeks. And Brenda knew that Fancy liked nice things. She didn't know what made her son turn her back on them so abruptly. Even coming around today with the measly two grand didn't make up for how distant he had been.

"Nah, we good," Nasir tried to explain. "We got more girls than we actually need. But you good, right, Fancy?"

"I'm always going to be all right, Nasir." Fancy just cut her eyes at him.

"Good. Then we out." Nasir gave his mother a kiss and bear hug before they all left.

# CHAPTER 32

Fancy wanted revenge so badly, she could taste it. She knew that it came with a price. Nothing came for free. You either paid with cash, your soul, your life, something.

Coolly she dialed Shoe-Shine. "We need to talk," she stated.

"A'ight, kick it."

"Not over the phone."

"Come on now, I ain't got no paper for you to borrow."

"Excuse me?"

"Yo, I'm in the middle of some shit right now. I gotta go!" *Click.* Shoe-Shine hung up.

A furious Fancy called right back.

"Why the fuck you keep hittin' my jack?" he barked.

"You're a dead man, and you don't even know it. Keep thinking you're untouchable. When you get touched, you better hope you got nine lives!" Fancy hung up.

Shoe-Shine called right back, several times, and Fancy allowed him to continually go to voice mail.

**✳✳✳**

At three o'clock in the morning Shoe-Shine showed up at Brenda's crib to see Fancy. He shook her violently out of her sleep.

"Yo, what the fuck you was spittin' earlier?"

Groggily, Fancy adjusted her eyes. Finally, she whispered, "I got the connect."

Shoe-Shine smirked. "So you call me all the way over here for that shit? As you can see, I'm doin' good without the connect."

Fancy shrugged. "Okay, fine. If you think car money makes you special, then continue on with your life. But when you wise up and want to become wealthy, come holla at me." She turned over and gave him her back.

"Wait. Be easy. You sure your father gave you the connect?"

"What kind of asinine question is that?"

"Well, why now? Why give it to me now?"

"First off, I ain't giving him to you, Alex is. Second, you have to promise to make me your partner, as we've always discussed, or else no deal."

"Oh, no doubt. I would do that anyway!" Shoe-Shine was so excited, his grin stretched a yard. "With this connect and what I already have on lock, I'ma be bigger than your father, Nasir, Tone . . ."

"Sure. If you say so," she said dryly.

"Oh, you don't think so?"

"I honestly don't know, and I honestly don't care about your ego."

Shoe-Shine stood to leave. "Yo, what was that about my life being in danger?"

"It is."

He grimaced. "Yo, when did this become twenty questions? If you got something to say, say it."

"Lucky made a deal with Shaheem. And before you ask, he's Devon's connect. They've now recruited Nicholas. Those thirty ki's you walked away with, they were his. Devon had them on consignment. There's a bounty on your head, and any day you're gonna die."

Shoe-Shine tried not to show fear, but he wasn't doing a very good job. "I told you we got robbed for that work."

"No, you didn't." Fancy was almost disinterested as she told her ex-lover he was as good as dead.

"I swear on my mom's life. May she drop dead if I'm lying."

"Well, if you keep it up, she will be. Look, Lucky already dropped dime. The jig is up."

"Lucky wouldn't do that to me. He's my man. We go way back."

"That's exactly what he did."

Shoe-Shine jumped up.

"Sit down," Fancy commanded.

"I'ma kill those niggas!"

"You can't."

"Like hell, I can."

"If you touch them that will, and I repeat, most certainly will murder your mother, your sister, and your sister's children. On this I put *my* life."

"So, I'm just supposed to give up my life?" Shoe-Shine looked at her with wild eyes.

Fancy could see the selfishness in his eyes. His heart never skipped a beat for his family; his hands only trembled for his life.

"No, you could shut the fuck up and listen. You will deliver the locales of Lucky and Nicholas to Shaheem's peoples in exchange for your life. You cannot let on that you know about their betrayal. If you jump the gun, you die."

"But how will that save my life?" Shoe-Shine asked. "How do I know that once I give up my mans that they don't come and do me? At that point, I'll be weak."

"My father convinced Shaheem that it's Lucky and Nicholas who not only are rats but also the ones who got the drop on Devon and tried to pawn you off as bait."

"And he believed him?"

"Why would he second-guess my father? You know how much clout he holds. My father and my mother are facing the death penalty, and neither one of them thought twice about informing on anyone, despite what the streets are saying. They are about to go to trial and I'm still breathing. Truthfully, if they even think about snitching I am as good as dead. Dead! My father's connect will murder me. So if my father says that he knows who was behind the Devon massacre, then his colleagues will listen. He's already *earned* his respect."

"Why is your father getting involved?"

"Are you stupid? It's because I was involved. And you and your dumb-ass crew have put my life in danger running around buying extravagant cars and tricking on bitches."

"Didn't nobody know where that paper came from."

He had a point. Fancy almost gave herself away. "Lucky told them where it came from. Have you not been listening?"

"How do you feel about this?"

"What do you mean?"

"You about to be a part of two more murders."

"My hands ain't getting dirty on this one. So I guess I ain't losing any sleep. You feel me?"

Shoe-Shine stared into her cold eyes. "Yo, you know we was gonna cut you in on the take. We got your cut put up." He began to think about his role in playing her. What would her father do to him for violating his daughter?

"Oh, no doubt. I know when the time's right I'll get mine."

Either Shoe-Shine was too high or purposely wanted to overlook the ominous threat.

Fancy said, "Now let me ask you a question. How will you feel about giving up Nasir as well to Shaheem?"

Shoe-Shine smirked. "Why Nasir?"

"He could try to do a deal with Shaheem, just as Lucky and Nic. We're not safe, as long as he's a loose end."

Shoe-Shine looked at Fancy and she made his steel heart shudder. Whether she knew it or not, she was one grimy, heartless bitch. There had to be a name for someone like her.

"You would really kill your own cousin?"

"If it meant saving my life I would."

"First, Nasir wouldn't ever sell us out to Shaheem because he didn't have anything to do with what went down after we all separated. That whole fake ambush was all my idea." For a split second, Shoe-Shine had the nerve to brag. He continued, "And I know you a little salty about killing shorty, but Nasir didn't know you really would. I keep tellin' your dumb ass that."

"I'm not salty, I'm cautious."

"You both!"

Fancy pushed further. "Then where did Nas get all those ki's from? And all that money to splurge on cars and trick on his bitch?" Fancy hated to admit it, but part of her anger came from Nasir falling for some broad and leaving her behind.

"You think I'm a fool? After we cut y'all out of the money and ki's, we soon realized we couldn't spend that shit. So, I set up the Haitians and we came up off that too. Those are the ki's you were unloading."

If he could have taken her temperature it would have been off the thermometer; that's how heated she was.

"For now, he lives, but I'm not making the decisions."

Shoe-Shine stood to leave but not before one last test.

"Yo, let me hit that," he said, rubbing his dick.

"You could eat my pussy, but I ain't fuckin' you."

All of a sudden he actually got turned on. He was only trying to see if she was setting him up. If she had refused his request, he would have thought he was being played.

"And why you ain't fuckin' me? What I do to you?"

Fancy feigned jealousy. "Come on now, I don't know where your dick has been. You running 'round with all these chickenheads."

He sat back down and stuck his finger in her pussy and began playing with her clit. He leaned over and started to kiss her neck softly. "I ain't fuck nobody in months. I swear."

Fancy allowed him to get her hot and spew lies. "You really want this pussy?" she purred.

"You know I do." He had already pulled her panties down and began to suck on her clit.

"We have to be quiet. We can't wake up my aunt or the kids."

Shoe-Shine nodded.

Moments later, he wrapped up his dick with a condom and Fancy slid on top and rode him until he came. The sex was quick and unsatisfying to Fancy, but she knew it was necessary.

Shoe-Shine left with reassurances to help take out one half of his crew. Born and raised in Bed-Stuy, his motto was do or die.

✳✳✳

In the dead of night two hired assassins casually walked into the Harlem tenement building as if they were residents. It was quiet, and the streets were desolate. Always professional and cautious, both men wore dark-colored jeans and jackets with concealed pistols tucked in their waistbands, a .357 for Big Mike, and a .45 for Fernandez.

They moved stoically, the task occupying their minds, Fernandez with a deadpan gaze, and Big Mike looking aloof. At the elevator they both perused their surroundings, checking how many exits the building had and the best escape routes, just in case things went different than they had planned.

Fernandez pushed for their floor. The door slid open, and the two stepped out to blaring music. They knew there was a party or something going on, but they weren't sure if their intended victim lived in the apartment where the party was being held. They scanned each door until they found 6C. The silencers screwed on to the barrels of their guns, they were ready to punch a few tickets.

"We're only getting paid for Lucky," Fernandez commented.

Big Mike shrugged. "The way the music is blaring, there's gonna be a lot of collateral damage."

"Just hope we got enough bullets."

"It only takes one to the temple. And I got at least seventeen."

Fernandez raised his fist and banged hard on the door. Nothing. He knocked again, much louder this time.

A short moment later, the door swung open, and a young chick said, "I hope y'all brought some liquor."

"Nah, we ain't bring shit but our Puerto Rican asses," Big Mike replied.

The young girl looked up and down at the eye candy that just walked in. She wanted first dibs on the taller one. "That sounds good to me."

Fernandez locked the door behind them and then casually asked, "Where's Lucky?"

"He be right back. He went to go and get some more weed, but now we done ran out of the drinks."

As the three walked deeper into the apartment, Fernandez and Big Mike assessed the situation. There was only one way for this to play out.

Big Mike leaned over and whispered into his partner's ear before pulling out his burner. His actions were quick, swift, and accurate. He shot the pretty female in her left temple, and as her body hit the floor, all hell broke loose.

The people inside the apartment were suddenly besieged with fear. The laughter and the good times were over.

A few dudes tried to reach for their burners, but they were cut down. A few women screamed, but instantly were silenced. *Poot! Poot! Poot!*

The bodies began to drop. It only took one shot, and they were down. The music was still playing, muffling the screams, which quickly turned into pleas for their lives as gunpowder filled the air in the small apartment.

Within the blink of an eye, the two men had the room under control. In total, six people were cut down.

Big Mike disappeared down the hallway, methodically checking each room for any stragglers. He came back shaking his head, indicating it was all clear.

While they waited for Lucky, Big Mike systematically went around checking pulses. No sign of life was found. Impatiently they both waited for their mark, who arrived moments later with a bonus—Nicholas.

Nicholas and Lucky walked into the living room and saw the carnage. Lucky's reflexes were delayed due to the large amount of weed he'd smoked. He looked at the two strange men, and his heart lurched. "Yo, what the f—"

Fernandez smirked and squeezed the trigger. *Poot!*

One shot to the dome silenced Lucky. The three additional body shots were just for the hell of it, and he fell dead to his feet, blood pooling around his head.

Nicholas was frozen with fear. He couldn't reach for his burner if he wanted to. The hot liquid running down his leg was indicative of the dread he experienced witnessing his partner murdered amid a room full of dead bodies.

Fernandez and Big Mike watched as the guy peed on himself. Fernandez almost felt sorry for the young dude but then remembered what had happened to little Devon and why they were there.

Big Mike recognized him first. "Yo, we ain't gonna hurt you, shorty. What's your name?"

# KIM K.

"Who? Me?"

"No, him," Big Mike replied sarcastically, pointing toward Lucky.

"Nicholas."

Big Mike nodded. "A'ight, Nic, you gotta promise to forget what happened in here today. You can't rat us out even though you saw our faces. Can you promise me that?"

"Sure, sure. I promise I won't tell a soul."

"That's what's up. Yo, you should go and clean yourself up."

Nicholas hesitated for a moment and then turned toward the bathroom. As he did that, Big Mike raised his pistol to his head and fired. *Poot!*

The body dropped to his feet.

"This guy just saved us a trip to Brooklyn."

"I didn't even recognize shorty. You got a good eye," Fernandez said. "Let's make the call and let them know we completed the job and go and pick up our paper."

And the henchmen left just as quietly as they'd arrived.

# CHAPTER 33

The news hit Fancy like a Mac truck. Did MCC just call her and tell her that her father was found murdered—stabbed to death with an ice pick in his cell? It couldn't be true. Who would want Alexandro dead? And who would be brave enough to do the hit? So many questions swirled through her head. It had to be Jesus! And if that were true, her life was in danger.

"What are you hollering about?" Brenda came running into the living room with a look of pure panic plastered on her face. "Is it Nasir? Has something happened to my baby?"

Fancy didn't even realize she'd let out a guttural moan. Her body was shaking so violently her aunt had to embrace and nearly pin her down on the sofa.

"Fancy, please, speak!"

She couldn't. She could barely see. The tears were so heavy her view was obstructed. Brenda couldn't take the agony anymore. She knew something had happened to her son. Immediately she grabbed the phone and called her oldest child. When he picked up waves of relief washed over her.

"You need to get here. Something's happened to Fancy."

Without hesitation, he said, "I'm on my way!"

In less than an hour, Nasir was in the living room comforting his cousin. He continually wiped her tears away, gave her a glass of water, and held her in his strong embrace. Finally, she squeezed out, "They killed my father . . . they killed him . . . he's dead." Her voice cracked from despair.

Now everyone in the room was somber. That was the last thing they thought they would hear. Alexandro Lane was a made man. He was respected and a legend. Who would want to get at him? And a better question was, Who *could* have gotten at him?

Fancy cried for hours with Nasir right at her side.

"I need to go and see my mother," she whispered. "Today. She has to hear this from me."

"You sure you're strong enough to go up there now?"

She nodded.

She didn't want to tell him her thoughts, which were, was she next? Fancy knew that Belen would have the answers, if she were still alive.

On the drive to MCC, Nasir's phone began blowing up, and when he answered the news nearly stopped his heart.

"Who was that?"

"That was Lucky's moms. There was some kind of hit last night, and both Lucky and Nic got murked. She said it's all over the news."

"Nasir, what's going on?"

He shook his head. "I don't know. But I know what the fuck ain't gonna go on! Ain't nobody gonna touch me or mines!"

Nasir dialed Shoe-Shine.

"Yo, Shine, shit fucked up. Somebody got at Lucky and Nic last night."

"Whatchu mean?"

"What the fuck you think I mean? Our li'l niggas got body bagged."

"By who?"

Nasir roared, "How the fuck should I know!"

"A'ight, so what we gonna do?"

"We gonna not discuss business over the phone, muthafucka. I got some business to handle and I'll hit you up later. Meet me at my crib so we can politick. One."

"One."

Nasir looked at Fancy. "This shit ain't no coincidence. Something ain't right. I can feel that shit."

Fancy didn't have any soothing words to offer because she really didn't give a fuck about Lucky and Nicholas meeting their demise. They both had it coming. Her only concern was saving her own ass and speaking with her mother. She needed reassurances, and only Belen could give her that.

As they approached the jail, Nasir was back on the phone. He told his mother to get the kids and get out of that apartment and go to the Hyatt hotel in Nassau County and not to tell anyone. He didn't know if goons would come after his moms and siblings, but he wasn't taking any chances. Nor was he leaving Fancy's side until he knew she was safe.

Fancy sat before Belen with puffy eyes. She bit her bottom lip in an effort to keep her composure. She knew her mother hated tears.

"Mommy—"

"Your father was murdered."

Fancy was shocked. "You already know?"

"Isn't it obvious?"

Fancy paused. "I should have known that you would find out quickly, right? Because in jail, as Pop-Pop said, y'all get news federal expressed."

Belen tossed her eyes in the sky. "So what you think should have been obvious to you is that I get news quickly? Out of everything we've discussed, that's what you glean from my omission?"

Fancy's heart began to palpitate. "Please tell me you didn't."

Belen leaned in close and gave Fancy a deathly glare. "Do you still feel you can walk in my shoes?"

She wanted to be as intelligent, devious, and ruthless as her mother, but Alexandro was her father. Fancy exhaled. "Yes, I can walk in your shoes if you shadow me."

Belen nodded. "Brace yourself. We got shit to discuss. You ready?"

"I am."

"I sanctioned the hit on your father. He had to go, Fancy. Alexandro had lost his mind the time he sat in jail. He grew paranoid and resentful."

Fancy nodded as if she was unaffected.

"My associates want me back out on the street. I'm a valuable commodity. We tried to nudge him, softly, through you, to take the weight, but he was defiant. When I got word that he was trying to set up a hit on me—"

"I don't believe that," Fancy snapped. Her father said he would never hurt her mother.

"As I said, when I got word that not only was he trying to have one of these bitches take me out in the shower room, he was also about to cooperate with the feds against a lot of dangerous people, which, as we've already told you, would cost you your life."

Now that was incredulous, but Fancy listened, intently.

"I got a message to Jesus and offered him a life for a life. I explained that if he murdered you that wouldn't stop Alexandro from testifying because from day one he already knew that they would kill you and he was going to testify anyway."

"Mommy, I hear you and I respect you. But there's no way my father was going to allow my life to be put in danger, let alone have some cartel murder me for his freedom."

"Fancy?"

"What?"

"He's not your father. Jesus is."

Fancy felt like she had vertigo. The room began spinning out of control. It was like she was caught between reality and a dark fairytale.

"I look just like him," she whispered.

"No, you don't. You just have a lighter skin tone than me. But we both know your features are my features. You look like a biracial woman, which you are. Alexandro is Colombian, and so is your real father, Jesus."

She sat there in stunned silence for a moment. "Does he know?"

"He does now. He always suspected it, but I confirmed it."

"So what does all this mean?"

"If you're asking if your real daddy is going to welcome you with open arms, the answer is no. You're safe for now. But don't push him or give him any reason to hurt you because he will treat you like a complete stranger and bury you six feet deep and won't lose a moment's sleep." Her mother actually showed a little fear in her eyes. "And this secret stays between us. No one must know."

"Did Pop-Pop know?"

"He always suspected it, but he never wanted to face it."

Though Fancy's head spun in utter confusion with all of the information Belen had just given her, she couldn't help but wonder how this was going to change the plan. "So what now?"

"My trial starts next Monday. Should take a couple weeks, and I will most likely be found guilty. But there's still hope. I can always appeal this, Fancy, and that's why I'll need you."

"Me?"

"Yes, you. I'm going to need money for proper counsel. Big money to hire the best lawyers for an appeal. I can't spend the rest of my life in jail unless I absolutely have to."

"But why can't Jesus pay for your counsel? You just said they want you out, and he definitely has the money."

"Fancy, everything comes at a price. You don't think I've broached the subject in my mind?" Belen shook her head. "It's too risky. If I allow Jesus to pay for my lawyer, and God forbid I lose my appeal, they're going to want repayment—perhaps even with interest. And if I am in here, how will I be able to come up with the money?"

"You won't."

"Exactly. So who do you think they'll go after for my debt?"

"Me?"

"You! And any nigga you fucking with. So, baby girl, do you. Stack your paper and get me the fuck up outta here. Debt free."

Fancy nodded. "I'll get you out of here. I promise."

Belen exhaled, and then switched course. "They missed the hit on Shoe-Shine last night."

"They tried to get at him last night?"

"Bullets were exchanged, but he narrowly escaped."

Fancy's eyes grew large. "Nasir called him and told him about Lucky and Nicholas and he never mentioned that niggas tried to get at him too."

"Where's Nasir now?"

"He's downstairs waiting on me. He felt like my life was in danger. But after we leave here he's supposed to go and meet with Shoe-Shine."

Belen hated to admit that she felt safer with Nasir looking after Fancy.

"Shoe-Shine knows that the hit had to come from you on his life, so that's a good call by Nas. He'll want to take you both out, but he has to get at Nasir first. He'll feel Nasir is a bigger threat."

"How did they let this happen? If their only job is to do murders, then do the fucking murder. What's so hard?"

Belen shrugged. "If these were my men, Shoe-Shine would be ghost. But Shaheem is running the show and his men fucked up."

Fancy listened as her mother explained how she should move forward to get rid of their problem.

Fancy called Shoe-Shine and told him that Nasir had to go. She explained that in a couple hours the streets would all know that her father was dead, which meant that Shaheem and his crew had double-crossed them. She told him that she was sure that Shaheem had someone get at her father in jail, and now they wanted to kill her over Devon Junior.

"The only person who could have convinced Shaheem that my father lied and that I really did pull the trigger on the kid was Nasir. They would believe him because we're blood."

Fancy told Shoe-Shine that Nasir had found out that she had the connect and had plans to take over the streets with Shoe-Shine as her right-hand and that they were going to cut him out.

Shoe-Shine was skeptical. "How would he know all that?"

"That night, in the apartment when we thought everyone was asleep, Aunt Brenda was listening. Lisa told me the whole story with her big-ass mouth."

Shoe-Shine felt Fancy was beating him in the head. It didn't matter, though, because he knew at the end of the day both Nasir and Fancy would be dead.

"So you telling me that you want to put a bullet in your cousin's dome?"

"Just get him to the place and I will do it."

# CHAPTER 34

As Nasir and Shoe-Shine fought for their lives in the street alley, Fancy stood in the shadows, gripping her pistol.

She'd already come to terms that sheep had to die in this drug game in order for the wolves to survive. Fancy went back and told Nasir the plan and said that she had one condition. She wanted to take out Shoe-Shine. It had always bugged Fancy that he'd essentially fucked her, taunted her after she murdered that little boy, and then took all of the blood money for himself. Nasir and Fancy walked away with blood on their hands while Shoe-Shine, Lucky, and Nicholas walked away with the ki's and the money. And the fact that he had done that grimy shit while they all were starving didn't sit well with her. She also reasoned that had she not questioned him the way she did, Nasir would have been the first to meet the assassin's bullet. She realized he didn't give a fuck about anybody but himself. All those talks about how he wanted to ride with her and be on her team were all just lies. He never had any respect for her because she was a woman.

When she went back to speak with Belen to convince her that she needed someone thorough by her side, if she was going to rise in the drug game, Belen finally agreed that it had to be Nasir. Belen gave her the blessing and told her that if she could prove herself, come up on her own, then in one year's time she would give her the connect, Jesus.

When Fancy stepped out of the shadows and finally pulled the trigger, she felt nothing, as Shoe-Shine fell to the ground. Nasir's strong arm enveloped her and then she heard a pop and felt his body jerk once, then twice. Nasir stumbled backwards only to see another gunman point his gun toward Fancy.

Fancy was shocked and frozen from fear. Her eyes were glued on yet someone else she thought she loved. Tone. He'd come out of the shadows with murder and vengeance on his mind. Fancy closed her eyes and braced for impact, and in one swift movement Nasir pushed her out of the way and leapt in front of the bullet. He took yet another hit.

Thinking quickly, Fancy scrambled for her pistol and let off numerous shots. As each bullet dislodged from the gun she was screaming like a crazy woman. Tone's body ate up each bullet until he eventually succumbed. Three men, all her former lovers, all lay on the dirty pavement as their lives drained from their eyes.

She cradled Nasir's head in her lap. Tears streamed down her face.

"I love you, Nasir. You hear me? You can't leave me," she cried. "I need you . . . I need you to live."

He couldn't speak, but his eyes told her he felt the same way. They could hear the sirens in the distance moving closer. With his last ounce of strength, he pushed her away and closed his eyes.

She knew he wanted her to leave him. She leaned over, gave him a soft kiss on his lips, and quietly slipped out of the alley.

# EPILOGUE

The whole neighborhood was abuzz after their friends were found slain in the streets. Apparently, Shoe-Shine hooked up with Tone and told him how Nasir had tried to assassinate him once upon a time ago. As Fancy stood stoically at the funeral of Lucky, Nicholas, and Shoe-Shine, she felt nothing.

Days turned into weeks, and winter turned into spring. Fancy finally had enough paper stashed to get her mother a good lawyer and go out and purchase a brand-new house in Deer Park, Long Island. She and Nasir were making a great team. She stepped directly into Nasir's shoes, after he'd gotten shot up; immediately contacting all the buyers she'd sold to in the past. Fancy immediately took the lead and began running their empire, just as her mother had done with Alexandro.

One day at the hospital, when they thought they were all alone, they shared an intimate kiss, only to be busted by Brenda.

The incestuous couple thought that a dirty little secret was revealed, however, Brenda had a secret as well. Nasir wasn't her biological child. It turned out that when she got with Nasir's father, he was six months old. His mother had gotten taken out in a home invasion robbery, and when Brenda met his father she agreed to raise him as her own. Subsequently, when Nasir's father was murdered, Brenda decided to keep the facts surrounding his real mother to herself.

At first, Nasir was a little disappointed realizing he would never get to meet his real mother. But then he realized that Brenda was more mother than he could have ever asked for, despite her shortcomings. She risked losing him as a son so that he wouldn't have to live his life with the shame of falling in love with Fancy.

✳✳✳

On the day of the move, Fancy gave her aunt ten stacks to hold her over, and gave her cousins, Lisa and Al-Saadiq, a hundred dollars each. They thought they were rich.

"So you and Nasir really gonna play house, huh?" Brenda asked, smiling.

"Don't say it." Fancy grinned. "We ain't having no babies."

"Well, you know that's next, right?"

"Not on my watch."

"I guess all those murders were a blessing in disguise for you."

"Well, God probably thought it was time I got a little good luck."

"God ain't have nothin' to do with this."

Fancy turned to face her aunt. "If you have something to say, just say it so I could go."

Brenda inhaled on her cigarette, debating whether or not she should push the envelope. Finally, she said, "You know, Nasir told me about what happened in that apartment."

"What apartment?"

Fancy could feel beads of sweat about to form around her hairline.

"In Queens, with that young boy you murdered."

Fancy's heart almost stopped. "Nasir told you that I murdered a kid?"

"That's exactly what he told me."

"And you believed him?"

"Nasir never lied to me."

Fancy's voice dropped a few octaves. "Answer my question—Did you believe him?"

Brenda almost couldn't face her, but her heart wouldn't let it go. She needed answers, and she felt she'd remained silent way too long. So many lives were snuffed out over that incident. Not to mention, she could have lost Nasir. "What happened in Queens happened in Queens. That's not my concern."

"Good answer. Look, I have to go. I have a delivery coming to the house in a couple hours." Fancy grabbed her Gucci bag and headed toward the front door.

Brenda called after her. "Fancy!"

She exhaled. "Yes, Aunt Brenda?"

"Did you have anything to do with Alexandro's murder?"

"Oh, God no. I could never do something so grimy." Fancy looked her dead in her eyes. "That would make me a *monster*."

A chill ran down Brenda's spine. It took her back twenty years. "You remind me of your mother."

"Well, I am her child."

*Follow*
# Melodrama Publishing

www.twitter.com/Team_Melodrama

www.facebook.com/MelodramaPublishing

# Order online at
bn.com, amazon.com, and
MelodramaPublishing.com